THE REGENCY
LORDS & LADIES
COLLECTION

**Glittering Regency Love Affairs
from your favourite historical authors.**

THE REGENCY LORDS & LADIES COLLECTION

A POOR RELATION

Joanna Maitland

First published in Great Britain 2001
Large Print Edition 2009
Harlequin Mills & Boon Limited,
Eton House, 18-24 Paradise Road, Richmond, Surrey TW9 1SR

© Joanna Maitland 2001

ISBN: 978 0 263 21033 0

Set in Times Roman 17¼ on 20 pt.
083-0309-67661

Printed and bound in Great Britain
by CPI Antony Rowe, Chippenham, Wiltshire

Chapter One

'Carriage stopped up ahead, m'lord.'

Lord Amburley did not spare a single sideways glance as he took his curricle past the stationary vehicle at the gallop and raced towards the bend in the wooded road.

'M'lord—' The groom made a move to look back.

'Keep your eyes on the road ahead, Brennan,' said the Baron sharply.

Brennan gave a grunt of surprise and turned to stare at his master, but Lord Amburley clenched his jaw grimly, ignoring the unspoken question. A moment later, they had rounded the curve and the groom was grabbing wildly for the side of the curricle, as the team was brought from headlong gallop to steaming halt in the space of a few yards.

'M'lord—' began the groom, sounding agitated.

'Keep your voice down. If he realises we've stopped, we'll never take him by surprise.' Lord Amburley reached under the seat with his free hand as he spoke. 'What are you waiting for?' he added in an exasperated whisper. 'Go to their heads, man. I've got my hands full as it is.' Extracting a pistol from its hiding place, he jumped down and started to make his way cautiously into the trees that now hid the curricle from the carriage.

Just before he disappeared into the thick cover, Lord Amburley threw a final instruction over his shoulder. 'Get the other pistol, Brennan. That ruffian may well be armed— and he may have accomplices, too. If you hear any shots, bring the curricle back up the road—at the double. And don't be afraid to shoot if you have to.' He did not wait for a reply. He knew his groom would obey his orders to the letter, whatever the risk.

It was probably no more than a few hundred yards to the stationary vehicle, but it took Amburley an infuriatingly long time to pick his way through the neglected woodland. The snap of the smallest twig among the dense leaf litter might betray his presence. And he was determined to retain the advantage of surprise. He had seen only one assailant raising his hand to attack the woman by the carriage, but the man was unlikely to be alone. Since the end of the war, the roads were full of bands of starving, desperate men, preying on unwary travellers, especially women. Nothing could excuse such crimes, in Amburley's view, even though many of the robbers were ex-soldiers, thrown on the scrap-heap by a wickedly ungrateful country.

He crept forward, silently cursing his failure to remove the white driving coat that might so easily betray his presence. He would need to use all the available cover, just as he had learnt to do when he was a soldier in Spain. Pity he had no troop of men at his back, this time.

At last he could see the outline of the carriage through the trees. Taking refuge behind a gnarled oak, he strained his ears. Only one low voice—a woman's—sounding neither distressed nor anxious. Remarkable, in the circumstances. In Amburley's experience, gentlewomen usually had a fit of the vapours at the first hint of danger. Perhaps she was only a servant, after all.

However much he tried, he could not quite make out what the woman was saying. Then he heard a second voice—male, deep, a little hesitant.

Amburley risked a quick glance from his hiding place. There was no one else among the trees. The assailant must be alone. Strange— but certainly welcome. It stacked the odds in his own favour.

Levelling his pistol, he walked slowly towards the stationary vehicle.

As he emerged from the trees, the woman started and gave an audible gasp. Everyone else turned, saw, and froze—the coachman on the box, the groom mounted behind, at least one other female cowering in the dark recesses of the carriage—and the woman's assailant.

Confronted by this petrified tableau, Amburley had time to wonder why neither coachman nor groom had made any move to overpower a single attacker who—he could now see—was neither young nor strong. The two servants appeared to have left the woman— a plain, worn-looking person of indeterminate age, her face hidden by the poke of her faded bonnet—to fend for herself. Odd, unless—

'Pray, what *are* you about, sir?'

On hearing her educated voice, Amburley's first thought was that this woman must be much younger than he had supposed. And fully in command of herself.

'Would you be so good as to put up that pistol, sir?' A slight edge of annoyance had crept into the shabby young woman's voice. This was surely no mere servant.

Keeping his pistol steady, Amburley half turned from the would-be assailant, who was looking increasingly shifty, as though he might take to his heels at any moment.

'Certainly, madam,' Amburley said evenly, not taking his eyes off the man. 'Just as soon as I have an explanation as to why this man was assaulting you.' He raised his pistol a fraction, so that the man would be in no doubt of his willingness to use it, if he attempted to escape.

The accused man took two steps back, eyes suddenly wide with fear at the sight of the gun's menacing little black muzzle. He made to speak, but no words came out.

The woman moved smartly between Amburley and his target, turning her back on the pistol and putting her hands reassuringly on the older man's arms. 'Don't worry, Jonah,' she said gently. 'I'll deal with this. Nothing will happen to you, I promise.'

She turned sharply then, shielding Jonah with her body. Fixing her gaze on the pistol, she said, in a voice that had lost all trace of gentleness, 'By your speech and your dress, sir, you are a gentleman. So I ask you again to put up your pistol. I have not been assaulted. And I have no need of your assistance.' She glanced up at his face for a second—without meeting his eyes—and then resolutely returned to staring at the pistol. 'Whatever you thought you had seen, sir, you were mistaken. Thank you for attempting to rescue me—but there really was no need.'

With that, she turned her back once more and began to reassure Jonah, who had not yet fully recovered from his fright.

Amburley stood for a moment before letting his pistol hand drop. By gad, she sounded anything but grateful for his attempted knight-errantry. Indeed, she reminded him of his mother's companion—sharp and shrewish, as most poor relations became, given half a chance. What a farce he had blundered into. He had been so sure the man Jonah was about to strike her—but it seemed he had been totally wrong. If his old comrades could see Major Amburley now… For a second or two, annoyance warred with amusement. Then he smiled to himself and shook his head resignedly. Heaven help him if this story ever got about. He would never live it down.

The woman had continued to busy herself with the man Jonah. She seemed to be intent on avoiding any further discussion. 'My apologies, madam,' Amburley said. 'Obviously, you do not stand in need of my assistance. I shall not trouble you further.' Still, she did not face him.

Amburley concluded wryly that he had attempted to rescue a mannerless harpy. Next time he saw a lady under attack, he would do well to drive past, if this was the thanks he could expect. He started back towards the trees but could not resist adding, with exquisite politeness, 'I wish you a safe onward journey. Good day, madam.'

'He's gone, ma'am.' Jonah's voice was a half-strangled whisper.

Isabella Winstanley forced herself to straighten her shoulders. There had never been any danger—so why was her stomach still turning like a frightened child's? And why had she been insufferably rude to a man who was trying to help her? Had she even thanked him? She could not remember. She realised that she had barely looked at him. Would she recognise him if she met him again? He was tall, certainly, and she fancied his hair had been quite dark—but she could not be sure. In the shadow of the trees, the light could play tricks.

'Miss Isabella.' Isabella's abigail, Mitchell, was pushing open the door of the carriage and sounding agitated. 'Miss Isabella, it's Miss Sophia…'

Isabella took in the situation at a glance. Sophia Winstanley, her pretty but penniless young cousin, had taken one look at the man with the gun and fainted clean away. How ironic. Only two days earlier, Sophia had been rhapsodising about romantic adventures—handsome strangers lurking in shrubberies, or ghosts and hauntings to send shivers down the spine. Sophia had fancied it would be quite agreeable to meet a ghostly apparition—provided, of course, that it drove her into the arms of an eligible gentleman who just happened to be nearby. Poor Sophia. She would never forgive herself, for this gentleman had certainly been eligible.

Heavens, how can I tell that, Isabella wondered, when I hardly know what he looks like? Was there something—?

At that moment, Sophia stirred, groaning. Her eyelids fluttered, and then snapped wide open. Obviously she was remembering the sight of the gun that had terrified her.

'He has gone, Sophia. There is nothing to be afraid of now.' Isabella's voice was gentle and reassuring once again. She reached into her reticule and offered her vinaigrette. 'Try this. It will make you feel better.'

Sophia took a cautious sniff. 'What happened? I don't understand…'

'Neither do I,' said Isabella. 'I can only surmise that, when the gentleman with the pistol saw Jonah hailing the carriage for me, he somehow assumed that I was being assaulted, and so he rushed gallantly to my rescue—terrifying you, and everyone else, in the process. However, he has gone now. And we, too, must be on our way, or we shall be late arriving at the posting house.'

'But, Winny—' began Sophia.

'I must just say my farewells to Jonah,' said Isabella matter-of-factly, ignoring the nickname she had repeatedly asked Sophia not to use. The last thing she wanted at present was a dispute about names—or a host of questions about her would-be rescuer.

'Thank you for your company today, Jonah. I could not have visited such a remote village without your escort—nor achieved half as much with the children without your help. I am only sorry that your kindness should have led to such a scene. It was my fault. I should not have chosen such an isolated spot to meet the carriage, however convenient it might have seemed.' She pressed some coins into his palm and he smiled, revealing a gap in his front teeth. 'You'll take care of those little ones, won't you?'

'Don't you worry, ma'am. No harm will come to 'em, I promise. And a blessing on ye for the help you've given to our poor orphans. Ye're a saint, that's what ye are, and—'

'Jonah,' began Isabella, blushing, 'I am nothing of the sort, as you know very well.' She put one worn black boot on the step of the carriage before the groom could climb down to assist her. 'But thank you, all the same, and God bless you. Goodbye, Jonah.'

* * *

Silence reigned in the carriage at last. It had taken Isabella more than half an hour to answer enough of Sophia's questions to pacify her. In the end, Isabella had forbidden all further discussion of it. The gentleman would certainly wish to forget their absurd encounter had ever happened. He was probably mortified by it.

And so was she.

She settled back in her seat once more, trying to focus her attention on the Yorkshire scenery. It was no use. She could not stop worrying about what had happened. She had always taken such care not to be seen in her 'poor relation' guise by anyone from her own station in life—it was the only way of being sure she could keep her philanthropy a secret—and now she had been caught out. Admittedly, the gentleman in question had been a complete stranger, but that could not guarantee her anonymity. If the gentleman came to London for the Season, he was bound to meet her somewhere.

And Isabella would have to be there. Flight was impossible. For she had agreed to chaperon pretty, portionless Sophia for this one London Season so that the child might have a chance of making a good match. Such a promise could not be broken. If they encountered the unknown in London, Isabella would just have to brazen it out, relying on the fact that her usual elegant appearance was a world away from the part she was playing today.

Sophia interrupted Isabella's painful reverie. 'How long will it take us to reach London, Winny dear? I am so looking forward to being at Hill Street again, especially as, this time, I shall be *out*. How many balls do you think we shall attend? Shall I have many partners, do you think? What about—?'

Isabella found herself smiling at Sophia's infectious enthusiasm. 'Sophia, please do stop to draw breath,' Isabella said. 'If you keep asking so many questions all at once, people will think that you are not at all interested in what *they* might say in reply.'

'You mean I talk too much. That's what Mama says,' replied Sophia, without much evidence of remorse. 'I am much more circumspect with people of consequence, I promise. Oh, and Winny—'

Isabella felt she dare not let that pass again. 'Sophia dear, *must* you call me "Winny"? It's such a very odd name for a lady.'

'But you said that your brother uses it quite often,' Sophia protested. 'You do not really mind, do you?'

'I concede you are merely copying from my quite incorrigible brother—so, yes, I give you leave to continue. But pray,' she added with a laugh, 'not in company. I should not like to be widely known as "Miss Winny Winstanley".'

'I shall try to remember,' said Sophia in a small voice, looking down at her clasped hands. After only a moment's silence, she began again, on the subject that Isabella had been hoping to avoid. 'Who do you think he was? The man with the pistol, I mean. Do you think that he—'

'That encounter is not to be discussed,' said Isabella flatly. 'Not with anyone. Do you understand, Sophia?' She waited for the girl's nod of agreement before continuing, 'You must see that it could be disastrous for my reputation—and yours—if it were known that I went about the countryside alone, visiting destitute soldiers and orphans.'

'But you are helping them,' protested Sophia hotly. 'How can that destroy your reputation?'

'My motives would be of no account, I'm afraid. Ladies of the *ton* do not consort with the lower classes—not for any reason. You will learn that they never go anywhere without a servant in attendance, either. And they certainly do not dress like servants.' She glanced down at her drab brown dress and fraying shawl. 'If I were discovered, I would never be admitted to Society again. You must never betray, by so much as a look, that you have seen me like this. Promise me, Sophia!'

'I promise. At least, I promise to try,' said Sophia.

Isabella felt the tension relax in her shoulders. 'I shall be satisfied with that. And now, let us talk of something else.'

'Yes, let's,' said Sophia more eagerly. 'Tell

me about your first Season—er—Isabella. Did you have many offers?'

Isabella smiled resignedly. 'I only ever had one Season, I'm afraid, and no offers, so there is little to tell.'

'But why?'

Isabella shrugged. Although she had avoided telling the story until now—over the years, she had learnt to be content with her single state, but it still hurt too much to discuss the deaths of her parents—she knew that Sophia would pester her until she gave in. 'My Season was cut short because my papa became ill and had to return home,' she said quietly.

'But surely there was no need to pack you all off back to the country?'

'I was only too happy to go, Sophia, I assure you. Mama needed my help to nurse Papa.'

'Oh.' Sophia seemed to have realised, at last, where the story was leading. She sat for a moment, thinking. 'Could you not have had another Season? Later, I mean, when…' Her voice trailed off.

'It suited me to remain on the family estate

with my brother, Sophia. He could not run it alone.'

'But surely he runs it alone now,' protested Sophia.

'He is a grown man now—and married. He does not need an older sister looking over his shoulder.'

'Is that why you went to live with Lady Wycham?'

'Partly.' Goodness, the child was certainly persistent. Isabella knew she was going to have to embroider the truth from now on. To the outside world, it was Lady Wycham who had the money and Isabella who was the poor relation. It was a fiction both worked hard to maintain.

'I don't understand,' said Sophia.

Isabella sighed. 'Great-aunt Jemima invited me to join her in Hill Street last year. She would have been alone, otherwise, so it suited us both. I can enjoy as much as I wish of London Society—and she has company about the place. Even more, now that you are joining us,' she added, with a gentle laugh.

'And I shall be as good as gold, I promise,'

said Sophia. 'It is so very generous of Lady Wycham to frank my come-out—' Isabella hoped she was not blushing '—and I intend to make her proud of me. Wait and see!'

'I'm sure you will. Aunt Jemima is looking forward to taking you to our French modiste for your new gowns. Your dark colouring is all the crack these days, you know. Fair hair is sadly passé, I'm afraid,' she added with a mischievous glance across at the abigail who spent so many hours arranging Isabella's honey-gold curls. 'Should I cover it with a turban, do you think?'

A moment later, they were engulfed in laughter.

In the late afternoon, the carriage arrived at the Bell in Barnby Moor where they were to spend the night. Isabella alighted first to see that all was in order for her party, leaving Sophia, chaperoned by Mitchell, to make a more leisurely descent. Sophia was just re-marking on the unusual degree of bustle in the inn-yard, when Isabella returned, grim-faced.

'It is too vexing,' she declared. 'The rooms

that were bespoke for us are not available, it seems. The inn is full of gentlemen, here for some sporting event about which I did *not* enquire. The landlord appears to have preferred the immediate custom of these *gentlemen* to the prior written instructions of a lady. You will please return to the carriage, Sophia, while I try to resolve matters.'

With firm tread, Isabella returned to the inn to do battle with the landlord for the promised rooms. By the time he eventually appeared, looking hot and flustered, she had been kept waiting for more than ten minutes and her patience had worn extremely thin. Her eyes had lost their usual grey-green calm to become very stormy indeed; her foot was tapping in a rhythm of irritation; and, with her threadbare clothes enhancing the effect, she knew she must appear a veritable harridan. She fully intended to make the most of it in this encounter.

The landlord, however, seemed to be in no mood to acknowledge the justice of her claim. He stated flatly that no rooms were to be had, either in his inn or for several miles around and, furthermore, that the locality was no place for ladies at present, with so large a gathering of sporting gentlemen in residence.

Isabella would have none of it.

Their heated discussion was beginning to attract the attention of the gentlemen assembled in the coffee-room behind her. Isabella could not help but notice that the level of their conversation had become muted as they listened avidly to hers but, driven by the justice of her cause, she would not be deterred. 'Two chambers and a private parlour were bespoke for Miss Winstanley, besides accommodation for the servants. I insist they be provided immediately. If you have been so lax in your duty as to let them to some of these gentlemen, you must simply require them to move elsewhere. I shall wait here until you have made the arrangements.'

By this time, the coffee-room was almost silent. Isabella coloured a little but stood her ground, wondering whether the men now staring at her defenceless back would have been so reluctant to come to her aid if she had appeared in her normal elegant guise.

The landlord was in a quandary. 'I'll ask among the gen'lemen, if you wishes, ma'am, but I don't see as 'ow I can do what you says. T'wouldn't be right.'

'Nor is it right to fail to undertake your commitment to two ladies,' flashed Isabella.

The landlord shrank a little before her fiery look. His hesitant response was forestalled by the arrival of a young gentleman from the inn-yard who immediately said, 'Landlord, you have wronged these ladies. I insist that you look to their needs—immediately!'

Isabella's stormy gaze softened a little at the sight of the young man. His intentions were good, certainly, though they were of little practical help. And the landlord was looking thoroughly mutinous.

The landlord's response was interrupted by movement from the coffee-room—one of the gentlemen there strode out to join the little group in the hallway.

Isabella swallowed a gasp at the sight of that tall dark figure. She recognised it at a glance. Somehow—impossibly—his powerful outline had become deeply etched in her mind.

It was her would-be rescuer—again!

Chapter Two

Isabella found herself confronting an imposing figure, dressed now in immaculate riding dress and top-boots. She was struck by a sternly handsome face, dark eyes of unfathomable depths, and curling black hair that seemed to invite a woman's fingers to touch it. This time, she found she could not drag her gaze from his face. Suddenly, she forgot to breathe.

The newcomer paused for a moment alongside Isabella's frozen figure, raking her from top to toe with a long, appraising glance that seemed to search out every shabby, demeaning aspect of her appearance. She felt as if he had stripped her naked. Then, with a tiny shake of his head, he simply turned away without a word.

Isabella remained motionless, though her heart was pounding now at the extent of the man's disdain. He was dismissing her publicly. But what else could she expect? In the light of her behaviour earlier, it was hardly surprising that he would not even acknowledge her. She wanted to sink.

Isabella thought she saw the merest hint of a condescending smile on his lips when he turned away from her. In a trice, mounting fury had overcome her embarrassment. How dare he treat her so? First, he pretended to be a knight in shining armour, and then he treated her like a…like a common doxy. This was no gentleman. For no gentleman would look at a woman as he had looked at her. The man must be a libertine. A man of his stamp would doubtless prefer to gaze on women with more opulent, and visible, charms. Isabella told herself she was glad of her dowdy appearance if it protected her from a handsome ladykiller. Isabella Winstanley would never have truck with such a man.

She forced herself to assume her normal

outward calm, but her wayward thoughts continued to whirl. Her heart was still racing. And the strangest feelings assailed her.

She was still trying to recover her inner composure when the tall gentleman began addressing his friend. 'I had not pictured you in the role of knight errant, Lewiston, I must admit—but I am sure *your* offer will be appreciated.'

Isabella felt the colour rising in her cheeks at the slight but unmistakable emphasis in his words. Her would-be rescuer was clearly determined to make her feel thoroughly ashamed of her earlier behaviour. And he was succeeding.

He did not so much as glance in her direction as he continued, 'I imagine you were about to offer the ladies one of our chambers and our private parlour. And without so much as a "by-your-leave", either,' he added wryly. 'If I were introduced to this lady, I might be more amenable on that subject, you know.'

Isabella was hard put to hide her astonishment. The man now spoke as if he had never set eyes on her before.

Mr Lewiston's relative youth was evident in

his response, for he coloured and stammered a little, before admitting that he himself had not yet been introduced to this particular lady.

The tall gentleman immediately took charge of the discussion, turning a sudden and devastating smile on Isabella that did the strangest things to her knees, much as she steeled herself to resist. 'I hope you will forgive my friend's shocking want of manners, ma'am. I gather he very much desires to be of service to your party in your present difficulties...though I do not fully understand what they might be. Perhaps you could explain a little more, Miss...?'

A number of unflattering descriptions arose in Isabella's mind, of which 'dissembler' was probably the least insulting. Unable to voice her opinion of him without lapsing into impropriety, she swallowed her wrath before explaining, in her best poor-relation manner, that she was Miss Winstanley, en route for London with her young cousin, Miss Sophia Winstanley. But she could not resist adding, with a touch of asperity, 'You are, I fancy, already well acquainted with the details of our predicament, sir. The landlord's views on our arrival must have been heard by every one of the gentlemen in the coffee-room.'

She knew she was yielding to her worst impulses by saying such a thing, but she felt so strange in the presence of this man. Somehow, she felt impelled to provoke a reaction from him.

It did not come, because the landlord could no longer contain himself. He burst into vehement self-justification. 'My lord,' he began, 'you knows that this b'aint no place for ladies just now, with so many sporting gen'le-men staying here. I only—'

Isabella cringed inwardly. Good God—not merely a libertine, but a peer as well. It was worse and worse.

The landlord's excuses were cut short by the unnamed lord. 'However well-meant your concern, landlord, the fact remains that rooms were bespoke for this lady and you have let them elsewhere. Furthermore, it is already too late for any of your guests, male *or* female, to journey on in search of accommodation elsewhere.' With a sidelong glance at Isabella which confirmed that he had indeed heard all of her discussions with the landlord, he concluded, 'Since this lady's instructions predate those of the sporting gentlemen, it is clear that the gentlemen must make way for the ladies. So, what do you propose, landlord?'

In truth, the landlord had nothing much to offer, since all his rooms were taken and it was not in his interest to offend the free-spending sporting guests. At length he ventured, 'If some of the gen'lemen might be willing to share, summat might be done, p'rhaps. But I don't know…'

'We have already offered the ladies the use of our sitting room and one of our bedchambers.' He looked blandly across at his friend. 'And since Lewiston would not really enjoy sleeping in the stables, he may share my room. That leaves, I think, only one more chamber to find. You can do that, surely, landlord?'

Isabella's senses were reeling. Why should a rake put himself to so much trouble for someone he obviously considered beneath his touch? And someone who had spurned his help once already that day. Perhaps… But no. Doubtless he had caught sight of Sophia— who looked, for all the world, like a pretty young heiress. Just the sort of prey that such a man would seek to fasten on. Pity the hapless female who was unwise enough to fall into his clutches. He was charming, too, no doubt about that. She would not easily forget that devastating smile and its effect on her. She was feeling it still.

Isabella straightened her spine, waiting until she felt sufficiently in control of her emotions to speak. 'You are most kind, gentlemen,' she said, carefully addressing her remarks to the space between the tall unknown and Mr Lewiston. 'I am sure my cousin will agree that she and I share a chamber also. There will be no need for further inconvenience to the guests on that score. I take it the landlord can find accommodation for the servants?'

The landlord readily agreed that he could. Then he fled from the scene, ostensibly to see to the readying of the rooms.

Isabella, now relieved of the immediate worry, felt some sympathy for him. It could not be easy dealing with a forceful lady and an arrogant lord at one and the same time. Arrogant? No, it would be unjust to call him so, however much she might detest his libertine ways. He was simply very firm about what was to be done. His manner was certainly daunting, but he was self-assured rather than arrogant, a man who was used to issuing commands and who expected them to be obeyed. It would probably be unwise to cross him, too, for there was something in his demeanour that suggested ruthlessness as well as strength. He… Enough! What on earth was she about, letting her mind wander so in the hallway of a posting house?

Isabella's tumbling thoughts were interrupted by the arrival of Sophia in her usual tempestuous fashion. 'Winny, dear,' she began, and Isabella's heart sank as she recognised a gleam of sardonic amusement in the tall gentleman's eye, 'Mr Lewiston has so kindly offered to resolve all our problems for us. I have—'

Clearly, Sophia must be stopped before Isabella was even further embarrassed. Her predicament was already wretched enough. 'Yes, I know, Sophia. Thanks to the kind offices of these two gentlemen, we have somewhere to sleep tonight, even if we are constrained to share a bedchamber. My lord,' she added pointedly, 'you must let me make you known to my cousin, Miss Sophia Winstanley. Sophia, this is Lord…'

'Amburley, at your service, Miss Sophia Winstanley,' he continued coolly, as if Isabella had known the name all along. He favoured Sophia with a brief, hard smile and bowed over her hand. Then, turning to Isabella, he took her hand also, adding, with another bow, 'And at yours, Miss Winstanley, of course. The burdens of a companion on a journey such as this are not lightly borne. I hope I may have helped to relieve them in some small way. If there is any other service you require of me, ma'am, please do not hesitate to ask. And now we will leave you. I am sure you will wish to assure yourselves that your accommodation is adequate.'

With a further bow, he released Isabella's hand and left them to return to the coffee-room, followed by a rather reluctant Mr Lewiston.

Isabella looked dazedly at her hand. It felt as if it were burning, yet there was no outward sign of heat. Her face, too, felt as if it were on fire. Was this an example of how a rake's practised charm was exercised? She shook her head, vainly trying to clear her disordered thoughts. She longed for solitude so that she might attempt to make sense of what had happened. But, of course, sharing a room with the effervescent Sophia would prevent any opportunity for calm reflection. It was hopeless.

Isabella now wished with all her heart that she had never succumbed to the urge to visit that rural orphanage. It had led her into two encounters with a man who affected her composure as no other had ever done. Not that it mattered, for he clearly regarded her as a poor, used, spinster companion, put upon by all and an object to be pitied. She felt deeply embarrassed and somehow shamed. Her only refuge was in the hope—earnestly felt—that she would never set eyes on Lord Amburley again. She did not see how her injured self-esteem could survive a third meeting.

'You carried that off perfectly, Winny,' said Sophia. 'But for you, we should be sleeping in the stables.'

Isabella smiled weakly in response. At least Sophia had not recognised Lord Amburley.

'Shall we retire to our parlour now?' continued Sophia. 'I so much want to tell you about my conversation with Mr Lewiston.'

Isabella nodded agreement. It would certainly not do to learn Sophia's views about the perfection of Mr Lewiston's figure and address in the hearing of the coffee-room gentlemen. That would be the final humiliation of an absolutely dreadful day. Fortunately, the landlord returned at that moment, and so they were soon ensconced in a comfortable parlour with easy chairs and a welcome blaze in the hearth. With a sigh of relief, Isabella removed her all-concealing bonnet and sank into a chair. Privacy, at last.

'I must tell you, Winny, about my encounter with Mr Lewiston. He must have witnessed our arrival, for he was seeing to his horses in the yard. They are very fine, by the bye, so I collect he must be a rich young man.'

'That need not be so,' interposed Isabella. 'Many a young gentleman of address is deeply in debt and hanging out for a rich wife to solve his problems.'

'I do not believe Mr Lewiston is such a one. How can you possibly suggest such a motive for the young man who helped to rescue us?' Sophia stopped short as the full import of Isabella's words struck home. 'Besides, I am not rich.'

'No, Sophia, you are not rich but, just for the moment, you have every appearance of it. You ride in a fine carriage with an abigail and servants in attendance. Your shabbily dressed cousin is naturally assumed to be your companion, while you yourself are dressed in the latest fashion. No one would guess it is thanks to your own nimble fingers, you know. No, indeed, you seem to have all the outward trappings of an heiress.'

'Oh!' Sophia blushed to the roots of her hair. 'Oh, dear! What shall we do?'

'Nothing. Tomorrow we shall wait until the gentlemen have left before we emerge as ourselves. And even then, I shall ensure that there is not so much difference in my own appearance as to cause comment. Then we can forget all about this unfortunate occurrence...and start preparing for your London Season. We must have you do justice to the Winstanley looks.' Her mischievous smile lit up her eyes.

That final sally was not enough to restore Sophia's spirits. 'But what if we should meet Mr Lewiston or Lord What's-his-name in London? I should die of mortification.'

'If you should meet either Mr Lewiston or Lord Amburley, you will behave as if nothing had happened, my dear. After all, *you* have done nothing, except to be your true self. The imposture, such as it is, has been mine, and *I* shall have to deal with the consequences if we should meet either gentleman again. However,' she added consolingly, 'I do not believe we shall. Although I do not go into Society very much, I have lived in London for almost a year now, and I have not heard of either of them. No doubt they are northern gentlemen who do not come to London for the Season.'

In a bedchamber further along the corridor, Lord Amburley was changing his coat, musing abstractedly on his two encounters with the elder Miss Winstanley. She was remarkably sharp-tongued—but perhaps that was not surprising, considering how shamefully she was treated by her young employer. It was not a fate he would wish on any woman, however poverty-stricken.

His valet's voice intruded insistently. Peveridge was clearly determined to indulge his irrepressible taste for gossip, now that he had an audience of two. 'Miss Winstanley is a real lady, m'lord, and a considerable heiress to boot, by all accounts.'

'Is she, begad?' said Mr Lewiston, who was reclining at his ease in a chair and nursing a glass in his hand. 'Well, well.'

'Pray do not encourage him, George,' said his lordship. 'I have been trying for years to persuade him out of his reprehensible tendency to gossip, and now you are like to undo all my hard work with a careless sentence or two.'

The valet grinned at Mr Lewiston, as if to say that no amount of effort on the part of Lord Amburley would ever cure that particular malady.

'Come, Leigh, I will have the truth out of you. Are you not at all curious about the circumstances of the lovely Miss Winstanley?'

'I know all I wish to know about that young lady,' countered his lordship. 'She is young and quite pretty, I grant you. If you listen to Peveridge, she is also rich. You could have concluded that yourself from her mode of travelling, without recourse to Peveridge's sources.' Peveridge cleared his throat at this point as if preparing to intervene, but subsided at a warning glance from his master. With barely a pause, his lordship continued evenly, 'Peveridge can no doubt give you detailed information on her family, her financial circumstances and her marital ambitions. I know nothing of those, nor do I desire to. The rich

Miss Winstanley is empty-headed, frivolous and spoilt. No doubt she has been indulged from birth.'

'How can you suggest such a thing, Amburley?' growled Mr Lewiston. 'You yourself admitted you know nothing about her.'

'I know her kind very well. Did you compare the poverty of the poor relation's dress with the expense of the young lady's? The cost of that single fashionable outfit was probably more than the companion receives in a year. And to address her as "Winny"… If there had been the least doubt as to her lowly station in life, that would certainly have settled it.'

'It could be her name, you know. Winifred, perhaps?'

'I take leave to doubt that, George. Did you not notice how she blushed? I believe she was quite put out.' Until the words were spoken, he had not been aware that her reactions had registered with him at all.

'She did seem a little strained, I admit, but I put it down to the difficulties of the situation. However, you went out of your way to be kind to her, I noticed. Indeed, you were much more solicitous to the poor companion than to the lady.'

'Since the lady had you to defend her, my friend, she clearly had no need of me. The companion, by contrast, had no one, not even her charge. She is—' He stopped in mid-sentence. For some reason, he did not feel able to share his assessment of the poor companion, even with his friend. Deliberately, he pushed her shabby image to the back of his mind, before continuing, 'I sought only to allow her to recover her composure a little. If I succeeded, I am glad.'

'You are very much your mother's son,' said Lewiston, after a thoughtful pause, 'with your concern for the poor and disadvantaged. Perhaps you should set up a foundation for impoverished spinsters?'

Lord Amburley smiled enigmatically. 'I have not the means, George, as you know very well—and, in any case, one philanthropist in the Stansfield family is quite enough. My mother does my share, I think—though only among the orphans.' His eyes narrowed suddenly. 'You, by contrast, could certainly afford to support such a worthy cause. Why not adopt your own suggestion?'

'I have not the taste for it,' came the prompt reply. 'I fear I fall into your category of empty-headed, frivolous and spoilt.'

The following morning was wet, which dampened everyone's spirits. Isabella waited anxiously in her chamber for the gentlemen to leave the inn. She had exchanged the hideous brown dress for a simple but modish travelling gown of deep green, which she planned to hide beneath a plain dark pelisse when she emerged. There was also a matching hat, but Isabella would not dare to put it on until she was safely in the carriage and miles from this unfortunate inn. For the present, she would continue to hide her hair completely under the battered brown poke bonnet.

Her main concern now was to avoid any further meeting with Lord Amburley. Until she was sure he had left, she dared not even venture into the parlour, lest he call to see how they did.

She had suffered mortification enough, she told herself. She was resolved to leave without meeting him again, even if she had to resort to ill-manners to achieve it.

Isabella returned to the window to check again on the departure of the gentlemen. To her relief, she saw that the curricle Sophia had described was standing ready in the yard. In spite of her preoccupation, she could not help noticing that the horses were quite as fine as Sophia had supposed. Mr Lewiston had a good eye, then, and might be wealthy after all. What a pity Isabella's actions had ruined everything for Sophia.

The sound of voices in the parlour next door distracted her from this depressing train of thought. Sophia's voice, conversing with a man. Thank goodness Mitchell was present as chaperon, so that Isabella need not join them.

She drew near the connecting door and, without *quite* putting her ear against it, found a position from which she could overhear all that was said. She told herself sternly that it was her duty to listen. Was she not, after all, the guardian of Sophia's virtue?

The voice proved to be Mr Lewiston's. Isabella breathed again.

Mr Lewiston was advising the ladies to delay their journey until the rain eased. He feared Miss Sophia might catch cold if she travelled in such weather.

'But what of you, sir?' responded Sophia. 'Are you not about to set out for your prize-fight, or whatever it is you are all here to see? I thought I saw your horses standing in the yard?'

'They are Amburley's horses, I am sorry to say,' admitted Mr Lewiston ruefully. 'I should give much to own them.'

'But they are not for sale,' put in a deeper voice.

Behind the door, Isabella smothered a gasp. A shiver ran down her body and she swayed on her feet. Amburley was there, just a few feet beyond the door. And it was all his—horses, wealth, everything. Surely a titled man of means would be bound to appear in London at some stage, whatever reasons had kept him away in the past?

Light suddenly dawned. What a fool she had been! Of course, he must have been with Wellington's army. How could she have missed something so obvious? His bearing, his air of authority, everything about him betrayed the soldier. He would be recently returned from the wars. There must be estates somewhere, she supposed. Oh, she prayed they were a long way from London and in need of his constant supervision. She could not *bear* the thought of meeting him again. A rake—and a hero too, no doubt. There could not be a more dangerous combination.

Chapter Three

Sophia looked around with glowing eyes. 'Oh, Isabella,' she breathed, 'I have never seen such beautiful fabrics. It's...it's like Aladdin's cave.'

'Just wait until you have seen Madame's designs.' Isabella smiled.

Sophia's dark eyes opened even wider, as Madame Florette's elegant black-clad figure re-entered the room, followed by a bevy of attendants carrying yet more bolts of splendid silks. Madame waved them into the background, before inviting the ladies to seat themselves on her delicate spindle-legged chairs.

'*Bien*, mademoiselle.' Madame was beaming at Isabella, no doubt in anticipation of a very large order. 'I am at your service.'

'Come, Sophia, let us make a start by choosing some simple morning dresses.' Isabella smiled encouragingly. 'Madame Florette has impeccable taste. You may trust her judgement.'

'Mademoiselle Winstanley is most generous,' responded the modiste with a self-satisfied smirk. 'Mademoiselle Sophia will be a pleasure to dress. Such colouring, such a figure.'

Over the course of the morning, a bewildering collection of gowns was selected for Sophia. Isabella was glad she had taken pains to ensure that there was no mention whatever of price, for it was vital that Sophia's feckless parents should not find out how much was being spent on their eldest daughter. What little they had was devoted to educating their five sons—and paying their debts. They did not seem to care that Sophia and her sisters were destined to become penniless old maids. As a spinster herself, Isabella had determined that Sophia, at least, should have the best possible chance of making a good match. And she was quite prepared to conceal the expense of the

Season from Sophia's stiff-necked parents, knowing that they would welcome a wealthy suitor with open arms.

'And for you, Miss Winstanley,' urged Madame, 'I have just received the most beautiful jade-green silk shot with gold. With your colouring, it would make an exquisite ball-gown.' With an imperious wave of the hand, she dispatched a hovering attendant to fetch the bolt of cloth.

The jade and gold silk was irresistible. 'With a lighter green underdress, mademoiselle, in this aquamarine satin, to bring out the colour of the silk…and then a gold gauze scarf for your arms.' Madame was sketching rapidly. 'We will fashion a special ornament for your hair too, I think, to pick up the greens of the gown and of your eyes. It will look ravishing, I assure you.'

'Isabella, it is too beautiful for words. You must have it, truly.'

Isabella yielded. She knew just how well the gown would become her. Partly as a result of Madame's beautiful creations, Isabella

Winstanley could hold her own among the best-dressed women in London. She was now wearing a carriage dress of emerald green, with a jaunty little hat of the same colour perched on top of her honey-gold curls. Even though Sophia's dark colouring was the prevailing fashion, it was Isabella's striking looks that had drawn every eye since their arrival in London.

Isabella was laughing gently with Sophia as they emerged to return to their carriage. Sophia, concentrating on their conversation, failed to notice a gentleman in her path and almost collided with him.

'Oh, I do beg your pardon, sir,' she began. 'Why, it is Mr Lewiston! Oh!' Her face was suffused with the deepest blush, and she began to stammer uncertainly, 'I…I had not thought… to see you in London. I…' Her voice trailed off; she was unable to utter another word.

Mr Lewiston saved her, at least for the moment. 'Miss Winstanley, how delightful to meet you again. I cannot think how I was so remiss as to fail to ask you for your direction in London. I hope you will permit me to call?'

Sophia had no choice but to acquiesce. 'I am staying in Hill Street with my godmother, Lady Wycham,' she said. 'I am sure she would be delighted to meet you.'

'And would you do me the honour of making me known to your companion?' asked Mr Lewiston, casting an appreciative glance at Isabella.

'Com...companion?' stuttered Sophia, suddenly ashen.

'I do not think I have been introduced to this lady,' said Mr Lewiston patiently, ignoring Sophia's apparent want of wits.

Isabella intervened to save the situation. She extended her hand, noting with satisfaction how steady it was. 'I am Isabella Winstanley, Mr Lewiston, a distant cousin of Sophia's. Lady Wycham would welcome a chance to meet you, I am sure. We have heard about your chivalrous rescue of Sophia in the north.'

It was Mr Lewiston's turn to stammer as they shook hands. 'Indeed, ma'am, I...I did nothing more than any gentleman would have done for a lady in distress, I assure you.'

Recovering his composure, he continued gamely, addressing Sophia once more, 'I shall call tomorrow, if I may?'

Sophia answered with a smile and a slight nod. She was still incapable of speech. With an elegant bow, Mr Lewiston handed them into the carriage and stood watching as they drove off.

Sophia sank into the cushions, as far as possible from the window. She had turned extremely pale. She sank her head into her hands, pushing her modish new bonnet askew in the process, and began to sob weakly.

Isabella, too, was a little pale, but she despised such missish behaviour. Her keen intellect was busy searching for a solution to their dilemma. Mr Lewiston had not recognised her, she was certain. If she was careful both in her appearance and her behaviour, she could continue to dupe him. She could not afford to fail.

'Do not distress yourself, Sophia,' she said firmly, grasping Sophia's shoulder and giving her a tiny shake. 'He did not know me. Nor will he, if we are careful. I shall continue to act as though he and I had just met, and so shall you. If he should ask after your "companion"—though I dare swear he will not so lower himself—you will say that she is with her family.'

'Oh, I could not,' protested Sophia, trying to dry her tears with a scrap of lace. 'I have not your talent for acting a part. Pray do not ask me to, Winny.' Her voice was quavering; the tears threatened once more.

'But I require you to,' replied Isabella resolutely, giving Sophia a stern look, which stopped the gathering tears immediately. 'Remember, Sophia—what I am asking you to say is no more than the exact truth. "Winny" *is* with her family.' Isabella softened her gaze with a slight smile as she continued. 'However, you *must* now cease to call me by that name. It would certainly betray us.'

They did not have much time to reflect on the possible horrors of the forthcoming visit from Mr Lewiston, because they were preoccupied with the preparations for Sophia's first party—

Lady Bridge's soirée—that very evening. Although London was as yet quite thin of company, Isabella had judged it wise to allow Sophia to make some acquaintances at a few small gatherings, before launching her into her first grand occasion.

For this first party, Sophia chose the prettiest of the evening gowns she had brought from Yorkshire. None of Madame Florette's creations could arrive for some days yet, however many seamstresses she might set to work on them. But Sophia's home-made gown would by no means disgrace her, since she possessed real skill both in cutting and in stitching.

'Thank you so much for lending me your pearls,' said Sophia, as soon as she joined Isabella in the hall.

'You look lovely,' replied Isabella warmly. 'Pink does indeed become you.'

'While you look quite beautiful,' responded Sophia promptly, casting admiring glances at Isabella's classical gown of old-gold silk, and the necklace and earrings of intricate gold filigree. 'You look like a princess from a fairy-tale.'

Secretly pleased, Isabella thanked her cousin demurely. 'But you should not say such things, you know. At my age, I am more likely to be the wicked witch than the good fairy.'

'Nonsense,' chimed in an older voice. 'You do yourself an injustice, as ever, Isabella. You look very well indeed, my dear.'

'Oh, Aunt,' protested Isabella. 'How can I retain my countenance, if both of you put me to the blush?'

Lady Wycham ignored that protest completely. 'Come, my dears, the carriage is waiting.' The elderly lady, clad in imposing purple and leaning lightly on an ebony cane, led the way to the steps.

Barely ten minutes after their arrival, Sophia was chattering gaily with their host's two nieces, while the hostess herself was seated by Lady Wycham, enjoying a comfortable coze.

'Will you favour us with some music, my dear?' asked Sir Thomas. 'It is always a delight to hear you sing.'

Isabella inclined her head towards her host and moved to open the pianoforte. First she played a German minuet, its demure rhythm making little impact on the hum of conversation in the salon. Then she turned to a book of Italian songs, accompanying her low, rich singing voice with soft arpeggios. Almost as soon as she started to sing, the level of noise in the room fell, as the guests stopped to appreciate her beautiful voice. Sir Thomas watched her with a beatific smile on his face. Hardly anyone moved.

At the end of three songs, she made to leave the instrument but was met with a chorus of requests for an encore. She felt the warmth of a flush on her cheeks as she nodded her acquiescence. 'Very well,' she smiled, 'but just one more.' Her choice this time was completely different, a sad Italian ballad, which she sang very quietly, but with great expressiveness. The room remained totally hushed until the last note had died away, and then there was a burst of enthusiastic applause.

Isabella felt pleased; she knew she had performed well. She raised her eyes from her music to acknowledge the applause—and

looked straight into the hard, dark eyes of
Lord Amburley.

For a moment she sat immobile, stunned.
How could this be happening? She felt her
flush return and deepen under his gaze, while
she strove both to regain her composure and to
find an escape route from this nightmarish encounter. What could she do? It was so terribly
difficult to order her thoughts with his penetrating gaze resting on her face. Had he recognised her, perhaps? Heavens, he was coming
over to the pianoforte. She rose hurriedly in an
attempt to avoid him, but it was too late. Sir
Thomas was before her.

'I think you cannot have met Amburley,'
began her affable host. 'He has not been in town
for some years. The wars, you know. He arrived
a little late this evening but, luckily, in time to
hear you sing. May I make him known to you?'

Isabella nodded dumbly, trying to recover
control of her decidedly wobbly limbs. Her
mind was still in a whirl. Foremost among her
thoughts was the awful certainty that he could
not possibly be the libertine she had earlier

judged him to be. Rakes were not received by the upright Lady Bridge.

'Miss Winstanley,' continued Sir Thomas formally, turning slightly to be sure of including his lordship, 'may I present Lord Amburley?'

'Your servant, ma'am.' His lordship had stopped by the far end of the instrument, Isabella noted, just near enough to avoid being impolite. He now bowed distantly to her, without moving forward to shake hands. 'My compliments on your performance. You have a most…unusual voice.' His voice was cool and expressionless, his manner stiff.

Curtsying politely, Isabella contrived a slight smile which did not reach her eyes. Inwardly, she was suddenly seething, her anger forcibly expelling her earlier weakness. She had been much too generous in her previous assessment of this man. Not a rake, perhaps, but both arrogant and overbearing in the extreme. She had received many compliments on her singing in the past, but a cold and patronising 'unusual' was certainly not one she would cherish. Better that he had re-

frained from voicing his evident disdain.
Hateful, hateful man!

She would not allow him to overset her. Let
him begin the polite conversation, if he dared.
The spark of challenge was unmistakable as she
raised her head proudly to look him in the eye.

If Lord Amburley observed that fiery spark,
he gave no outward sign of recognition as far
as Isabella could tell. Indeed, he seemed to be
completely devoid of any human feeling—he
just stood motionless by the pianoforte, surveying Isabella through half-closed lids.

Isabella refused to be cowed. Clearly his
lordship did not desire to prolong their conversation. *She* certainly had no wish to do so. 'If
you will excuse me, gentlemen, I must rejoin
Lady Wycham,' she said politely, turning to
leave. Sir Thomas nodded genially. Lord
Amburley responded with only the slightest
bow, keeping his hard eyes fixed on Isabella
throughout. She could feel his gaze boring into
her back, as she moved away to join her great-
aunt once more, keeping her pace measured
and deliberate. She might feel like running from

him, but nothing—nothing—would be allowed to betray her inner weakness to such a man.

'Why, Isabella,' exclaimed Lady Wycham, 'whatever is the matter? You look quite ill. Have you the headache, my dear? You really should not have agreed to perform for so long.'

'I am quite well, truly. It is just a little warm with so many people in the room. I shall be recovered in a moment, I assure you.' Taking a deep breath, Isabella raised her eyes to survey the company and discovered, with a sigh of relief, that Lord Amburley was no longer anywhere to be seen. A little of her colour returned.

But she had forgotten about Sophia, who was signalling urgently from across the room. Isabella swallowed a moment of panic. What should she tell Sophia? She reminded herself sternly that he had shown no sign of recognition—with luck he had completely forgotten his encounters with 'Winny'.

Sophia drew Isabella into a shadowy alcove, desperate to know what had happened. 'What did he say? Did he recognise you, do you think? Oh, what are we going to do?'

'Be calm, Sophia,' answered Isabella, doing her utmost to appear so herself. 'There is no reason to be agitated, I am sure. Lord Amburley did not know me. We were introduced by Sir Thomas, that is all.' She cut Sophia's protest short, lest the child fret herself into an attack of the vapours. 'He will, of course, recognise you when you meet, and you must acknowledge him, as you would any other gentleman. Remember that your "companion"—"Winny"—has gone to stay with her family. You may say, quite truthfully, that you are staying with your godmother and your distant cousin *Isabella*. Can you do that, do you think?' She laid a gloved hand gently on Sophia's arm.

'I shall try,' promised Sophia, looking pale and strained.

The inevitable meeting with Lord Amburley took place at supper, towards midnight, just when Isabella had begun to hope that he might have left. Isabella and Sophia were seated in the midst of the same group of young people they had joined earlier, and all were enjoying Lady Bridge's generous hospitality.

Isabella felt, rather than saw, Lord Amburley's entrance. Turning her head fractionally so that she could observe the doorway out of the corner of her eye, she saw that he was lounging near the door, apparently engrossed in discussion. She clenched her hands together in her lap to stop them from shaking.

Let him not notice us, she prayed silently, and if he does, I will *not* blush. Heavens, why cannot I have more self-control? What can it be about that man that oversets me so? He may be used to intimidating others, but I refuse to let him do so to me.

Trying to hide her confusion, she sipped gingerly at her champagne flute.

'Miss Winstanley,' said the well-remembered voice immediately behind her, 'how delightful to meet you again—' Isabella started and turned, only to find that he was clearly addressing Sophia, not herself '—I beg your pardon,' he corrected himself, 'I should have noticed that both Misses Winstanley were present. Miss Sophia, I hope you are well after your ordeal on the North Road? Are you fixed in London for the Season?'

Sophia answered with commendable self-possession that she was. A short, polite exchange ensued, after which Lord Amburley quickly withdrew. Sophia visibly relaxed.

Isabella noted that his lordship had not enquired after 'Winny', nor had he favoured her with any further conversation at all. She concluded that he had not given her another thought. Unaccountably, she felt piqued.

'Lord Amburley is not much given to light conversation, it seems,' she said softly to Sophia. 'Perhaps that is just as well, in the circumstances.'

'I am glad he is gone,' confided Sophia. 'There is something about his eyes that frightens me. I felt as if he could read my very thoughts.'

Isabella's eyes widened in sudden recognition—for that was exactly how she had felt earlier, at the pianoforte. Then, she had not been able to put it into words. Now…now she had to admit that Lord Amburley would be a very dangerous man to cross.

Chapter Four

While society ladies were sleeping away the exertions of their late night, Lord Amburley was much occupied. He had never lost the soldier's habit of rising early, though nowadays he used the time to exercise his horses rather than to inspect his troops. He revelled in the solitary beauty of the park and the freedom he enjoyed there in the early morning. Later in the day, there were always too many prying eyes for his comfort—the rigid etiquette of the *ton* sat very uneasily on the shoulders of the man of action that he had been.

It was a beautiful, late spring morning, but Amburley barely noticed the birdsong or the budding trees. The huge grey he rode seemed to be itching to gallop across the fresh, dewy grass but was held to a sedate walk by an iron hand. The horse tossed his head in protest.

Lord Amburley was still in Sir Thomas's drawing-room, listening to a heart-stoppingly beautiful voice—and worrying at the riddle of the woman behind it. He had observed her closely while she sang. She was remarkably handsome—her glorious golden hair and her glowing complexion were a revelation to him. Only those unforgettable grey-green eyes confirmed her double identity—and her duplicity. She had been totally in control, too, until she caught sight of him. From then on, her agitation—and Miss Sophia's—had been apparent, though she had masked it well in the supper room. A good actress, he supposed.

But what—in truth—was she? On the road, he had met a poor relation with a sharp tongue and more concern for poor Jonah than for polite behaviour. Now, she was transformed into a lady of the *ton*. One guise must be false, of course—and, remembering her guilty reactions of the previous evening, he knew which it must be.

None the less, he found he could not help admiring her. She had more than beauty—she had spirit. No shrinking violet she, in spite of what she was. And yet, her inexcusable behaviour must surely be condemned by any right-thinking man?

The grey shook his head again, more forcefully. 'All right, old fellow. You've made your point. You think I'm good for nothing this morning, don't you? Well, we'll see about that.' He let the horse have his head. The grey needed to shake the fidgets out of his legs. If only Amburley's own concerns could be so simply resolved.

Around ten o'clock, while Lord Amburley was partaking of a light breakfast in his rented house in Jermyn Street, Mr Lewiston was announced. 'Good God, George, you are up betimes,' exclaimed his lordship, waving his friend to a chair. 'I have not known you to emerge before noon, unless there was a prize-fight to attend. What brings you here at this hour?'

'I have some news,' replied Lewiston. 'I must

tell you that I encountered Miss Winstanley yesterday, quite by chance. You recall the young lady we rescued on the North Road? Well, it was she. And I have discovered her direction in London. Quite wonderful luck! I mean to call on her today. Will you accompany me?'

Lord Amburley did not immediately reply. 'Did you, indeed? And was she still in looks?'

'Indeed she was. She looked quite lovely. And so animated, more so than before, I fancy. I think that that dowdy companion we met up north had a malign influence on her. Miss Winstanley seemed in much brighter spirits without her louring presence.'

'Miss Winstanley was alone?' asked Lord Amburley sharply.

'Of course not,' snapped Mr Lewiston. 'She was accompanied by a distant relation—a Miss Isabella Winstanley. She is much older than Miss Sophia and a perfectly proper chaperon. Though I should perhaps warn you that she is a most elegant female herself, not beautiful exactly, but certainly striking.'

Lord Amburley raised an eyebrow. Isabella

Winstanley was much more than striking, surely? But that was not a subject for discussion with Lewiston. 'And what has become of the poor companion? "Winny", was it not?'

'I have not the least notion. In any case, what has she to say to anything? You are not about to have another attack of philanthropy, are you, Leigh?'

'No. Merely curious.' Lord Amburley busied himself with the coffee-pot as he spoke. 'Tell me about your encounter, including the distant cousin.'

'There is little more to tell. Miss Winstanley—Miss Sophia Winstanley, I mean—almost collided with me outside Florette's. We exchanged a few words. Miss Sophia introduced me to her companion, and then she told me she was staying with Lady Wycham in Hill Street. Lady Wycham is her godmother, you know.'

'Well, no—in fact, I don't know her ladyship, I'm afraid,' responded his lordship flippantly.

'Sometimes, Leigh, you are quite exasperating. I did not expect you to *know* Lady Wycham, dammit; I was simply explaining how things are. If you'd just let me finish…'

'Oh. Is there more?' His lordship sat back, calmly drinking his coffee.

Lewiston continued doggedly. 'Kenley has told me all about the Misses Winstanley. Your man Peveridge was right about her being an heiress. Apparently Lady Wycham is very well-to-do, and Miss Winstanley is her nearest relative. She is expected to inherit everything. I dare say she will be the catch of the Season—beauty, breeding and a fortune into the bargain.'

'With Kenley involved, she will certainly become the centre of attraction—he is a gossip-monger of the first order. I have never understood why he spoils his own chances of winning heiresses by spreading the news all over London. After all, everyone knows he's mortgaged to the hilt. But you mean to be first in line yourself, I collect?'

Lewiston glowered in response. 'I have no need of her fortune, as you know perfectly well. I mean only to further my acquaintance with her and, perhaps, to warn her about some of those who may have mercenary motives.'

This was serious, Amburley realised. And there was an edge in Lewiston's tone that suggested… 'I trust you do not include me in that category, do you, George?'

Lewiston laughed. 'Why, no, of course not. I know you are not hanging out after an heiress for a wife…or indeed any wife at all, as far as I can see. And even if you were, I doubt you would choose someone of Miss Winstanley's tender years. The cousin, now, might be more to your liking. I'd say she is past five-and-twenty, but she is very well-looking, none the less. I gather she is a poor relation of some kind, though, and totally dependent on Lady Wycham's generosity, so you couldn't really afford to—' Lewiston broke off at Amburley's dark frown. 'What is the matter, Leigh?'

'I will thank you not to interfere in my private affairs, George. I know you mean well… However, what is important at present is that I prevent you from making a complete ass of yourself in this case.' Lewiston gave an audible gasp. 'As I said, an ass,' repeated his lordship. 'You clearly did not look closely at Miss Isabella Winstanley. If you had, you would have recognised the "malign" companion of our earlier encounter.' Lewiston now looked as if he had received a blow in the solar plexus.

'I chanced to meet both ladies at Lady Bridge's soirée last night,' continued Lord Amburley evenly. 'Miss "Winny" is attempting to pass herself off as a lady of fortune, no doubt in the hope of catching a husband. Your Miss Sophia, probably abetted by Lady Wycham, has clearly put quite some investment into her companion's appearance, for she appeared as a very fine lady indeed. Miss "Winny's" manners are irreproachable, of course, but then that is often the last resort of the impoverished. It's a pity she is indulging in such a shameful masquerade. She would have been better to take honest employment as a governess. She is certainly well qualified for that. She plays and sings delightfully.'

Lewiston put his cup down with a clatter. 'I don't believe it,' he gasped.

'What other explanation can you offer?' countered his lordship grimly. 'We both met Miss "Winny". There can be no doubt of her lowly station in life. Unless I am mistaken in my identification of her as Miss Isabella—and I assure you I am not—there can be no other explanation. Your Miss Sophia is not only rich, frivolous and spoilt, she is also prepared to perpetrate a disreputable fraud upon you and other unsuspecting gentlemen of the *ton*. I have to say I am not surprised. Heiresses tend to have little regard for morality.'

He rose from the table and strode to the window, frowning out on to the busy street. 'I see that you doubt me. It is understandable, perhaps, that you think my judgement has been swayed by my own experience of society ladies. However, once you have paid your respects in Hill Street and looked upon Miss Isabella Winstanley with new eyes, you will doubt no longer, I promise you.'

'I am sure you are wrong, Amburley,' said Lewiston coldly, making to rise from his chair, 'and I shall take pleasure in telling you so, as soon as I may. Such a delightful and well-bred girl as Miss Sophia would never be party to so base a deception. It is not possible.'

'As you wish,' replied Amburley calmly. 'But since my opinion cannot be put to the test for some hours yet, let us turn to happier pursuits. I was intending to take a turn in the ring at Jackson's parlour this morning. Will you join me? It might improve your temper to plant me a facer.'

'No doubt it would, if I could do it,' admitted Lewiston, forced into unwilling laughter, 'but I know very well that I cannot. You are much too skilled for me, and I prefer not to suffer your left again, thank you. I will gladly accompany you, though.'

Good humour temporarily restored, they left for Gentleman Jackson's boxing parlour.

Although Mr Lewiston's dress was the height of fashion and his coat owed its immaculate fit to the artistry of Weston, he nevertheless looked nothing out of the common way by comparison with the tall and imposing figure of Lord Amburley at his side. Mr Lewiston kept fingering his cravat—a mathematical that he had laboured over for nearly two hours. It felt too tight. 'I think, perhaps, we should not go in, Leigh,' he suggested, tugging at it yet again.

'Do you tell me you do not care to catch Miss Sophia in her outrageous behaviour, George?'

'What? Oh, heavens, no! This cravat of mine. It's not, I fear, quite what I should like. Perhaps I should—' At that moment, the great door swung open to reveal the uncompromising stare of Lady Wycham's butler. Retreat became impossible.

Lady Wycham greeted them amicably from her place on the sofa in the blue drawing-room. 'Sophia has told me all about your gallant rescue, Mr Lewiston. Believe me, we are most grateful to you both.'

'It was nothing out of the ordinary, ma'am, I assure you.' Mr Lewiston blushed. 'I was glad to be of service,' he added with a smile for Sophia, sitting beside Lady Wycham.

The elder Miss Winstanley was seated on

the other side of the room, entertaining another guest. Mr Lewiston could hear her voice fairly clearly, but was unable to study her face without turning round. Surely this voice was different—lighter, younger?

After a few minutes, Lady Wycham asked Sophia to present Mr Lewiston to those other callers with whom he was unacquainted. 'Forgive me if I do not rise to make the introductions myself, sir. I am afraid I am no longer as spry as I once was.' While Lord Amburley, looking faintly amused, remained in conversation with Lady Wycham, Mr Lewiston accompanied Sophia to the window where Sophia performed the introductions, first to Miss Isabella Winstanley, with the reminder that they were 'distant cousins, you will recall', and then to the Earl of Gradely, who bowed and left.

Mr Lewiston appraised Miss Winstanley with some care. She was the same height, pretty much, he admitted, but 'Winny' had been thin, while this lady, though slim, was elegantly formed. No. Amburley *must* be wrong.

'Is this your first visit to London, Mr

Lewiston?' enquired Isabella, looking into his face and determined to maintain the bright, youthful character that had successfully deceived him so far.

He did not immediately reply. For a moment, Isabella fancied his mind was elsewhere. She hastened to fill the silence. 'Have you visited Westminster Abbey since you arrived in London, sir?' she said quickly. 'I assure you it is a magnificent edifice and repays a journey. Sophia and I attended divine service there on Sunday last. It was truly moving. The music in particular was most beautiful.'

Mr Lewiston looked suddenly nonplussed. He stammered a little as he made to answer Isabella. Then he paused for a moment, as if trying to collect his wits, before finally responding to Isabella's inconsequential conversation in much the same vein. When Lord Amburley strolled over to join them, some minutes later, the conversation was still centred on such delights of London as might properly be discussed before ladies.

Mr Lewiston tried to bring his friend into

the discussion. 'You must have seen all the sights, of course, Leigh?'

'Too many years ago,' agreed Lord Amburley, making no attempt to include Isabella in his remarks. 'I am more familiar now with the great churches of Madrid than of London, I fear. I shall be forced to reacquaint myself with them, now the war is finally over.'

Isabella was incensed. She determined that she would no longer be ignored by this arrogant man. She would force him to acknowledge her. 'Were you many years in the Peninsula, my lord?' she asked innocently.

'I joined Wellesley in eighteen ten, ma'am,' he replied tersely, directing a stern gaze at Isabella.

She swallowed, refusing to be intimidated. 'And your family was content for you to go? I fancied it was more usual for the heir to kick his heels at home, and that only younger sons joined the colours. I collect your parents did not share the received opinion?'

'No, ma'am, you are mistaken,' he rejoined sharply. 'The heir did indeed remain at home. I was the younger son merely, and required to make my own way in life. I inherited the title only in eighteen twelve, on the death of my elder brother.'

Isabella paled with anger at his condescending manner. How dare he? He had purposely made her simple question sound impertinent. 'Did you leave the army then, sir?' she continued calmly, refusing to be daunted by his hard eyes.

'No, ma'am. I remained until Boney was sent to Elba.'

'Even then, he was afire to be off again when Boney escaped,' interposed Mr Lewiston, ingenuously, 'and would have gone, had it not been for Lady Amburley's entreaties.'

'You allow yourself too much latitude in interpreting my motives, George,' returned his lordship, with a generous smile that softened his features markedly. In that moment, he seemed to Isabella to reveal a character totally different from the hard, taciturn man she had judged him to be. 'My mother's wishes happened to coincide with my duty. I was not in a position to quit the estates again, however much I might have been tempted.'

'But you have yielded to temptation now, my lord, have you not, in coming to London?' Without pause for thought, Isabella had decided that, if he would condemn her for impertinence, she would give him cause. She fixed an innocent smile on her lips.

Lord Amburley turned back to Isabella and surveyed her slowly. It was exactly the same calculating look he had given to 'Winny' on their encounter at the Bell inn. Then suddenly, he laughed. '*Touché*, ma'am. I have indeed yielded to the delights of the London Season. Though, before you reproach me further—' Isabella lowered her eyes, suddenly conscious of the impropriety of her outburst '—I should reassure you that my estates are now in good enough order to be able to survive without my ministrations for a month or two.'

Isabella raised her gaze again to discover that he was now laughing at her. Infamous! Her earlier embarrassment was replaced by righteous anger. She must—and would—find the means of repaying him in his own coin… and soon.

* * *

The door had hardly shut behind the two men, when Lewiston launched into a slightly incoherent recital of the stages of his enlightenment. 'What the devil do they mean by entertaining Gradely? He's the worst sort of fortune-hunter. Puts me in mind of some ravening beast, waiting to prey on the innocent and helpless. If *he* should make her an offer…'

Amburley waited patiently for the tirade to end before gently steering his friend back to the question of Isabella's identity.

'I would not have believed that they were one and the same, but for her eyes. They are a most unusual colour. I noticed that at the inn. But she did not guess that I had rumbled her, I'd swear to that,' Lewiston added, with obvious self-satisfaction, 'so we still hold all the cards.' He paused. 'It's a devilish tricky situation, though, Leigh,' he added uncertainly. 'You are quite justified in saying they have practised a disreputable deception on us, yet I cannot readily believe Miss Sophia is truly guilty. She is such an innocent… In the circumstances,' he continued, after a moment, 'I thought it best to say nothing, at least for the present. To be honest, I wanted time to think.'

'Very wise, George,' agreed Amburley. 'Revenge is a dish best eaten cold.'

'What the devil do you mean, "revenge"?' exclaimed Lewiston. 'What need have I, or you for that matter, to wreak vengeance on that poor girl?'

'Easy, George. Remember that they set out, quite deliberately, to dupe us. Let us consider the situation dispassionately, before we pronounce upon the appropriate retribution. The facts are simple. Miss Sophia Winstanley, the heiress, has a distant cousin, Isabella, also called "Winny". Said cousin is only a poor companion, but has now been dressed to the nines in order to appear as an equal. We do not know why, nor who is responsible for this disreputable scheme, though I must say that it is much more likely to have originated with the rich Miss Winstanley than with the poor relation.' He cut short his companion's attempted defence of Sophia. 'However, I attach the largest part of the blame to the elder Miss Winstanley. A lady of her years and experience should never have consented to such a bird-witted escapade, however tempting the bait. It was always bound to fail.

'By the way, George,' he added, 'I think you owe me an apology, for doubting my ability to detect a fraud.'

Lewiston's jaw dropped momentarily.

'Do not bother to beg my pardon, old fellow,' Amburley said, with a sardonic smile. 'I understand that you are much more concerned about Miss Sophia's feelings than mine.'

'Leigh, you are quite outrageous,' returned his friend. 'Yes, of course you were right. But what are we to do?'

'For the moment, I think, we shall simply wait and observe developments. We could *easily* spread the tale now, of course. Nothing simpler. But I think—not yet. I confess to being intrigued by this potentially disastrous make-believe of theirs. I should like very much to know what occasioned it. Indeed, I intend to find out. Then I shall decide what is best to be done.' He paused. 'I beg your pardon. *You*, of course, will take whatever action you think is right. It is not my place to make decisions on your behalf.'

Lewiston shook his head. 'I have no present intention of betraying them, Leigh. Indeed, I rather think we should not unmask them at all, unless it is clear that mischief is afoot. To be honest with you, I cannot believe it is more than a silly prank.'

'Ladies of Miss "Winny's" age and background should not become involved in pranks,' declared Lord Amburley flatly. 'I may yet bring her to rue it, I dare say. However, I agree that, for the present at least, we should simply watch and wait.'

They turned the corner and approached his lordship's door. 'Are you bidden to the Duchess of Newcombe's ball tomorrow, George?' Lewiston nodded. 'Doubtless *both* the Misses Winstanley will be there. We shall have ample opportunity for spectator sport. It promises to be better than a prize-fight.'

Chapter Five

Sophia awoke early next day, the day of her
first ever ball. She made no attempt to go back
to sleep, scrambling out of bed and into her
dressing-gown without ringing for her new
maid. Then, eyes shining with excitement, she
hurried along the corridor to Isabella's room,
where she knocked briefly and entered,
without waiting for an invitation.

'Isabella, forgive me for…' Her words
trailed off, and she looked at her cousin in astonishment. 'Good God,' she exclaimed,
'whatever are you doing, dressed like that at
this hour?'

Isabella was not best pleased at the interrup-
tion to her plans, nor was she prepared to

indulge Sophia's curiosity. With a stern look, reminiscent of Lady Wycham at her most haughty, she replied sharply that her private business was of no interest to her young cousin.

'But those are the clothes you wore to visit the orphans,' protested Sophia, refusing to be silenced. 'If anyone were to see you, there would be a scandal. Surely—'

'Sophia,' interrupted Isabella sharply, 'I shall thank you to allow me to be the judge of what I may or may not do. And where I go is of no interest to anyone but myself.' She turned to her maid. 'Have you my gloves, Mitchell? Thank you.' Drawing them on, she spoke more gently to Sophia. 'Now go back to bed, my dear. It is much too early for you to be about. Even on the day of your first ball,' she added, with a slight smile. 'Say nothing to anyone about what has happened here, even to me. And ask no questions. They will not be answered.' With a quick nod, Isabella opened the door and was gone.

It was still quite early when Sophia entered the breakfast room. Even so, Isabella was before her, now dressed in a light morning dress of cream cambric trimmed with green velvet ribbons and calmly pouring coffee. Sophia's mouth formed an *O*, but no sound came out.

'Good morning, Sophia dear,' beamed Isabella. 'I hope you slept well, for it will be a long night, I fancy. Will you have some coffee? Or shall I ring for chocolate?' Isabella was quite determined that no allusion to their earlier encounter would be permitted, but Sophia surrendered with only token resistance.

As the day wore on, Sophia's excitement visibly increased, until Isabella at last managed to persuade her to rest in the late afternoon. Relaxing on her own chaise-longue, Isabella abandoned herself to thoughts of her own attempted début, nearly ten years before. Then, with her father still alive, she had been viewed as a potential heiress, but it had not brought happiness, merely a train of grasping fortune-hunters. She shuddered at the memory. She and her brother had been wise to pretend that everything had been left to him.

Better to be an old maid than to be pursued for money alone. Isabella had no regrets, now, about pretending to be dependent on Aunt Jemima. Her life was her own, and she could live it in comfort, even though she would die a spinster.

She smiled with sad irony at the memory of her come-out. White and pastels were all very well for brunettes like Sophia, but pale-complexioned blondes tended to look merely insipid. And gentlemen were unlikely to be enamoured of a lady who looked them straight in the eye, or worse, overtopped them when she rose from her seat. Lord Amburley, now, was a much better partner for a tall lady. She would not even reach his shoulder. Dancing with such a tall gentleman—waltzing, perhaps?—might be delightful. She would put her hand on his shoulder, where the warmth of his body could be felt through the fine cloth of his coat. His gloved hand would rest in the middle of her back—perhaps even against her bare skin— while he guided her firmly through the throng of dancers. She would feel his warm breath on her face as he complimented her on the lightness of her dancing. His dark eyes would…

Isabella checked herself severely before her musings advanced even further into the realm of daydreams. A man should not become the subject of missish fancies just because he happened to be rather taller than the ordinary. He certainly had little, other than height, to recommend him. Unless, perhaps, that underlying sense of humour which had betrayed itself when she taunted him? Resolutely, Isabella put his lordship from her thoughts and rose to begin her preparations for the ball.

Madame Florette's jade creation was a wonder of expensive simplicity, allowing the beautiful shot-silk overdress to fall in graceful folds from a high waistline below a deeply scooped *décolletage*. The neckline and the tiny sleeves were edged with the aquamarine satin of the underdress. The open edges of the overdress were similarly trimmed and finished with tiny aquamarine satin buttons and loops.

Isabella was more pleased than she was prepared to admit. She had almost persuaded herself that she was now past the age when a lady hoped to be admired, and that she should settle quietly into spinsterhood. But faced with the fairy-tale gown, she knew a moment of youthful excitement ill-suited to an 'ageing spinster'. Let us see whether he can ignore me now, came the unprompted thought.

Soon Isabella was standing in front of the pier glass, critically assessing her reflection. Mitchell's new way with her hair was most becoming, she decided. The rather looser knot of curls on top made her look very young. And Mitchell's suggestion of aquamarines was right too, mere trumpery though they might be.

Answering a light tap at the door, Mitchell admitted Lady Wycham's maid. 'Can you come to my lady, please, miss? She's took bad.'

Isabella immediately hurried to Lady Wycham's apartments. She found her great-aunt lying on her bed, partly dressed for the ball, but with a silk dressing-gown over all. She was very pale, and a hand was pressed to her throat.

'Oh, Aunt,' gasped Isabella, 'is it one of your spasms? Shall I send for Dr Ridley?'

'I shall be well again in a moment. Parsons should not have fetched you.' She looked severely at her faithful maid, but it had no visible effect. 'Only I fear I may not be able to accompany you tonight.'

'But we shall stay here with you,' exclaimed Isabella. 'We cannot possibly go when you are unwell.'

'Nonsense, Isabella. I am quite recovered now.' She attempted, unsuccessfully, to sit up. 'Perhaps not quite enough to accompany you, but certainly enough to be left in Parsons' care. I *insist* that you take Sophia to the ball. You must simply make my excuses to the Duchess.'

Isabella was torn between her duty to her aunt and her desire not to disappoint Sophia. Her indecision must have been apparent.

'Isabella,' said Lady Wycham curtly, 'what *is* the matter with you? Have you windmills in your head, child? I take it you will do as I ask?'

'Dear Aunt, I should rather stay here to see to your comfort—' Lady Wycham drew breath sharply, as a preliminary to another biting retort '—but I know that you will not tolerate it. So, if you insist, I shall chaperon Sophia to the Duchess's ball.'

'I do wish it, my dear. Thank you. I know I can trust you to ensure she behaves as she ought.' A sudden look of concern shadowed her face. 'You will make sure she does not waltz?'

Isabella smiled reassuringly. 'Have no fear, Aunt. I have been drilling Sophia for weeks on the subject of the waltz. She knows she may not dance it until she has received permission at Almack's. And that is one rule she will not dare to break.'

Lady Wycham gave a sigh of relief and smiled lovingly at Isabella. 'You look quite beautiful in that gown, my dear child. Do not waste your looks among the chaperons tonight. Promise me that you, too, will dance.'

Isabella knew that, if she was to be Sophia's chaperon, it would hardly be proper for her to dance. Chaperons did not do so. A small voice whispered that chaperons did not dress in gowns of shot silk either, but she pushed that thought to the back of her mind, while she grappled with Lady Wycham's request. She could not refuse without upsetting the old lady, so she agreed, consoling herself with the thought that, at her age, she was unlikely to be asked to dance at all.

Having made her curtsy and Lady Wycham's excuses to the Duchess, Isabella led the way into the huge ballroom, where thousands of brightly coloured flowers were already beginning to wilt in the heat of the banks of candles. The ballroom was full to overflowing with beautiful ladies and elegant gentlemen, some in scarlet regimentals, and the noise of their conversation was so loud that it was barely possible to hear the orchestra. Sophia was soon laughing and chattering in the midst of a gathering of young people. Isabella watched contentedly for a few moments, prior to joining the chaperons at the side of the ballroom.

She was startled out of her reverie by a voice in her ear. 'Miss Winstanley, do you tell me you are become a chaperon? And do you plan to assume the turban too?'

'Why, Lady Sefton,' laughed Isabella, 'how

you have found me out. I am guilty, I fear, though not yet of the turban. My aunt, you must know, is rather poorly this evening, and we could not deny Sophia her first ball.'

'I see. You are both very generous. Which is she?'

'The dark girl in white, with the pink roses and the lace shawl.'

Lady Sefton's sharp gaze assessed Sophia. 'Hmm. Yes. I dare say she will do very well. What is her background?'

Isabella felt the need to dissemble a little here, in front of one of the influential patronesses of Almack's. Lady Sefton believed Isabella to be Lady Wycham's pensioner. It would not do for her to suspect that Sophia was penniless, too—especially as, in Sophia's case, it was true. 'We are distant cousins, ma'am. She is from the Yorkshire branch of the Winstanleys. Her father's seat is Locke House, near York.' Isabella hoped she had said enough to divert Lady Sefton from the uncomfortable subject of Sophia's expectations.

'A pretty chit, indeed. I like her style. Shall

I send vouchers for Almack's for you?' Lady Sefton smiled, clearly conscious of the prize she was offering. 'We never did have the pleasure of seeing you grace the floor there, my dear, which is a pity.'

'You are very kind, ma'am. Thank you, on behalf of Sophia. I know she will be delighted. And if my dear aunt is well enough to accompany us,' she added with a twinkle, 'I may yet avoid the turban.'

'But you must not await a visit to Almack's to dance. Why, you look radiant tonight, my dear Miss Winstanley, and such looks must not be wasted on the dowagers.' She made an unmistakable signal to someone out of Isabella's line of vision and, hardly a heartbeat later, Lord Amburley stood before them, bowing to Lady Sefton with a quizzical smile on his face.

'Miss Winstanley,' announced Lady Sefton, 'may I present to you Lord Amburley as a suitable partner for this dance?'

Isabella knew a moment of indescribable panic. Dear God, why did she have to choose *him*? She forced herself to curtsy to his lordship, while racking her brains for a suitable means of refusing him. She could not possibly dance with him—touch him… 'You are most kind, ma'am,' she stammered eventually, 'but I am truly unable to dance this evening, since I am here as chaperon to my young cousin.' With growing embarrassment, she noted how Amburley's jaw tightened at her rebuff, while he raised his glass to survey her slowly from head to foot. His incredulity was obvious. Some chaperon she!

Lady Sefton, however, was not so easily diverted from her object. 'Nonsense,' she protested. 'Your aunt's indisposition should not prevent your enjoyment of the evening. I insist you dance. And if it sets your mind at rest, I will keep an eye on that chit of yours. You will oblige me in this, Amburley?'

Lord Amburley bowed his acquiescence and offered his hand to lead Isabella into the set that was just forming. Isabella stared at his gloved fingers. Her stomach turned molten, generating a wave of heat in her lower body.

For a moment, they stood in embarrassed silence. Then Isabella forced herself to put her hand in his, praying he would not notice the slight quivering of her fingers. He guided her to her place with a light, firm grip. She detected the faintest hint of a tangy cologne when he moved away to stand opposite her. The warmth from his hand seemed to have invaded her whole arm, which tingled strangely.

She knew she should speak, but she could not even look at him.

Lord Amburley's good manners prevailed. 'Miss Sophia looks charmingly this evening, ma'am. She does you credit.'

His routine politeness broke the spell that had gripped her. She was mistress of herself once more—and horrified at her momentary loss of control. 'Thank you, sir.' She paused uncertainly, searching for a safe topic, for it was clearly her turn. 'Is Mr Lewiston here this evening, perhaps? Sophia would be glad to meet him again, I think.'

'He is before you, ma'am,' said his lordship. 'Look towards the group around Miss Sophia when you come down the set. He is already among her bevy of admirers, begging for her hand for this dance.'

A moment later, she saw that this was true. A host of young men was flocking around Sophia. Isabella wondered idly how it was that Sophia had become quite so successful, quite so quickly. But she could not pursue that puzzling thought while engaged on the dance floor—especially not when partnered by Lord Amburley.

Above all, she must not lose control again.

His voice broke into her thoughts. 'And may I add, ma'am, that Miss Sophia is not the only Winstanley lady to attract admiring looks tonight?'

Isabella was surprised to find that his words did not overset her. She was blushing a little, she was sure, but she was still in control. For the first time that evening, she dared to look into his face. The disdain he had shown before did not seem to be there. His dark eyes—the colour of rich chocolate, she decided—seemed to have lost the hardness she had flinched from on every one of their previous encounters.

Obviously, he could be absolutely charming when he chose. But why should he be? Not simply to oblige Lady Sefton, surely? No. It was more than charm. There was something indefinable in his look, too. Humour, perhaps? Or was it pity for an old maid? Please, no. That would be too much. She knew well enough that she was destined to end her days as a spinster, but no one—no one at all—would be allowed to pity her for it. She could feel the anger rising in her throat at the very thought.

The movements of the dance parted them then, for which she was thankful. It gave her time to bring her tumbling thoughts into some kind of order. For the next twenty minutes, nothing more was said, and Isabella took care to avoid his eyes. She breathed a silent sigh of relief when, at last, the dance was over.

'Thank you, ma'am,' he bowed. 'It is quite delightful to dance with a lady who has such stimulating conversation.'

Oh, how dare he? Now, he was roasting her in tones of studied politeness. 'You are too kind, sir,' she replied quickly, mimicking his manner. 'One has little chance to exercise one's wit in country dances when one is so often parted from one's partner. It is important to save one's breath for the exertions of the figures, lest one fail to do them justice. Do you not agree?'

Lord Amburley smiled dangerously. 'A veritable hit, ma'am. I collect I should not fence with you, for I am like to be bested. However—' he raised the dance card at her wrist '—I fancy there may be an opportunity later for a lengthier interchange. I shall look forward to it.' He scribbled on her card, bowed again, and left her.

Before Isabella could check to see what he had done, Sophia returned, pink and a little breathless, but glowing with animation. No wonder all the young men had been milling round her. It had clearly been right not to deny her this ball.

'You were dancing with Lord Amburley.' Sophia seized Isabella's dance card before she could reply. 'And he has taken the waltz for his second,' she exclaimed. 'I am not at all surprised, for you look truly beautiful tonight. Now that they know you will dance, all the other gentlemen will be queuing to fill your card. It is strange that Mr Lewiston should be so wrong, however. He told me Lord Amburley does not dance.' She lowered her voice to a conspiratorial whisper as she scanned the ballroom. 'His lordship has disappeared,' she said. 'He is most often to be found in the card-room, I believe.'

'Sophia, that is the worst kind of gossip,' bit out Isabella, in a sharp undertone. 'You must not repeat such things.' There was no opportunity to pursue the matter, however, for Sophia was soon led off to the floor by another young cavalier.

Sophia's predictions proved right. Isabella's dance card was soon so full that she felt a pang of conscience at neglecting her duties as chaperon. However, she reassured herself that she could still keep a wary eye on Sophia from the floor and, since she was in no way troubled by the cut of the young men who partnered her charge, there was unlikely to be any cause for concern.

Just before supper, Lord Amburley reappeared to lead Isabella into the waltz. This time she was ready for him. 'You did not give me a moment to tell you, sir,' she said quickly, 'that I do not dance the waltz.'

He quirked an eyebrow but said nothing, fixing his direct gaze on her face.

'Forgive me. It is…you see…'

He continued to stare.

Isabella's embarrassment was finally converted to anger by his steadfast refusal to make the polite response that any reasonable man would have offered. 'I cannot dance the waltz, my lord, because I am here as chaperon to my cousin and *she* is not yet permitted to do so. If you had asked my permission before writing on my card, I should have told you so at the time.' She knew that her sharp tone had betrayed her annoyance. Damn the man! Why could she not keep her temper under control where he was concerned?

Lord Amburley still said nothing, but raised her dance card to peruse it. 'And what a pity that your card is now full, so that there are no others for which I may ask the favour of your hand. I am quite at a stand.' His piercing glance suggested he was nothing of the kind. His next words proved it. 'But you will, I am sure, favour me with your company, if I invite you to sit here while the others waltz? May I procure you a glass of champagne?'

Chapter Six

Isabella perched rather uncomfortably towards one end of the sofa. His lordship lounged at the other, apparently quite at his ease, watching her. He had removed his gloves and stretched his free arm nonchalantly along the back of the sofa so that his fingers were within inches of her bare shoulder. She could almost feel the heat of his skin. She wrenched her eyes away. She appeared—she hoped—much calmer than she felt. Inside, she was a turmoil of conflicting emotions—though anger, indignation and embarrassment were the only ones she was prepared to put a name to. She had been adroitly manoeuvred by Lord Amburley into a distinctly improper speech and then into an awkward, though mercifully public, tête-à-tête. She had much rather have been almost anywhere than sitting so close to him, wondering what his next move would be—for she still found it impossible to predict his actions, or to gauge his motives.

Steeling herself, she resolved not to help him to begin a conversation. Since he had desired her company, he must make the first move.

'I am sorry to learn that Lady Wycham is indisposed. A sudden turn, I collect?' He was regarding her ball-gown pointedly.

Isabella refused to lose control of her temper again. 'Lady Wycham suffers from spasms, sir, which come on without warning,' she responded stiffly. That should surely be enough for any gentleman to acknowledge the need to change the subject.

Apparently unabashed at her words, he bent his quizzical gaze on her. Clearly he was wondering why she had come to the ball at all. What kind of hard-hearted woman did he consider her to be? Isabella could feel her anger rising again, like bile in her throat. She would not demean herself to make excuses for her behaviour. Let him judge her as he chose. She deliberately returned his frank gaze.

For several moments, neither moved. Then, since he was clearly not going to speak, Isabella was forced, in common politeness, to turn the conversation herself. 'I did not see you dance again, my lord. Indeed, I concluded that you had been so *stimulated* by my conversation that you had left to seek stimulation elsewhere.' She permitted herself a slight smile.

He quirked that infernal eyebrow again, surveying her coolly. 'You are right, but only in part, ma'am. I certainly had no intention of missing this *waltz* with you. But, in the meantime, I did retire to the card-room. It is not my habit to dance with young and foolish girls.'

Isabella bridled. How dared he? 'It is true that I cut my wisdoms years ago, sir, though it is unhandsome of you to remind me of it. Am I also to take it that you do not class me as foolish?'

'There can be only one polite answer to that question, ma'am. And yet I hesitate to give it.

Your having asked it at all does suggest a certain…shall we say, lack of forethought?'

However indignant she might be at his high-handed behaviour—and she was—Isabella had to admit the justice of that rebuke. An involuntary gurgle of laughter escaped her, as she realised the absurdity of her position.

'That's better,' he said, with a sudden smile that made her heart begin to race. 'Anger makes your eyes sparkle magnificently, but I think I prefer the twinkle of laughter. You should laugh more often.'

'Oh, how dare you say so! You are outrageous!' But, in spite of herself, she smiled still.

'Indeed I am, ma'am. But it was worth it to see that radiant smile. It outshines even the golden radiance of your gown.'

Now *that* really was too much, even for him. 'Come, my lord, let us speak of other things. I am neither young enough nor foolish enough to listen to such flummery. Tell me—' she clasped her hands demurely in her lap '—what do they play in the card-room?'

'Piquet. And whist, I believe. Do you play?' He seemed genuinely interested.

'A little. Especially piquet. My late father enjoyed it very much, particularly towards the end of his life, when more active pursuits were denied him. We were used to play almost every day. Lady Wycham enjoys a game too, although she is not as skilled as my father was.' She caught herself up then. Now, why had she volunteered so much information to him about her private life? Something to do with his quiet way of listening, perhaps? But dangerous, and to be avoided. She must take more care. She had not the least idea of what his object might be, but she was sure that he had singled her out for some purpose of his own.

'It sounds as if you are a practised player, ma'am. Do you care to enter the lists against me?' He favoured her with a half-smile and that quirked eyebrow again.

Every line of that sternly handsome face challenged her to accept. Every instinct of her own urged her to run. In her heart, she could admit she was afraid to meet his challenge—

but her pride would not allow her to let him see her weakness. She refused to let him triumph over her, even in such a small thing as a game of cards.

'By all means,' she replied smoothly, determined not to lose the advantage to him this time. 'And the stakes?'

Her prompt response had clearly surprised him. After a moment, he said, 'The usual stakes would not be right for such an encounter. May I suggest—?'

'Indeed, sir, I have no wish to offer you less than any other opponent. And I play to win, I assure you. Why do we not play for the same stakes as you were playing for earlier, in the card-room here?'

'Do you know what they were, ma'am?'

'No. But I feel sure they would be equally appropriate for a match between your lordship and myself. May we agree on that?' She was perversely pleased to see that he was frowning now. No doubt, he was more used to dealing with demure damsels who hung on his every word.

'First I must tell you, Miss Winstanley, that

Gradely and I were playing for a guinea a point. I believe that we—'

Isabella stretched out a hand to stop him in mid-sentence. 'Forgive my interrupting you, sir. I collect you were about to propose some lesser stake for our game. Pray do not embarrass me by suggesting any such thing.' She was further gratified to see him flush slightly at that. 'I should like to play for the stakes you mentioned. Are we agreed?'

That hard, calculating look had returned to his eyes. 'I do not pretend to understand you, ma'am, but at your insistence I will agree. I warn you that there will be no quarter given.'

'No, sir, none. Nor is any expected.'

'If you will favour me with your company at supper, ma'am, we can agree the time and place for this contest of Titans.'

'You are too kind.' She threw him a look that suggested she thought him quite otherwise, but he did not react at all to her veiled sarcasm. 'Unfortunately, I already have a supper partner for this evening. As to the venue…' she paused, mentally reviewing her calendar '…I believe Lady Morrissey's soirée on Friday would serve very well. Provided, of course, that we allow any onlookers to believe we are playing for chicken-stakes.'

'As I would be more than happy to do,' he countered hotly. 'Why do you insist on such stakes?'

'It must be in the blood, do you not think? Excuse me, here is my supper partner.' She rose and, with the slightest bow to his lordship, turned to take the arm of an elderly gentleman who led her off towards the supper room.

It was some moments before his lordship could gather his scattered thoughts. She had surprised him again. And his admiration had grown, in spite of his best efforts to condemn her. There was something… He shook his head in vexation. He did not understand her at all. But he could not but be impressed by her cool poise in the face of such enormous financial risks. She must feel very sure of herself—and yet he knew that there was not the least possibility of her matching his skill with the cards, since he was widely acknowledged as one of the finest players in London. What's more, she could easily lose a fortune.

He explained as much to his friend Lewiston who, frustrated in his desire to escort Sophia to supper, had come to join him on the sofa. 'I challenged her to piquet and she insisted, positively insisted, on playing for a guinea a point. She must feel very certain of winning. Even on a single rubber she could lose several years' salary.'

'Perhaps she fuzzes the cards,' suggested Lewiston.

'A female Captain Sharp?'

'Why not? She is trying to foist herself on Society as something she is not. If she cheats in that, may she not also cheat at cards?'

'No, I think not,' responded Lord Amburley immediately, 'not a lady of her breeding. Besides, there is no man alive—or woman— who can cheat me at cards and remain unde- tected. And if you should prove to be right in your suspicions, believe me, I should expose her on the spot.' As he spoke, he felt absolutely certain that he would not be called upon to honour that promise. He did not seek to wonder how he knew.

Lewiston, well aware of his friend's remarkable skill at the table, did not pursue the matter further. He turned the subject instead to something that was obviously much nearer his heart. 'I could not obtain more than one dance with Miss Sophia, no matter how I tried. The news of her expectations seems to have travelled fast. Kenley's doing, probably. Every gazetted fortune-hunter in London is after her. She is such an innocent that she is like to be taken in at every turn.'

'Do not tax yourself about that, my friend. With a duenna as *sharp* as Miss "Winny" to protect her, she will come to no harm. More likely that you impressionable young men will need protection from her.'

'What? That's gammon, Leigh. I am in no danger from Miss Sophia.'

'No, of course not. Young ladies of her stamp look for a title as well as a fortune. You fail to qualify on the first count, even if not on the second.'

'Leigh, I fail to understand you,' Lewiston said tetchily. He seemed to be in no mood for such banter. 'Why is it you can never see any good in females?'

Amburley refused to be ruffled. 'You exaggerate, George,' he drawled. 'I see much good in females who are useful according to their station. It is just the simpering, empty-headed ones I cannot abide.'

'Now it is you who exaggerate. I have seen many an empty-headed piece on your arm over these last months. You seem to have both time and tolerance for *them*.'

'I referred to *ladies*, George, not members of the muslin company. They, however empty-headed, fulfil a role in life. They make no secret, either, of their designs on a man's pocket-book. If the blunt is not forthcoming, then—' he made a gesture as of blowing away a feather '—such *ladies* will be gone too. It is better so, I believe.'

Lewiston looked quite horrified at his

friend's bleak verdict on womankind, but he was too well-mannered to prolong such a discussion, especially at a ball. Raising his champagne glass, he gave a short, forced laugh and said, 'Come, Leigh. Let us drink a toast to your success against Miss "Winny" on Friday.'

Silently they drank. Then, arm in arm, they descended the stairs.

Although it was early morning when the Winstanley ladies returned to Hill Street, Isabella visited her great-aunt before retiring. She found her sleeping peacefully, watched by the faithful Parsons.

'She agreed to take a few drops of laudanum, miss, and she fell asleep around midnight. You'll visit in the morning? She will be agog for news of the ball. Would have stayed awake for your return, if I'd let her.'

Isabella smiled. 'Then I shall not ask you how you *persuaded* her to take the laudanum. You were quite right, of course, but I had better be here early to give her the news. Goodnight, Parsons, and thank you.'

Isabella returned to her own room. Her body was tired—she was not accustomed to dancing so much—but her brain was on fire. Every time she tried to focus her thoughts on Sophia's astonishing success, a hard and handsome male face intruded.

Why on earth had she done it? If he should prove to be the better player, she could easily lose several hundred guineas. Not that the money mattered a jot, of course, to someone in her position. But to lead him to believe she was an inveterate gambler...she must have been out of her mind. Or was it, perhaps, an unconscious desire to demonstrate, by a highly circuitous route, that she was neither poor nor a companion after all? She shook her head. It was impossible to straighten her ravelled thoughts. Why was her peace of mind so affected by what one rather haughty lord thought of her? Why this ungovernable desire to outface him?

I am *not* developing a *tendre* for him, she told herself firmly. He is the last sort of man to attract me. He is far from truly handsome—

and his want of address is lamentable. He hardly ever speaks and, when he does, it is usually to say something outrageous. How could I even begin to like such a man?

Memories of their encounter at the inn crowded in on her. There, he had been equally strange in his manners, but she could now admit that he had proved generous in assisting a poor, plain companion. Truly, the man was a riddle.

Isabella tossed and turned for some hours, unable to exclude Lord Amburley from her thoughts or to resolve her own feelings. Clearly, sleep was impossible so, giving in to the inevitable, she rose and donned her comfortable old riding-habit.

'A brisk ride in the park will blow the cobwebs away,' she replied to Mitchell's suggestion that she return to bed. 'And I promised to visit my dear aunt as soon as she wakes this morning. I cannot be a slug-a-bed today, Mitchell.' Seeing the abigail's concern, she added, 'But if it will please you, I will rest this afternoon. Now, where are my riding gloves?'

Some twenty minutes later, Isabella was

trotting off in the direction of Hyde Park, accompanied by her groom. She felt strangely exhilarated. She told herself it was the combination of early morning air and sunshine on her skin. As she neared the park, the raucous sounds of awakening London receded and the fresh scent of young leaves surrounded her. On such a morning, it was good to be alive.

'I have neglected you shamefully these past two days, Princess,' whispered Isabella, stroking the neck of her big bay mare. Princess twitched her ears in response. 'If every morning is as glorious as this, we shall certainly ride out together, I promise you.' Turning to the groom behind her, Isabella said, 'I am going to give Princess a good gallop this morning. She is much in want of exercise.'

'Are you sure that's wise, Miss Isabella? It's all very well in the country, but ladies don't go galloping in Hyde Park.' He spoke with the familiarity of one who had known her when she sat her first pony.

Isabella smiled generously at him. 'Come, Tom, you have no need to be concerned today.

You can see for yourself that there is no one about. It is much too early. Anyone who might recognise me is at home sleeping off the effects of last night's ball. Shall we race?' She was as animated as a mischievous child enjoying a forbidden treat.

With a sigh of resignation, Tom nodded. 'It'll be no race though, miss, not my old nag against the Princess.'

Recognising the justice of that, Isabella gave the groom a good start, then touched her heel to the mare. The big bay changed almost instantly from gentle amble to powerful gallop. Her long raking strides covered the ground easily and she gained steadily on the groom in front, with Isabella bent low over her neck, urging her on. Isabella was quite unconcerned when her hat slipped and part of her hair came down. There was no time to stop for such trivial matters. Winning was all-important.

Isabella reached the winning post, a large tree, fractionally before Tom. She turned to him, half-dishevelled, her eyes sparkling with laughter and her bosom heaving. 'You were quite right,

Tom,' she gasped. 'Princess is not to be bested. But, ah, what a splendid run. We must do this every morning.' She leant forward in the saddle, clapping her mare's neck. 'Well done, my Princess. I knew you could do it,' she cooed.

Absorbed as she was in communion with her beloved mare, Isabella did not at first see the gentleman on horseback sitting quietly among the trees watching them. At length he stirred his mount to a walk and the movement caught her eye.

Amburley again! Devil the man! He appeared everywhere, especially when she was least prepared for him. Well, on this occasion, she simply did not care. She had been behaving like a hoyden and looked it. Let him take her as she was.

Isabella lifted her chin a little as she turned towards him. Still somewhat short of breath from the race, she hailed him gaily. 'Why, good morning, my lord. I had not thought to meet any of last night's guests so early. You are about betimes.'

Lord Amburley walked his horse forward to

join her, surveying her carefully all the while. Isabella tried to look unconcerned, but was very conscious of her rather shabby green habit and her unkempt appearance. She knew her hair was half-tumbled down her back, but she did not realise how beautiful it looked, glinting like guinea-gold where it caught the early morning sunshine. Nor did she realise that, with her jaunty hat askew and her green eyes sparkling, she had an endearing look of impish youthfulness.

'Well met, Miss Winstanley,' he replied politely, touching his crop to his hat. 'I might say the same of you, might I not?'

'Why, yes, sir. I suppose you might. But I have no intention of pulling caps with you over which of us has the right to be more surprised by this encounter. Such a wonderful morning is not to be so squandered.' Smiling to herself, she rose slightly in her saddle to look round at the beauties of the almost empty park. She felt so wonderfully free this morning. Nothing—and no one—would be allowed to spoil her pleasure.

'I should always give way to a lady in such a discussion,' he returned with a slight bow.

'Thank you, sir. I had not thought to win that bout so easily.' She half-bowed in acknowledgement, looking up at him through her dark lashes.

'There is, however, a small impediment to your complete victory, I fear, ma'am.'

Isabella raised her head and looked him full in the face. His rich chocolate eyes were glinting strangely, but—yet again—she found his expression impossible to read.

'You do not ask about the impediment, ma'am. Very wise, but I shall tell you, none the less. Since I returned from the wars, I have been unable to revert to my lazy old ways. I cannot break the habit of rising with the dawn and, since there is little else to entertain me at such an hour, I exercise my horses in the park.' His expression remained resolutely impassive while he delivered this master-stroke. There might have been a fleeting glimmer of humour in his eyes, but it vanished so quickly that it was impossible to be sure it had ever been there.

Isabella was baffled. The man was a riddle.

She could not begin to divine his motives, even in a mere battle of words. But she was determined not to be bested, even in so trivial an encounter. 'I yield, my lord, immediately,' she said quickly. 'I do hate to see a man struggle so to hide his triumph.'

Lord Amburley's lips twitched a little ruefully at her sharp wit. Then, recovering himself, he commented, 'That is a very fine mare you are riding, Miss Winstanley. Many a gentleman would envy you such a mount.'

'Lady Wycham keeps an excellent stable,' lied Isabella. 'But I doubt Princess is up to your weight,' she added, casting an ironic eye over his tall person and the huge grey he rode. 'She may be fast, but she is a lady's mount.'

'I did not think to ride her myself, ma'am,' he said ruefully. 'I recognise the difficulties of mounting a man of my size.' He ran his gloved hand down the grey's neck. 'Did you enjoy the ball last night?'

Isabella was not one to resort to the usual comments about 'a shocking squeeze'. 'Yes, sir, I did,' she said frankly, 'though I have not danced so much for a very long time.' Behind her, Tom's horse was growing restless. 'Forgive me, I am neglecting the horses. After such a mad gallop, we must walk them.' With a slight bow, she started away.

Lord Amburley urged his grey into a walk also. 'Will you not permit me to ride with you for a space, ma'am? There can be nothing to concern you, surely, accompanied as you are by your groom?'

'I fear that is not quite how some would choose to view the matter, sir,' she said with mock severity. 'It is not usual for single ladies to ride with gentlemen when the park is thus deserted. It would have the appearance of an assignation.'

His lordship continued to walk the grey at her side. 'I promise to keep my distance, lest prying eyes observe and make improper deductions. Would you have me search the bushes?' he added, with a slightly quizzical look.

Isabella burst out laughing. 'I fancy you are trying to roast me again, sir,' she gasped.

'Yes, it is quite outrageous of me, as you

have said before. I plead the same defence. You look splendid when you laugh.' He favoured her with a long, admiring look, which brought so much colour to her cheeks that he immediately offered an apology. 'Forgive me, ma'am, for speaking out of turn. It was not my intention to embarrass you in any way.'

Isabella reddened even more. Heavens, what was she about? Determined to prevent this dangerous conversation from continuing, she swallowed hard and challenged him to a gallop. He agreed, apparently with relief. He did, however, insist on giving her an advantage, to allow for her mare's shorter stride and earlier exertions. For once, Isabella did not attempt to argue.

On this occasion, Princess did not win. The big grey overhauled her easily. Lord Amburley was not even breathing hard by the time Isabella reached the winning post, looking rather more tousled than before.

Pulling off her precariously perched hat and letting the last of her hair tumble down her back, she admitted defeat. 'Even when she is fresh, the Princess could not outpace your grey, sir. We were quite outclassed.'

'You were defeated but not, I think, outclassed, Miss Winstanley,' he conceded. 'You and your mare make a fine pairing.'

Isabella felt herself blushing yet again and quickly made to turn her mount towards the park gates. 'I think I must now be returning to Hill Street, sir, before I am cried a hoyden all over London.' With no little difficulty, she pinned up most of her hair and replaced her hat. She refused to consider how disreputable she must look.

He raised his hat in polite farewell. 'It would be my pleasure, ma'am, if you should again choose to ride in the park unreasonably early.'

Was that an invitation? Isabella was not at all sure what to make of him in this strange mood, but she did know that she would risk her reputation by meeting him again in such a way. Whatever she had earlier suggested to Tom, it must now be forgotten—no matter how tempting the thought…

'It is not my habit to ride quite so early, I fear,

but thank you for your company, none the less. And now, if you will excuse me, sir?' With a genuine smile, she bade him farewell and trotted towards the exit, closely followed by the groom.

His lordship sat motionless astride the big grey, watching her receding back. His dark eyes narrowed as they followed her passage, and a thoughtful frown creased his forehead.

This was a completely different woman from the poor relation—or the enigmatic lady of the *ton*. This Miss Winstanley was utterly captivating, with her frank, open ways and her manifest joy at simply being alive on a beautiful spring day. He found himself wishing that he had not met her at all before today, that he knew nothing of her deceit. The glorious creature who had laughingly raced him across the park was the kind of woman who could haunt a man's dreams.

Chapter Seven

Although still early, it was later than she had planned when Isabella arrived back in Hill Street.

Mitchell took one look at her and briskly set about bringing some order to her hair, muttering darkly as she combed out the tangles. 'Her ladyship is already awake. She has been asking for you,' she chided.

'Oh, dear. I had hoped to be there when she awoke. Make haste with my hair, Mitchell. And I shall have to change out of this habit.'

'I should think so, indeed. I cannot imagine why you chose to go riding in that shabby old thing, when you have two others hanging in the clothes press. Her ladyship would be shocked to know you had worn it in Hyde Park.'

'But her ladyship will not know, Mitchell, will she?' said Isabella with emphasis. 'I wore the old habit because it is comfortable. The newer ones are designed for displaying oneself at a gentle amble. They are not suitable for taking real exercise.'

'I just hope nobody saw you dressed like that, miss.' Mitchell pursed her lips in disapproval. 'I would never live it down.'

Isabella fervently hoped that Tom would not betray her in this. 'You surely did not expect me to meet anyone so early, did you?' she asked innocently.

Mitchell merely grunted and began to unbutton the offending garment.

Barely five minutes later, properly attired in a simple morning gown, Isabella was by Lady Wycham's bedside. 'Dear Aunt, are you recovered this morning?'

'Much better, thank you, my dear, though no thanks to Parsons, who will insist that laudanum is the cure for everything.'

'It did allow you to sleep, however. And I fancy it will have eased the pain?'

'Well, yes,' admitted the old lady grudgingly. 'But tell me about the ball. Was Sophia a success?'

'Much more than I dared to hope, though she did look lovely. She was surrounded by admirers, almost from the moment we arrived. She may yet become a toast.'

'Sophia? I beg leave to doubt it. You, rather— especially looking as you did last evening.'

'Oh, Aunt, how can you? At my age?'

'Nonsense, child. You are only twenty-six—still young enough, I'd say. Did you keep your promise?'

Isabella plunged into a vivid description of how often she had danced and with whom, casually mentioning Lord Amburley's name among her list of partners.

'Amburley is the only personable one among them,' pronounced Lady Wycham. 'An interesting gentleman, I would say.'

'I know very little about him,' volunteered Isabella, trying to tempt her great-aunt into continuing, 'except that he was with the Duke in Spain and inherited on the death of an elder brother.'

Lady Wycham closed her eyes, frowning in concentration. 'There was a scandal some years ago, I seem to remember. He would have been about twenty-five, then. Ah, yes.' She nodded to herself. 'You were in mourning at the time, I think. Amburley's fiancée jilted him. He was forced to leave England.'

'Why? Was there a duel?' Isabella had paled.

'Hardly. The lady jilted him for his brother, the heir. The two brothers were at daggers drawn, as you can imagine. The old lord sided with the heir, of course—he was bound to, I suppose—and shipped young Stansfield out of the country. He eventually made his way to the Peninsula and joined the army. And he never saw his father—or his brother—again.' She gave a short, mirthless laugh and opened her eyes once more. 'The irony of it is that— as it turned out—the lady married the wrong brother. I understand she is left with almost nothing now, except her title and her very small jointure. It would have been different if she had produced a son, of course.' Lady Wycham was overcome by a fit of coughing, and Isabella hurriedly fetched a glass of water.

Isabella knew she should not tax her aunt's strength, but she found she was longing for more. 'I collect it is not a rich estate, then? Yet Lord Amburley does not seem to lack for funds.'

'A façade, I suspect. It could be a good estate, I believe, with some investment, but it is still heavily mortgaged. And, besides the widow, there is the Dowager—the present Baron's mother. She is much given to good works, which must be a further drain.' Lowering her voice even more, she added, 'I had heard that he finances her from his winnings at cards.'

Isabella choked.

'Good heavens, Isabella, are you all right?' cried Lady Wycham.

'Yes, Aunt,' coughed Isabella weakly, 'perfectly, I assure you. I cannot think what came over me.'

'Too much dancing and not enough sleep,' concluded Lady Wycham sagely. 'You look very pale, my dear. Are you sure—'

'Yes, dear Aunt, truly I am quite well. But I

am a little tired. Perhaps I should lie down for a while.' That was not really true—but Isabella knew that it was the best way of avoiding Lady Wycham's increasingly difficult questions.

It was early afternoon when Isabella awoke. She lay on her back, gazing sightlessly at the window through the open bed-curtains. Amburley's face was not to be banished from her mind. Heavens, she had even been dreaming about him. Her body felt somehow different—soft and fluid, and aching for something that seemed to have been snatched away. She had been warm and melting in his embrace, thirstily drinking in the subtle male scent of him, twining her fingers in this thick black hair. And then he had—

No. He had not. He had been about to kiss her, but somehow it had not happened. Her practical side intervened to point out that it was not at all surprising. A woman who had never been kissed was bound to find it rather difficult to imagine how it felt, even in a dream.

However much she tried, Isabella was unable to drive thoughts of Lord Amburley completely from her mind. She found him unfathomable but—she had to admit, to herself at least—immensely attractive in his enigmatic way.

And Lady Wycham's intriguing description of his early disappointment… How on earth was it that an old lady who went about so little could be always so well-informed? Isabella smiled to herself. Her great-aunt never revealed her sources, but they were certainly reliable. It might even be possible to find out more about Amburley's past by that route. The tale of the rift between the brothers had been tantalisingly brief.

Relaxing back on her pillows, Isabella allowed her normally practical mind to muse on what little information she had. Jilted! And for his own brother! What a terrible blow to his pride, and doubly so when he was rejected by his father too. No wonder he seemed so unbending in his dealings with women. He had every reason to despise them all for causing him so much humiliation.

And, if he had been nursing a broken heart all these years...

Isabella's common sense reasserted itself. Sophia might fondly imagine a man sighing for years for his lost love, but she did not. Such a man would have made a pretty poor soldier. Besides, Aunt Jemima had implied—and her information was to be trusted—that the widowed Lady Amburley was living in straitened circumstances. If Amburley had any feelings for her still, he would surely have seen to her comfort? Or had she been too proud to accept his 'charity'?

Enough! There was no way in which she could divine his feelings by indulging in idle speculation. And she was quite as foolish as Sophia, even to begin to allow her thoughts to wander in his direction.

Flinging back the covers, Isabella jumped out of bed and pulled the bell for Mitchell, silently vowing that she would keep herself so busy over the next few days that she would have no time to think about anything, especially not about Lord Amburley.

* * *

Isabella remained true to her word until Friday morning, when Lord Amburley was forced back into her thoughts by an innocent enquiry from Mitchell as to what she would wear to Lady Morrissey's soirée.

Isabella turned quickly and walked to the window, taking several deep breaths as she did so. Then, in a passable imitation of her normal voice, she said, 'I am not sure. What do you suggest?'

Mitchell seemed to have noticed nothing. 'It will be quite a large affair, Miss Isabella, so you'll need to look your best. What about the blue crepe? I finished the new trimmings yesterday. Nobody would recognise it now.'

'That sounds splendid, Mitchell,' said Isabella, turning from the window. 'Would you fetch it so that I may see?'

The blue crepe gown had been transformed. The rather old-fashioned blonde lace trim had been removed and replaced by ruched ribbons in shades of blue darker than the dress itself. And instead of the old underdress to match the lace, Mitchell proffered a silk slip of deepest ultramarine that picked up the shade of the darker ribbons. The ensemble was exquisite.

'Shall you wear your mother's diamond collar, Miss Isabella?'

'No, I think not. You know I never wear it. The stones are too fine for a poor relation. No, I think the aquamarines again. They are such a pretty colour...and will look interesting against the deep blue, do you not agree?'

'The necklace certainly becomes you, but surely you wore it just a few days ago? What about the sapphires instead?'

'I do not care to flaunt the contents of my jewel case, Mitchell. Too many questions would arise. The sapphire pendant would suit, I admit, but I prefer the more unusual colour combination, I think.'

Mitchell dutifully fetched the aquamarines to set against the dress. The combination was striking—so the discussion of jewellery ended there.

When they arrived at the soirée, Lady Morrissey greeted Lady Wycham with real concern, enquiring after her health. Isabella felt a twinge of guilt. She would not for the world have wished ill on Lady Wycham, but the old lady's presence tonight deprived Isabella of the excuse of chaperoning Sophia. Clearly, the meeting with Lord Amburley was fated. Isabella felt as if a dark cloud were looming over her. Even if she tried to escape, it would follow.

Hardly had their party established itself in a corner of the saloon than Lord Amburley himself was bowing over Lady Wycham's hand.

'I am delighted to hear of your recovery, ma'am,' he smiled. 'It is a pity you were not able to attend the Duchess's ball to witness the success of Miss Winstanley and Miss Sophia. I'd wager that neither of them lacked a partner the whole evening,' he added, looking pointedly at Isabella, who groaned inwardly. He seemed to have the old lady eating out of his hand. How was it that a man who was so cold and forbidding at one moment, could be so charming the next?

Lord Amburley was now devoting all his attention to Lady Wycham. 'I must tell you, ma'am, that I learned at the ball that Miss Winstanley is a fine piquet player. I have never pitted my skill against a lady, and I confess I am intrigued to try her mettle. If you permit, I should like to challenge her to a rubber or two.'

Lady Wycham looked inquiringly into his lordship's face, but his expression was inscrutable. He had made it seem as if this invitation were the most natural thing in the world.

Isabella knew her great-aunt would find some means of turning the challenge aside if she showed the slightest hint of reluctance. But it was now a matter of honour. She nodded bleakly.

'Well, sir,' said Lady Wycham a little uncertainly, 'if Isabella wishes to accept, I can see no reason to gainsay you.' She continued to look a little concerned as she added a hurried afterthought. 'I take it you will not play for high stakes?'

'I shall happily play for any stakes Miss Winstanley cares to name,' responded his lordship with an innocent smile. Lady Wycham visibly relaxed. 'Are you ready, ma'am?' He rose, still smiling, and offered his arm to Isabella.

'You make it very difficult to refuse you, sir,' she returned instantly, then immediately regretted her words. She must give her great-aunt no cause for anxiety. But Lady Wycham had already turned away.

Isabella rose gracefully. Placing the tips of her fingers on his arm, she discovered that the cloth of his immaculate black evening coat was infinitely smooth and soft to the touch. She could feel the warmth of his body through the layers of material, almost as if she were touching his skin. And that faint hint of his citrus cologne assailed her senses. Yet again, she found she was more aware of this man than of any other she had ever met. And from the merest touch!

Leading her towards the card-room, Lord Amburley lowered his voice to a conspiratorial whisper. 'There is no need to go through with this if you have changed your mind, Miss Winstanley. Indeed, I pray that you have.'

'Do you, my lord?' She prickled visibly. 'But

I am not so craven, nor so lost to a sense of honour that I would cry off, I assure you.'

Lord Amburley's expression hardened. Again, he bestowed that cold, calculating look on her, making her shiver inwardly. Again, she recognised the streak of ruthlessness that she had discovered in him during their first encounters.

In cool, correct tones, his lordship then informed her that he had at no time desired to question her honour or her courage. He would play, as he had promised, for any stakes she cared to name.

Isabella despaired of her own impulsive tongue. How could they be so easily at daggers drawing? Why had she set them at odds by bristling so, in response to his simple offer to let her withdraw? Her response had been purely instinctive. She barely understood her own motives, except that she had fancied she detected a note of pity in his offer. To be pitied—especially by Amburley—was intolerable. She would let him see she was a woman to be reckoned with.

'We agreed, as I recall, sir, to play for a guinea a point. Three rubbers?'

He nodded, drawing out her chair.

'And shall we say twenty guineas the game, besides?'

Lord Amburley barely suppressed a gasp. Isabella was not surprised—after all, she was insisting upon extraordinarily high stakes. He threw a penetrating look at her, holding her gaze. For a moment, she thought he was about to round on her. Then he seemed to take a renewed grip of himself, forcing calm back into his features as he took his seat opposite her. He dropped his gaze to the cards.

Watching his strong fingers expertly shuffling the pack he had just broken, Isabella became increasingly conscious of his skill with the cards. Everything she had heard about him—and her own common sense—told her she was likely to lose. Her instinct told her his lordship was now sufficiently piqued by her inexplicable conduct to give no quarter. Yet her irrepressible sense of humour whispered that, however much she lost, it was all in a good cause. After all, it would go to fund his mother's good works! The unbidden thought that losing would be an act of pious generosity brought a greener gleam to her eyes and a chuckle to her throat. She attempted to disguise it as a cough.

'May I fetch you a glass of wine, ma'am?' offered his lordship, with exquisite politeness. 'I should not want any dryness of the throat to disturb your concentration.'

The chuckle could no longer be contained, especially as a little of his hostility seemed to have disappeared. She allowed herself to laugh softly, hoping to dispel yet more. 'I shall certainly want for concentration if you roast me so, sir. I declare it is wicked of you.'

'I could not resist, I fear. And I meant to punish you for the joke you did not share. Will you tell me what it was?' He was gazing down at her now, invitingly.

Isabella could not tear her eyes away from his. 'I...' She searched for an acceptable half-truth. 'You will now think me a sad creature, since I alone am responsible for the situation we are in. On a sudden, I saw how ridiculous my actions have been.' She continued quickly, as he made to speak. 'Forgive me, sir, but, in spite of what I have just said, I am still determined to proceed as we have agreed. I beg you will simply accept that, however strange it may seem.' She might concede that her actions seemed inexplicable, but she would never withdraw. Isabella Winstanley was no coward.

Lord Amburley frowned. A hard shadow passed across his face and was as quickly gone. He looked into Isabella's limpid eyes. What did he see there? Isabella had no way of knowing. Her motives were impenetrable, even to herself. She thought he gave a little shrug, as if accepting that he had no choice but to continue.

'As you wish, Miss Winstanley. Will you cut for deal?'

Chapter Eight

The first hand was remarkably even. Both players lingered over their discards and over their play, feeling for the opponent's weaknesses. Eventually, Isabella won by a handful of points, but neither scored well.

'Well played, ma'am,' said Lord Amburley generously.

'I had the slightly better cards only, I think,' she admitted, dealing the second hand. To her surprise, he made only three of the five permitted discards. He must have very good cards, she supposed, though his expression revealed nothing at all. The remaining cards improved Isabella's hand markedly. This would be a real test. She waited expectantly for his first declaration.

'A point of six, ma'am?'

'That depends on its value,' she responded quickly, reckoning the total of her six hearts.

'Fifty-five?'

'I have fifty-eight.'

'I concede your point, ma'am. Do you concede my quint?'

Isabella's own sequence of five hearts to the ace could only be equalled, not beaten. His lordship conceded her fifteen points.

'I offer besides a quartet of aces,' she added quickly, since that too was unbeatable. 'Repique, I believe.' She then proceeded to take Lord Amburley's opening lead and to lay down her remaining eleven winning cards. 'And capote, also.'

His lordship threw down his cards. 'A splendid hand, ma'am. Unusual for the dealer to score so well against the major hand.'

Isabella raised her eyes from the task of recording her score, but there was nothing to be read into his expression. 'Even the dealer may have a share of luck sometimes, my lord,' she responded a little tartly, gathering up the cards to hand to him. 'Shall you see if you may do as well?'

With a slight nod he began to shuffle the cards. Luck did not favour either player, however. The four remaining hands of the first game were evenly matched and low-scoring. Isabella's first deal had given her enough points to win this game by a sizeable margin.

'I have exactly one hundred points, ma'am,' announced Lord Amburley, with some evidence of relief. No doubt the thought of being rubiconned by a female—especially this one—was singularly unpleasant.

In the second game, they won three hands apiece. But Lord Amburley scored well in his, while Isabella's scores were pitifully low: only ninety points.

'My game, I believe, this time,' he said, quickly leading his last winning card.

Isabella threw down her last card with a laugh. 'And as I have failed to reach the rubicon, you will be several hundred guineas to the good. Still, we are all square on games won.' She threw him such a rueful glance with this last remark that he was forced into an un-willing laugh. He summoned a footman with a tray of champagne.

'For my cough, sir?' she asked archly.

'No, ma'am, for your concentration. I won that game on the luck of the cards only. And the luck may always change.'

'You mean you would prefer an opponent who was less sharp?'

He seemed startled by her choice of words and paused a moment to search her face. 'I think I have met a redoubtable opponent, Miss Winstanley. I may need all the help I can get.' He placed a glass of champagne by her hand.

She raised it to her smiling lips. 'As do I,' she said, and sipped. 'It is your deal, sir.'

Isabella eventually pipped him to the deciding game and the first rubber. A quick reckoning, however, showed that, for all her efforts, the rubber had netted her only thirty-five guineas.

'An excellent rubber, ma'am. Clearly the champagne improves your play,' he observed with the merest hint of a smile. 'Another glass?'

'Thank you, no. I think I shall need a clear head if I am to win a second rubber. I should prefer lemonade, if you please.'

He nodded and rose to fetch it himself, leaving Isabella watching his retreating back as he strode out of the card-room. Abstractedly shuffling the cards, she found herself admiring the set of his broad shoulders and the easy grace of his long stride. He returned almost immediately to place lemonade by her, with champagne for himself. When she won the cut, he sat back, drinking his champagne and watching her deal.

Isabella felt his keen gaze and willed her hands to behave normally. She refused to consider why he paid such close attention to her movements, for that would undermine her confidence completely. Better to concentrate simply on one hand at a time.

The play proceeded in silence for several hands. At the end of the next game, Isabella breathed a sigh of relief as she recorded her winning score. With one rubber and one game under her belt, she now needed only one more game to win both the second rubber and the match. And she was nearly two hundred guineas ahead, to boot.

As Isabella shuffled the cards to begin dealing, Mr Lewiston came into the card-room, looking about him. Seeing the seated pair, he came across to join them, though he knew better than to disturb the players by speaking to them. He simply eyed Amburley's score-pad and grimaced.

'You may speak, if you are so minded, George,' invited his lordship curtly, 'provided it is not simply to remind me of how badly I am losing. I am already well enough aware of that.'

Isabella glanced up from her shuffling but said nothing. She smiled tentatively at Mr Lewiston.

'Forgive me, ma'am. I should not disturb your play. If you permit, however, I should like to watch for a space. It will be instructive to see Amburley beaten.'

'George—'

'Mr Lewiston—'

Their protests came in unison—his exasperated, hers embarrassed. But Mr Lewiston showed no sign of chagrin over his outrageous remark.

'Mr Lewiston,' repeated Isabella, in the patient accents of a governess to an irritating child, 'you must know very well that nothing is certain until the last card is played. There may yet be a very long way to go. I pray you will not embarrass me—or indeed his lordship—by suggesting that victory is certain to be mine.'

Mr Lewiston had the grace to flush, a very little. 'Apologies, ma'am,' he muttered in a low voice. 'I had no intention… I apologise—'

'Oh, for goodness' sake, George, do hold your tongue,' said his lordship testily. 'You are interrupting our game. Stay if you must, but, I beg of you, stop your chatter and let us concentrate!'

Mr Lewiston flushed hotly under this rebuke but seemed to take it to heart. He stationed himself silently behind Lord Amburley.

Isabella returned to the business of dealing, wishing that Mr Lewiston had not remained. She found his presence disconcerting. She should be grateful, she supposed, that he had not chosen to stand behind her and watch her every move. That would be even worse.

Isabella dealt for the opening hand of the next game feeling very tense. Although she tried hard to concentrate on nothing but the cards, her thoughts insisted on straying to Lord Amburley and his friend. What were they thinking? It was impossible to deduce anything from Lord Amburley's face for, in spite of the impatience and irritation he had just shown his friend, he appeared relaxed and unconcerned. A good actor, she concluded, as any fine card player must be. But I am sure he does not relish the thought of losing to me, especially in front of an audience.

As the game proceeded, neither player made any mistakes, but the cards rather favoured his lordship—with only one more hand to be played, he was nearly fifty points ahead of Isabella. She fancied his lack of concern had become less of a pose. No wonder. She would need very good cards indeed to win the game on this last hand.

Isabella picked up the cards he had dealt her, offering a silent prayer for good luck. She found she really did want this victory, even though she was still at something of a loss to explain why.

Her hand was fair, but by no means outstanding. She was unlikely to win with such cards. Instead, she consoled herself with the thought that she might still win the rubber by two games to one.

As Isabella led out the cards of her point suit, she realised that her hand was much stronger than she had thought—there was a real possibility that she might be able to take all twelve tricks. Such a clean sweep would give her the second rubber—and victory.

She won the first ten tricks quickly and paused to reconsider her last two cards: the queen of hearts and the eight of spades. The queen was a certain winner; the spade less so. Lord Amburley certainly held the ace of clubs; it was possible that his other card was a spade, though it was more likely to be a second club. She had planned to take the eleventh trick by leading her queen. Provided he retained his ace—as was to be expected—she would win the last trick with her spade.

She hesitated.

Raising her eyes to his face, she detected a tightness around his mouth that had not been there before. He must know that the odds were stacked against him. Perhaps he was even imagining how his friends would roast him when the knowledge of his defeat became public? No doubt he would be in some degree humiliated—yet another blow for a man who had already suffered so many blows.

She looked again at her cards. The players at the neighbouring tables were all watching them now. The atmosphere around the table had become tense and expectant. She felt again that it was somehow doom-laden, even as she recognised that she was ascribing momentous importance to a mere card-game.

And then she knew. Her decision was made. She could not do it—at least, not like this.

Before she could change her mind, Isabella led the eight of spades, giving him a clear opportunity to deny her the rubber.

Lord Amburley looked up with a start to stare into her face. After a moment, he took the trick with the nine of spades and led his ace of clubs to win the last. He smiled oddly as she dropped the queen of hearts on to it.

'My game, ma'am, I believe,' he said softly, 'though it was a close-run thing.' His matter-of-fact words did not match the scorching intensity of his eyes, searching her face. Mr Lewiston's presence was apparently forgotten.

Tearing her eyes from his, Isabella busied herself with her score-pad and responded that there was still much to play for; she hoped to emerge the winner from the next game.

But she did not. Lord Amburley won it comfortably to square the match at one rubber apiece. Then, to Isabella's vexation, he ran out the deciding rubber in two quick and very profitable games.

'Allowing for the additional points for games won, I make that a lead of 537 points, Miss Winstanley. Do you agree my figures?'

In Mr Lewiston's presence, Isabella contrived to remain light-hearted about her losses. After all, he did not know the level of the stakes. He would probably assume they were playing for pennies.

'My figures exactly, sir. A splendid win, I admit, particularly in the last rubber. And now,' she continued with apparent unconcern, 'I feel I ought to return to the drawing-room. I have neglected Lady Wycham for a very long time.'

To her relief, Mr Lewiston took that as a hint to leave them. She faced Lord Amburley across the card table, where the cards remained scattered as they had been at the end of the last hand.

'I shall need a little time—' she began, but was allowed to get no further.

'Miss Winstanley, I have no desire to press you for payment. I beg you will settle this matter when you are ready.' He was pushing the cards around as he spoke, without looking at her directly. Then he picked up one card and held it in his fingers, studying it intently. 'May I add, without any desire to indulge in idle flattery, that you are without doubt one of the finest players I have encountered? I have rarely met an opponent who judged the game so nicely. Or one who made so few mistakes.'

He let the card fall face-up on to the table. It was the queen of hearts!

For a long moment, Isabella's heart seemed to stop beating altogether, then it began to pound furiously. Good God! He knew! She gazed, mesmerised, at the card on the table. Then, with a supreme effort of will, she raised her eyes to his face, to meet the mockery there.

She did not find it.

'You are pale, ma'am,' he murmured, with obvious concern. 'I have kept you much too long in this hot and stuffy card-room. Let me escort you to where the air is fresher.' He rose, politely offering her his arm once more.

Isabella was numb. Without a word—for she was incapable of speech—she allowed him to lead her into the drawing-room. But he did not immediately seek out Lady Wycham, as Isabella had expected.

'I am sure you would welcome a turn about the room now, after sitting for so long.' It was a statement, not a question, and he moved her away from her party as he spoke.

After a moment's silence, he broke into Isabella's disordered thoughts once more. 'Would you do me the honour of driving in the park with me tomorrow, ma'am?'

Now *that* was the last thing Isabella had expected him to say.

'Or on another day, if tomorrow is not convenient,' he added smoothly.

What choice did she have? She could think of no reasonable excuse for denying him. 'Thank you, sir, I should like that,' she answered simply. 'Tomorrow will be quite convenient.'

'I shall call for you at four, then.'

Lewiston rejoined Amburley as he returned to the card-room. 'Well?' he asked cryptically.

His lordship raised an eyebrow. In truth, the last thing he wanted was a discussion now. But it could not be avoided, even though he was not at all sure of his own conclusions. She must have known something of his reputation as a card player, and yet she had persisted, poor though she was, in naming those astonishing stakes. And then losing.

Lewiston lowered his voice. 'I suppose you saw nothing... What we discussed, you remember? Did she...?'

'I saw nothing, George, nothing at all. And I do not believe there was anything to see. To be sure, I did wonder at the start, because of her luck as dealer. But I had the same odd luck myself, later on. No. There was nothing to see.' He paused to catch up another glass of champagne and take a long swallow. 'Besides—I won, and handsomely.' He grinned at his friend.

'You could have lost the whole bout in that second rubber.'

Lord Amburley clapped his friend on the shoulder. 'You mean, *you* would have done so in my place. Believe me, I knew pretty well which cards she held. I had every intention of winning that hand, even if she...even if she had not made that mistake.'

'Will she pay up, do you think?'

'She has asked for time. She intends to pay, I believe. It remains to be seen whether she can, and also why she...' He found he had no desire to discuss Miss Winstanley's play with anyone. It seemed unfathomable. If she had deliberately thrown that hand, as he suspected, her motives were obscure indeed. Better simply to accept that her excellent card-playing skills had deserted her for a second. There were still puzzles enough, deciding between the parts she played. Lord Amburley frowned into the middle distance, recalling the many riddles she posed.

His friend was looking inquiringly at him. 'Just what are you planning, Leigh? I've seen that look before. And the last time, I recall, no good came of it. No good at all.'

His lordship surveyed his friend with suddenly narrowed eyes and a half-smile. 'Do you care to take a small wager on that, George?'

Chapter Nine

Well before the gentlefolk were out of bed, Isabella was to be seen quietly making her way out through the mews at the back of Hill Street. Shrouded in a dark shawl and her battered brown bonnet, she climbed unaided into a hackney carriage that seemed to be waiting for her.

'Let us be on our way quickly,' she whispered urgently. The jarvey set the horses forward at a brisk trot.

The mews was almost deserted as the cab pulled away. Only a solitary street urchin seemed to be about. He was small, dirty and ill clad. He was huddled in one of the corners as if he were half-asleep and dreaming of better times, and he paid no attention to the cab and its occupant when it moved past him, starting to gather speed.

Then, all at once, the sleepy figure came alive. No sooner had the hackney passed beyond the spot where he stood, than he was no longer on it. In the blink of an eye, he had swung himself up on to the back of the cab and concealed himself there beneath the tarpaulin.

The cab and its passengers, the acknowledged and the stowaway, turned the corner and disappeared from view.

'There is a young varmint, my lord, asking after you most particular.' The butler's lofty disdain pervaded every syllable of the description. He seemed disappointed to find that Lord Amburley did not respond immediately in the same vein.

'Does he have a name, this young person?'

'Sam, my lord, I believe. Shall I send him about his business?'

'No, thank you, Wilson. Will you show him into the book-room?'

The butler's mouth opened and then shut

again at the sight of his master's expression. With a bow, he left the room.

The 'young varmint' was shown in. He appeared little abashed by his elegant surroundings and started across the turkey carpet.

'Did you wipe your feet downstairs, Sam?'

'Course I did, yer honour. Yon whey-faced cove wouldn't let me in the door 'til I wiped everyfink in sight: feet, 'ands—'

'Yes, thank you, Sam,' interrupted his lordship, with a grimace. 'I take your meaning.' He sat down behind the mahogany desk. 'Now, I take it you have learned something already?'

Sam took a deep breath and launched into his narrative. 'Ever so early this mornin', it were. Weren't nobody about, or nearly. So I sat meself round the back, out o' the wind. Then this jarvey drives up an' stops outside the back entrance o' the gentry ken, the one what you told me t' keep me glims on. So, I ups and says to meself, "Them's strange doings." Didn't give no sign, o' course. The jarvey, 'e didn't even notice I were there, I reckon.'

His lordship sighed. 'Might you just tell me what happened, Sam? I have no doubt you carried out your role to perfection, so let's not waste time on describing how good you are. The fact that you're here, and in one piece, speaks for itself.'

The urchin grinned, exposing a mouthful of broken and missing teeth. 'Right y'are, yer honour. As I were saying, the jarvey, 'e just sat there. Then, about ten minutes after, the gate opens and out comes the gentry-mort, all wrapped in a black shawl, climbs into the cab and they're off at the gallop.'

'Is that all? Describe this lady in the shawl. Was she alone?'

'She were uncommon tall, guv'nor, just like you said.' His lordship allowed himself a slight smile. 'Couldn't see 'er 'air, though. Wore a brown bonnet, pulled down around her phiz. Didn't 'ave nobody wiv 'er, neither.' He paused.

'You look remarkably pleased with yourself, young Sam. I take it there's more?'

'Aye, yer honour. I 'itched meself up on the

cab as it passed and settled meself down, all right and tight, ter go wiv 'em. And so I did.'

His lordship burst out laughing. 'Well done, Sam. Believe me, I have never doubted you. Now, tell me, where did she go?'

'You'll not believe it, guv'nor, but it's the truth, swelp me it is.'

'Sam…' Lord Amburley allowed the rising note in his voice to sound more than a little menacing.

'The Fleet.'

'What?'

'Honest to God, guv'nor, she went to the Fleet.'

In a calmer voice, Lord Amburley asked, 'Did she go *into* the Fleet?'

'Aye, yer honour, that she did. I see'd her. Stayed above an hour, I'd say.'

'What did the jarvey do? Did he wait? And where were you?'

'I weren't going to 'ang around there, not more'n I could 'elp. Not the jug, o' course, but stands t' reason, a man don't—'

'What did the jarvey do?' repeated Lord Amburley.

'He drove off, o' course. Came back again, though, just afore the gentry-mort come out again. So it must 'a been fixed 'tween 'em. She got back in and they was off. Didn't 'ave no chance ter go wiv 'em, that time. Sorry, yer honour.'

His lordship leaned back in his chair and allowed himself to smile. 'Sam, you've done well. Here.' He handed some coins to the boy, who beamed. 'There's more where that came from, if you keep at it. I want to know if she goes anywhere else, particularly dressed in that way. And I want to know whom she visits in the Fleet.'

'Could go yerself, guv'nor, an' ask,' suggested Sam cheekily. 'Mite difficult fer me ter go in there.'

'Do your best, Sam. There's a guinea in it for you, if you get me a name. No doubt you have contacts?'

Sam nodded. 'Best be off, yer honour.' He paused, a mischievous light in his eyes. "Ere, guv'nor, what's yer lay with this 'ere gentry-mort?"

'That, Sam,' responded his lordship coldly, tapping a finger along his nose, 'is not your business. And if I were to find you had been doing a little enquiring on that subject, I should be very displeased—very displeased indeed.'

Sam backed towards the door. 'Honest, guv'nor, I didn't mean nuffink. I'll do me best, like you said.'

'Good,' said Lord Amburley. 'Come back the minute you have anything. I promise it will be worth your while.'

With those encouraging words ringing in his ears, Sam made his way out.

Lord Amburley continued to sit at his desk, gazing unseeingly in the general direction of the morocco-bound copies of Latin classics on the book-shelves opposite and resting his chin on his steepled fingers. He could not understand this latest intelligence. Or, at least, the only conceivable circumstances which would fit were particularly unflattering to Miss Winstanley.

Why on earth had she gone into the Fleet? To be sure, it was less dreadful than the prisons for the common felons, like Newgate, or worse, the convict hulks moored offshore. They were feared by even the most hardened criminals. But the Fleet was still a terrible place where no gentlewoman—or gentleman for that matter—would ever willingly set foot. Some gentlemen had no choice, of course, if their debts caught up with them before they could vanish abroad.

Could she have a relative in the Fleet? She had said something about gambling being in the blood. A brother, perhaps? Or a lover? Somehow, that last idea was singularly unpalatable to his lordship, and he dismissed it instantly. She had gone to the prison unchaperoned, which no lady would do, except perhaps to visit her family. Miss Winstanley was unquestionably a lady, and so—

A discreet knock on the book-room door was followed by the entrance of the butler. 'Mr Lewiston has called, my lord. Shall I show him into the—'

'No need for all that formality, man,' said the gentleman in question, breezing past the butler. 'I can announce myself. Mornin', Leigh.'

For the second time that morning, the deflated butler was forced to retreat.

'You're not busy, are you, old man? Because we've got to do a bit of knight-errant work, and sharpish.'

Rising from his chair, Lord Amburley smiled at his enthusiastic young friend. 'A damsel in distress, I take it, George. May I ask who it is this time?'

'The heiress, Sophia Winstanley, of course. It's Gradely. He is planning to call in Hill Street to ask permission to pay his addresses to her. He must be stopped.'

Lord Amburley raised an eyebrow. George Lewiston was impetuous and unpredictable, but this behaviour was unusual, even for him. 'Must? You may want her for yourself, George, but you'll just have to enter the lists with everyone else, including Gradely. I dare say his title will count in his favour, though.' He narrowed his eyes. 'On the other hand, you're rich while he, by all accounts, is practically cleaned out. He needs a rich wife.'

'But he will not have Sophia,' Lewiston burst

out. 'You don't understand, Leigh. It's not that I want her for myself—though I'll admit she's a taking little thing. No, it's Gradely. He's a gambler, a hell-hound, a... Leigh, you and I don't really know him, but Kenley does, and he says Gradely has strange habits. He says... he says Gradely likes to hurt people, especially women.'

His lordship frowned. 'Do you believe Kenley? He may simply want the heiress for himself, you know, and be using you for his dirty work.'

'I've thought of that. He's promised to produce evidence, if necessary. One of the opera dancers, last year, still has the scars. And in any case, Kenley's no longer after Sophia. He's pursuing another interest now.'

'I see,' said his lordship slowly. He had never known Lewiston so serious about a woman before. 'What are you proposing to do?'

'I thought that I...that we might warn him off, let him know we know about his little "habits" and will make them public if he persists in this.'

Serious Lewiston might be, but his judgement had not improved one jot. 'Really?' said Lord Amburley witheringly. 'George, you are letting your enthusiasm overcome your reason. It's impossible to "warn him off", as you put it, without proof. And the word of an opera dancer won't do for this, not a year after it happened. No doubt he bought her off at the time, but he'd always deny it. He'd simply swear she was lying and you had paid her to testify. And, what's more, Gradely would be bound to call out his accuser. He's a crack shot, I believe.'

'So are you,' protested Lewiston.

His lordship laughed mirthlessly. 'I thought it might be coming to that. No, George, it won't wash. We can't warn him off. And I have no intention of meeting Gradely at dawn, in order to save your precious Sophia's pampered hide.'

'But we can't just—'

'However,' continued his lordship meditatively, 'there may be a subtler way. I have promised to take Miss Winstanley driving this afternoon. I shall somehow contrive to warn

her about Gradely's "predilections". She is a
sensible woman, too sensible to dismiss such an
allegation out of hand. She will be bound to take
steps to ensure Gradely's suit is turned away.'

'But you can't talk to a single lady about such
things. She could have the vapours—or worse.'

'Miss Winstanley? I doubt it. I should be
most surprised to find that *anything* would
undermine that lady's composure.'

'Does that include losing a small fortune to
you last evening?'

'Yes. Nobody would have known it from her
face. She was totally in control throughout.
And she is a very fine player indeed.'

'You said that before.'

'Well, it is none the less true. Don't play
against her, George. She would fleece you
shamefully.'

'Perhaps I should, though,' said the younger
man with a sudden grin. 'Then she could use
those winnings to pay her debts to you.'

'Don't you dare! I don't want her let off that
particular hook. I shall find out what her game
is eventually—and keeping her under pressure

to find so much money will *encourage* her to make mistakes sooner.'

'You could have her watched.'

Amburley prevaricated. 'Do you think that would serve? She is a lady, after all.'

'Perhaps not. She probably never goes anywhere without a maid or a groom.'

Lord Amburley smiled slightly but said nothing.

'Perhaps she will let something drop when you take her out later?'

'I shall try to ensure that she does,' promised his lordship.

Promptly at four, Lord Amburley reined in his greys in Hill Street and jumped down from his phaeton, throwing an instruction to Brennan to walk the horses while he waited. There was no telling how long he would be.

But Isabella Winstanley was not a lady in the ordinary style. When he was shown into the drawing-room, she rose to greet him dressed in a jade-green walking dress with matching hat and pelisse. The colour suited her wonderfully well. Lord Amburley was reminded of how enchantingly dishevelled she had looked at the end of that ride in Hyde Park. He determined to set a light note for today's encounter. It was just possible that she could be charmed into dropping her guard.

'Miss Winstanley,' he exclaimed in mock contrition, pointedly scrutinising her apparel, 'forgive me. I must have mistaken the hour. I had no intention of being late for our appointment.'

She was clearly not deceived. 'You are here precisely to the appointed hour, sir, as you know very well. Is it *so* unusual not to be kept waiting by a lady?'

Her quick wits had beaten him. It was quite impossible to make a reply that was both proper and truthful, so he simply bowed and offered his arm. 'If you are ready, shall we go?'

He noticed with approval that she was in no way daunted by his high-perch phaeton, which he had chosen to drive on this occasion, at least in part, to test her mettle. She settled herself calmly, while he spread a rug over her knees and gave his horses the office.

'Do you drive, Miss Winstanley?'

'I was used to, once, when we lived in the country. My father taught me.'

'If you drive as well as you ride, ma'am, I should like to witness it.'

'Oh, no,' she responded, then coloured in obvious embarrassment. 'I did not mean… My lord, you go out of your way to put me to the blush.' She swallowed and continued stiffly, 'Thank you for the pretty words about my riding. And as to driving—no, I do not pretend to be a whip.'

He raised an eyebrow and glanced sideways at her. 'What a pity. I had thought you might like to try my greys.'

She tried unsuccessfully to suppress a chuckle. It was a mannerism he found oddly attractive. 'Must you always roast me every time we meet, sir?'

'Yes,' he answered simply. 'Unless, of course, you were to learn to control your habit of rising to my bait. Then, I fear, the pleasure would wane.'

He could tell that she was refusing to allow herself to smile.

'There must be a better word than "outrageous",' she mused aloud, watching his hands as he deftly guided his greys through the crowded street. 'What about "abominable"? Or "unpardonable"? Yes, I rather like "unpardonable". What do you think, sir?'

'I think, ma'am, that you are roasting *me* unpardonably when you know I am too preoccupied with the traffic at present to give you full measure in return.'

'Oh!' She laughed aloud at this palpable hit. 'If that is the quality of your wit when you are preoccupied, sir, I shall take care not to cross swords with you when you are at leisure.'

They drove on in silence until they had completed a circuit of the park. Then Amburley halted his team.

'Would you like to take the reins for a spell now, Miss Winstanley?' he invited. 'They are no longer quite so fresh.'

'Are you sure, sir? After all, you have no reason to believe I am to be trusted with them.'

She was smiling up at him in the most disconcerting way.

'No? I have seen both your courage and your composure, ma'am, and I value your good sense. If you were not sure you could drive them, you would not make the attempt. Will you?'

She nodded, taking the reins and the whip he offered her in her gloved hands. He looked on approvingly as she felt the horses' mouths and started them into a walk. He was pleased to see that his judgement of her abilities was amply borne out.

'You have been well schooled, ma'am,' he said, as she completed the circuit and pulled up. 'I hope you noticed the looks of envy in all the carriages we passed.'

'No, sir, I did not,' she responded promptly, returning the reins to him. 'I was much too busy minding my team.'

'Well, no doubt the prime topic of conversation after divine service tomorrow will be how Miss Winstanley drove Amburley's greys in the park.' Immediately, he wished the words unsaid. They made him sound insufferably conceited.

But Miss Winstanley seemed to have missed the point completely. Her reply took him by surprise. 'I would hope to hear a more Christian subject aired on such an occasion,' she protested quickly. 'A little concern for our fellow-beings, perhaps, especially those less comfortably circumstanced than ourselves.'

'You speak with passion, ma'am. Not many ladies of the *ton* think as you do.' He started the phaeton into motion once more.

'No. I wish they did. There are so many poor souls who could be helped—orphan children, women fallen on hard times, families deep in debt, old soldiers with no means of support. The list is endless.' She seemed genuinely distressed at the thought of their plight. What an extraordinary woman she was—full of contradictions. Still, she had given him a chance to probe just a little.

'There are many who suffer through no fault of their own, I grant you, and we should help where we can. But, equally, there are many who have brought punishment on themselves, by running up enormous debts, for example.'

If he thought to provoke a reaction from her by that statement, he was disappointed. She said nothing at all. But he was heartened to note the figure of Lord Gradely, on horseback, coming towards them.

'And good families are affected quite as much as the poor,' he continued, with barely a pause. 'Indeed, they have further to fall. I can think of many of my acquaintance who are but one step in front of the tipstaff. One in particular who is like to be pursued both for the Fleet and for Newgate, unless he is very lucky.'

Miss Winstanley turned to stare at her companion.

'Why, speak of the dev—' Amburley said. 'Gradely, how d'ye do?'

The three exchanged pleasantries for a few moments before the phaeton drove on, its occupants bowing and smiling to their acquaintances. It was not long before they were on their way back to Hill Street.

Lord Amburley was delighted to note that his companion seemed suddenly preoccupied.

Thinking about what he had 'accidentally' let slip about Gradely, he hoped. But what if she failed to take the hint?

Chapter Ten

Isabella lost no time in visiting her great-aunt to ask about Lord Gradely and to wonder aloud why Lord Amburley should have taken such pains to give her a hint against him. Strange, strange man.

Lady Wycham was somewhat reticent on the subject of Gradely. He was an inveterate gambler, to be sure, and practically penniless, but she would not be drawn on any other vices, forbidding Isabella to press her further. 'It is of no account, in any case,' she concluded. 'He cannot be interested in Sophia, for she is not well-endowed enough for him. You are, of course, but there is no reason to believe he knows of your fortune. Besides, you are much too sensible to contemplate an attachment to such a man. It is a puzzle why Amburley should go to such lengths.'

Isabella agreed readily. She had felt not the slightest liking for Lord Gradely and, since her great-aunt clearly knew something to his detriment, Isabella would willingly avoid him as much as possible.

The Gradely puzzle deepened a few days later, however, when he called on Lady Wycham, just as Mr Lewiston had predicted. But Lady Wycham was more than a match for him. Lord Gradely had barely got as far as the fateful words about asking her permission to pay his addresses, when the old lady cut him short, with acid politeness. She regretted, of course, but she could not grant him the leave he sought. And, without actually being rude, she gave him to understand that further visits to Hill Street would not be welcome.

Lord Gradely left in something of a hurry, looking rather less collected than when he had arrived.

Lady Wycham immediately confronted Isabella. 'My dear, what have you done to make Gradely think you might welcome his addresses?'

'Why, nothing, Aunt. I have barely spoken to him.' She was blushing fiercely. 'Surely there must be some mistake?'

'I do not see that it could have been Sophia who interested him—though I admit he was in the middle of asking permission when I stopped him. I felt it was wiser not to hear him out— one of those interminable rehearsed periods about his feelings. Nonsense, all of it. No— somehow he must have found out about your money, Isabella. You *must* be more careful.'

Isabella acquiesced weakly, though she was certain that she had given Gradely no encouragement whatsoever. Yet Amburley— somehow, Amburley had known what Gradely planned. What on earth was happening to her? Since she had met Lord Amburley, her life seemed to be spinning out of control.

However much she racked her brains, she could not imagine how Gradely might have thought an offer might be welcome. Never had she shown even the slightest partiality for him. Of course, if Gradely were barely one step ahead of his creditors, marriage might be his only hope. Perhaps he believed that she was Lady Wycham's heir. Perhaps he thought that, at her age, she would be so desperate for a husband that she would accept any offer, even from a…even from a what?

Lord Amburley had hinted at Newgate gaol—something worse than debt, then. And Isabella had instinctively believed him.

I'm sure he deliberately went out of his way to warn me, she thought, smiling softly as Amburley's face rose in her mind. Why on earth should he do that? And how did he learn of Gradely's plans?

With a shudder, she realised that all the gentlemen of the *ton* might know. They might even be taking wagers on the outcome. And a wager could account for Amburley's behaviour too. After all, he was known to be a gambler.

Isabella gave herself a mental shake. She refused to believe it could be so. Surely

Amburley was too honourable to do any such thing? He must have been trying to warn her, to save her lest she might be tempted. But why?

Lord Gradely's astonishing visit had thoroughly disrupted Isabella's plans for the morning. She had intended to pay a call on her banker's, in order to arrange to settle her debts to Lord Amburley, and then to go riding in the park, perhaps with Sophia. She now felt incapable of either. Nor could she continue to struggle with the impossible Gradely puzzle. Isabella decided to turn her attention instead to reassuring practical matters—the final arrangements for Sophia's coming-out ball.

She and Sophia settled down to spend the rest of the morning poring over designs for the decoration of the ballroom and discussing colours and accessories. It was well past noon when they were interrupted by a message that Lord Amburley had called.

'Did he ask for me?' Isabella demanded a little crossly, not having the least desire to be interrupted at that moment—especially by the man she was trying so hard to banish from her thoughts.

'He asked for Lady Wycham or yourself, miss,' came the reply, 'but her ladyship is resting and is not to be disturbed.'

There was no help for it. After his warning about Gradely, it would be churlish to refuse to receive him. 'Tell his lordship that I will be with him directly. And have some madeira sent in.'

As she checked her appearance in the glass, Isabella considered what might lie behind this visit.

He must want to know if his warning about Gradely was taken to heart, she concluded, deliberately allowing her irritation to grow. And if he did make a wager, he may even want to know if he can collect on it. Well, he is doomed to disappointment, for I shall certainly not tell him. With a stubborn tilt to her chin, she made her way to the drawing-room to meet his lordship.

He was standing by the window, looking out on to the street. The madeira tray stood untouched on the side table. As the door opened, he turned quickly and bowed. His eyes did not leave her face, and a slight smile played around his firm mouth.

Isabella did not return it. She merely dropped a polite curtsy. There was no need to advance to shake hands after that. Her 'Good day, my lord,' had a hint of sharpness in it.

Lord Amburley frowned slightly at her un-accustomed reserve. She could feel his eyes assessing her in that calculating way of his. Yet his voice sounded quite normal. 'I dare say you will not believe me, ma'am, but I have taken your strictures to heart.'

Isabella's eyes widened in surprise. What could he be talking about? 'Indeed, sir?'

'Mindful of your words, I have determined to visit some of the London monuments which I have so neglected.' He smiled—but his eyes were still hard. 'I wondered whether you might care to accompany me this afternoon?'

Isabella refused to believe for one moment that this invitation had an innocent motive. All of his lordship's actions seemed to be carefully planned—even a drive in the park. 'Alas,' she responded smoothly, 'that is not possible.

Much as I would like to help you to make up for your earlier deficiencies—' in spite of the sharp look these words provoked, she managed to remain a picture of demure innocence '—I am not free this afternoon.' In response to his impertinently raised eyebrow, she added calmly, 'I am engaged to visit my banker's in the City. However, I—'

'I hope you are not visiting your banker's on my account, ma'am,' interrupted his lordship, with unwonted vehemence. 'You will recall that we agreed there was nothing pressing in the matter of our game last week.'

'You mistake matters,' replied Isabella hotly, feeling the colour rushing into her cheeks. '*I* agreed no such thing. Debts of honour have to be paid promptly—even by women.'

'Miss Winstanley…' Perhaps it was the stubborn set of her chin and the martial glint in her eye that gave him pause. Whatever the reason, he began again on a marginally softer tack. 'As it happens, ma'am, it was my intention to make my first pilgrimage to St Paul's. It would be my pleasure if you would accept my escort to the City. Perhaps you would enjoy a visit to the cathedral before you transact your business?'

Isabella pondered this suggestion for a moment, forcing herself to ignore his possible motives and to focus solely on the rational aspects of his unexpected invitation. By rights, a gentleman should not take a lady driving into the City, even in an open carriage, but a visit to St Paul's would allow her the satisfaction of paying every guinea of her debt to his lordship in person. She consoled herself with the thought that, after all, she was now of an age when the rules for single ladies did not need to be applied quite so strictly.

'You are most kind. I accept.'

'I shall call for you at three, if that is convenient?'

'Perfectly, thank you,' she responded with cool politeness.

He arrived promptly at three. Barely five minutes later, he was handing her into his curricle and spreading a light rug over her knees.

'You do not drive your phaeton today, sir?'

'No, ma'am. I thought you might like to try your skill with my curricle. It is better adapted for the city streets.'

Isabella threw him a frankly quizzical look. 'Have you something particular in mind, sir?'

'Quite so, ma'am,' came the enigmatic reply. He took his eyes from the greys for a brief moment to look down at her, apparently daring her to quiz him further.

She tried unsuccessfully to look outraged but, faced with that challenging gaze, she was quite unable to revert to her earlier coolness. After a moment, she collected herself enough to say, 'My lord, you will allow me to say that I have the strongest suspicions of your motives today. I believe they go beyond a desire to admire Sir Christopher's great work. I take it you do not propose to tell me your plans?'

'No, Miss Winstanley,' he responded curtly, but with the slightest twitch of his handsome mouth. He was concentrating on threading his team through the narrow streets.

Isabella was torn between indignation and laughter. And she knew that he was observing her inner conflict from the corner of his eye.

'Outrageous, ma'am?' he suggested coolly.

Her laughter bubbled forth. No doubt, just as he had expected.

'No, indeed. Abominable! Quite abominable!'

After some minutes, he said evenly, 'I have a proposition to put to you, ma'am.'

Isabella surveyed him quickly. Perhaps she should not have come. He would not, surely, make any improper proposal to a lady?

'I see I have roused your interest,' he continued. 'It concerns our earlier wager.' He pointedly ignored the darkling look she cast at him. 'I offer you a second challenge, ma'am. A curricle race—between us two. If you win, your debt is cancelled. If I win, you pay me double.'

Isabella was incensed. How dare he propose anything so improper? It was a moment before she was sufficiently in control to speak. 'You do not, surely, expect a lady to take part in such a scheme?' she asked witheringly.

'Few ladies would have the courage, I own…but I had thought that you, ma'am, were of that intrepid number.'

'Intrepid? Or foolhardy? Certainly not. I do not care to risk my reputation in a public race for such a stake.' The words were out before she understood their full import. He would think she was an out-and-out coward. She groaned inwardly, recognising—too late—how much his good opinion mattered to her.

After a moment's pause, he said, tantalisingly, 'Of course, it need not be a *public* event. It could be known only to ourselves.'

Isabella was now truly intrigued. Was he looking for an opportunity of losing to her, so that he would not have to collect on their earlier wager? She wondered how he had intended to manage the affair, however, and her inner devil prompted her to provoke him a little more. 'I do not see how that could be done, sir.'

He smiled knowingly, clearly believing he had hooked his fish. 'Trust me, ma'am, it can be done. A town race might serve, for example.'

Isabella did not understand him and allowed it to show on her face.

'Permit me to explain,' he said. 'We agree a course through the town from, say, St Paul's to Westminster Abbey. Then one of us drives it against the clock. The other does the same, and the better time wins.'

'But it would be bound to attract attention with two curricles—'

'Ah, no, ma'am. Not two. One. That is the beauty of it. Just one curricle, driven along the same course, but at different times.'

'It could not possibly be a fair contest, my lord,' she protested, forgetting altogether that it would be quite improper to participate in any kind of race at all. 'The traffic, the weather…oh, anything could happen.'

'Indeed so. And that makes the challenge all the more interesting. Let me tell you the rules. The first whip can choose both day and time as he—or she—thinks best. The second can also choose as he thinks best, provided only that he completes the course within the agreed time span. Two or three weeks is usual. Do you dare to test your skills, Miss Winstanley?'

'I have no curricle to race against you, sir. You must find another opponent.'

'Ah, but that is easily remedied. You may drive this curricle and this team.'

'Good God! You must think I have wind-mills in my head. *Your* curricle and *your* team?' She began to laugh at the absurdity of it all. How on earth had she allowed the dis-cussion to come this far? Surely, no lady would ever agree to such a proposition?

'You would be able to get to know my team before the event, of course,' he added silkily, as her mirth subsided. 'And there would be an appropriate handicap to take account of my greater experience. You would not need to better my time to win. Shall we say…anything less than double? With odds like those, Miss Winstanley, do you dare to refuse?'

Isabella was torn between a strong desire to accept his challenge and best him, and the inner promptings of her better self against such unladylike behaviour. The challenge seemed truly unavoidable if she were not to lose face completely. Yet, were her behaviour to become public knowledge…

He is sure, she thought, that I will accept. And he thinks he is totally in control. Well…

Looking full into his face—which seemed to show a degree of satisfaction already—she smiled sweetly. Then, with wide-eyed innocence, she agreed to the wager. 'However,' she added smoothly, 'I do not agree to the proposed stakes. Double or nothing? Paltry, my lord, paltry!' She was gratified, then, to see his jaw muscles tighten. 'If we are to race, sir, the stakes must be worth the candle, especially for a poor female against whom the odds will be very long indeed. If I should win, the prize shall be… Do you dare to hazard your matched greys?'

Lord Amburley's hands tightened involuntarily on the reins and his precious greys shied slightly in protest. 'I believe I have underestimated you, ma'am,' he said after a moment, in a strained voice. 'But as I issued the challenge, I cannot now refuse the stakes you suggest.'

'While if you should win—'

'Those stakes shall remain unchanged,' he stated flatly. 'Twice the original debt. I would not accept more.'

It was now much too late for Isabella to draw back.

Isabella tried to bring some order to her thoughts, pushing the promptings of her conscience as far as possible to the back of her mind. Simpler to concentrate on practical matters. In the circumstances, her visit to the City need not take place that day. Instead of St Paul's, they turned aside to visit Westminster Abbey, which would provide splendid cover for the necessary discussions about how the race was to be run without attracting the attentions of the *ton.*

'It cannot take place for some weeks,' said Lord Amburley, as they walked together down the great nave. 'You must have time to become accustomed to my team, and frequent excursions are out of the question, of course. That would excite all sorts of gossip.'

Isabella flushed slightly. She was beginning

to appreciate the enormity of what she had agreed to. Heaven help her! She could not draw back now.

'I suggest we drive out about once a week for the next two or three weeks and decide on the course and the timing after that. Would that meet with your approval, ma'am?'

She nodded helplessly. Devil take the man. He had it all too pat. And she was caught like a bird in lime.

'And since I shall be driving out with other ladies in the interim, the *ton* will conclude that Amburley has at last been converted to the pleasures of female company in his carriage. Do you think that will serve, ma'am?'

'That will depend on the ladies you invite, I fancy,' she replied acidly.

'Yes, you are right. I shall think carefully about that. I should not want to raise the hopes of any fond mamas… A ticklish problem, indeed.'

Isabella refused to consider what might be the implications of that.

He turned her away from the stained glass they had been admiring. 'And now, ma'am, will you be so good as to instruct me about the inhabitants of the Poets' Corner?'

By the time they were ready to return to Hill Street, Isabella's good humour was almost restored. She knew that he was deliberately exercising his charm on her, but she found herself quite unable to resist. He had gone out of his way to be entertaining during the remainder of their visit to the Abbey, and he had even encouraged her to drive the curricle for part of its return journey.

She thanked him prettily as she handed back the reins. 'Shall we see you at Lady Sefton's this evening, sir?'

'I am otherwise engaged, I fear. Such a pity. Musical evenings can be so…' He paused, clearly searching for a suitably ambiguous epithet.

'Soporific, sir?' She looked archly at him through her lashes.

'Viper!' he exclaimed with mock horror, stirring the greys into motion once more. 'I should not dare apply such a term to an evening arranged by one of our foremost hostesses. No single gentleman would risk his entrée to Almack's by such language.'

Isabella's silvery laughter burst forth.

'That's better,' commended his lordship. 'In point of fact, I am sorry to miss Lady Sefton's soirée. At least, I am, if I shall miss hearing you sing.'

Isabella blushed rosily, not only because of her companion's pretty compliment, but also because it gave the lie to her earlier conclusion that he did not like her voice. How many other times had she misjudged him?

Lord Amburley must have noticed her confusion, for he politely turned the conversation. 'Has Lady Sefton sent you vouchers for Almack's, Miss Winstanley?'

'I fear so.'

'Fear, ma'am? Why, surely it is the ambition of every young lady?'

'It is certainly Sophia's, and it will be gratified on Wednesday next. For myself...I shall go as chaperon to Sophia, nothing more.'

'Truly? Surely not. I count on your dancing,

ma'am. I particularly hoped to waltz with you there.'

'You are roasting me yet again, my lord,' protested Isabella, remembering how uncomfortable their last 'waltz' had been. 'Do you truly mean to attend the assembly at Almack's? I had thought you would certainly have a prior engagement then.'

'No, that would never do. Besides, I must seek out suitable ladies to drive behind my team for the next few weeks. And where better than Almack's?'

Lord Amburley dined alone after his return from the excursion to Westminster Abbey. He felt much in need of a period of calm reflection to consider what he had learned of the Misses Winstanley and—more pressing—to apply his keen intellect to the many puzzles which remained.

The two women could not have been more unlike—not only in age and appearance, but also in temperament and tone of mind. He had instantly characterised the younger Miss

Winstanley as 'empty-headed, frivolous and spoilt', not out of malice, but as a reflection of his experience of young and wealthy débutantes. He still believed he was right. He had never yet known one who was otherwise.

Amburley had paid little enough attention to Miss Sophia at the time—why should he?—but that was before George Lewiston had begun to take an interest in the chit. Lewiston *said* he wanted only to preserve her from Gradely. Well, that was done. For, if Sam's latest observations were to be trusted, Gradely had left Lady Wycham's house with his tail between his legs. But it still left Lewiston himself. Amburley was loath to see his friend leg-shackled to a woman of Sophia Winstanley's cut. He would regret it in a month.

It was too much to hope that Miss Sophia would prefer one of her other suitors, for none of them was as rich as Lewiston. Even heiresses—or rather, their parents—preferred wealthy suitors. Lewiston would have been the catch of the Season, had it not been for his lack of a title.

Might the chit be hankering after a title? Since she had wealth of her own, perhaps she could be lured away by a coronet? Amburley considered the possible field. Now that Gradely had fled the lists, there was only one unmarried peer available—himself. If Miss Sophia were to be tempted by a title, it would have to be his. It was only a barony, of course, but an ancient one, none the less. It would have to serve. Yes, he would have to test Miss Sophia, court her a little, prove that his assessment of her was a fair one. It was the least he could do for such a friend as Lewiston.

Lord Amburley wondered idly how Miss Winstanley would react, if he were seen to be aspiring to her younger cousin. As a loyal companion, she should be delighted at the prospect of a titled suitor, even a relatively impecunious one, for her wealthy charge. But her reactions were impossible to predict, just as they had been again today, on the question of the stakes for the curricle race. His proposal had been precisely and cold-bloodedly calculated to prolong his hold over her, and to provide a means of honourably cancelling her debt—if he should choose to use it. He had been quite sure she would accept his challenge, for she had too much spirit to hide behind the cloak of propriety. Indeed, he had counted on that, when devising his little scheme. But he had to admit he had underestimated his opponent's mettle—he had been too clever by half. Had she guessed his intention? She had certainly outmanoeuvred him very neatly. And with his prize greys now at stake, he could not afford to lose—so Miss Winstanley's debt would be doubled. God, what a coil!

He sipped meditatively at his port. It didn't really help. She was an enigma. Furthermore, he had yet to fathom out the secret of her double life and of her visits to the Fleet prison. On that subject, Sam was being remarkably slow.

He was still ruminating when Lewiston was announced. Lord Amburley realised, with a start, that he had forgotten their engagement to play cards at their club. He had allowed himself to become much too preoccupied with the Winstanley puzzle.

Rising, he greeted his friend affably, making no mention of his lapse of memory. 'Come and sit down, George. Will you take port or brandy?'

Lewiston, though keen to be off, allowed himself to be persuaded to a glass of port. 'Any news?' he said, as soon as the butler had closed the door.

'News?' Lord Amburley lounged back in his chair, still sipping his port.

'About Gradely.' Lewiston sounded anxious.

'Mmm. I think he called this morning and was rebuffed.'

'How do you know? Are you sure?'

'Pretty sure, yes. Your Sophia is safe from danger, from that quarter at least.' Lord Amburley could see the relief in his friend's face. He also noticed that Lewiston did not object to his use of the term 'your Sophia'. That seemed ominous, indeed.

'Shall we go?' said Lewiston, setting down his glass.

'A moment, George. There is something I need to discuss with you—here, in private.'

Lewiston looked surprised.

'It concerns Miss Sophia.'

Lewiston looked displeased. 'I do not wish to discuss her, not even with you, Leigh,' he said sharply.

Amburley hesitated. He had not prepared for this moment as well as he should have done. In all honour, he needed to give some kind of warning to his friend about what he had in mind to do. But how? He could say he planned to try his luck with the heiress, whose wealth would help him restore his estates; or he could say he planned to tempt her with his title, to demonstrate the faults of her character. In either case, he would be cutting Lewiston out, which could easily lead to a breach between them. And Lewiston would take little consolation from learning that his goddess had feet of clay, especially if that fact were publicly demonstrated by his closest friend.

His lordship resolved to try to find a middle way. He adopted his most nonchalant pose. 'I have no intention of saying a word against Miss Sophia, George. Who would dare, when she has you to defend her?'

Lewiston laughed rather unconvincingly.

'I have been thinking about her,' Amburley continued. 'It may be that I was too hasty in my judgement. After all, I hardly know her. I think, perhaps, I should make some effort to further my acquaintance with Miss Sophia. Why not, after all? She is young, pretty and rich; and—so far as I am aware—she has not yet indicated a preference for any of her many suitors.' Amburley cast a shrewd glance at Lewiston, to gauge his reaction, but he appeared to be studying the polished table-top.

Lewiston did not look up. 'Do I take it you intend to become one of them?' His voice sounded a little forced.

Lord Amburley did his best to sound light-hearted. 'I have no idea. Perhaps. It will depend on Miss Sophia. Of course, if your intentions are serious, I should not dream—'

Lewiston raised his head. 'I admire her, of course. And I am prepared to defend her against the likes of Gradely, as any man of honour must. But I do not believe she means to make her choice in her first Season. I think she is enjoying everything too much to form an attachment so soon. She is very young, after all. Being an heiress, she will always be surrounded by admirers. She can afford to take her time.'

Lord Amburley nodded sagely. How like Lewiston to underestimate his own chances with the heiress. He was too diffident by half. 'No doubt you are right. I shall become just one more of her bevy of admirers, I expect. I wonder, though—do you think the title might make a difference?'

Lewiston swallowed hard. 'It did not help Gradely,' he said stiffly, 'and he is an earl.'

'That puts me in my place, does it not?' Lord Amburley had been surprised into a laugh. 'Still, I am glad we are not at odds over this.' He rose quickly before Lewiston could decide to prolong the discussion. 'Shall we go now, George? I must say I have been looking forward to this evening. I feel lucky tonight.'

Lewiston groaned good-humouredly as they left the room. 'Heaven help the opposition then,' he said. 'It could be a very expensive experience.'

Chapter Eleven

The following Wednesday brought the all-important visit to Almack's.

Isabella had carefully instructed Sophia in everything she needed to know about the sacred portals of the Marriage Mart. Most important of all, Isabella stressed repeatedly, was the absolute injunction not to dance the waltz until Sophia had received express permission from one of the patronesses.

Sophia quaked visibly at any mention of those formidable ladies. She was obviously quite terrified at the thought that she might say or do something wrong in front of them.

Almack's was already fairly crowded when the party arrived. Luckily for Sophia's self-control, none of the patronesses she most dreaded was in view near the entrance. Having paid their compliments to Lady Sefton, Isabella and Sophia were able to move into the relative safety of the ballroom, leaving Lady Wycham in conversation with their hostess.

When she looked around at the frankly rather modest surroundings, Sophia's spirits lifted visibly. 'I really did not believe you, Isabella, when you said—'

'Hush. We can discuss that later, at home.'

Sophia nodded imperceptibly. 'Do you know everyone here, Isabella?' She was looking around, with interest, at the multi-coloured throng of young ladies and mammas, interspersed here and there with sober-suited gentlemen and scarlet regimentals. As yet, few of the gentlemen had arrived.

'No, dear, only a few of the older ones. I have been out of Society for a very long time. This is my first visit to Almack's too, remember.'

'But I thought that you and Lady Wycham—'

'You forget that I have not lived in London all that long, Sophia. And Aunt Jemima has not been well enough to allow of much entertaining. You saw that for yourself, when you visited last autumn.'

'It is such a shame,' protested Sophia. 'You wasted your youth nursing your parents, and now you are doing it all over again when you're—' She stopped, blushing fierily.

'An ape-leader?' finished Isabella tartly. She was gratified to see Sophia's blush deepen. Looking round to ensure they were not overheard, Isabella allowed herself to give vent to what she felt was righteous indignation. 'Whether or not I may be an old maid is of no moment,' she hissed. 'But understand that you are quite wrong about Aunt Jemima. I *chose* to come to London, to live a life of my own rather than being beholden to my brother and his wife, who were killing me with kindness. Aunt Jemima has given me a home and respectability—and a freedom which I could never have elsewhere. She owes me nothing—but I owe her a very great deal. You misjudge her shamefully.'

Sophia's contrition was clear to see. She

mumbled the beginnings of an apology, which was cut short.

'There is no need to say any more,' said Isabella, rather more gently. It was important not to undermine the girl's precarious confidence. 'Now, I wonder who will be the first to invite you to dance?'

That was not difficult to guess, since Mr Lewiston could be seen making his way towards them. Sophia visibly brightened at the approach of his familiar figure.

'Good evening, Miss Winstanley, Miss Sophia,' he bowed, smiling warmly at both ladies. 'With your permission, Miss Winstanley, may I ask for the honour of Miss Sophia's hand for this dance?'

Isabella smiled her assent and watched them join the set which was forming. They did make an attractive couple, he so fair and she so dark. She wondered whether Mr Lewiston might come up to scratch—and whether he was sufficiently wealthy to take on Sophia and all her impecunious family. She must make it her business to find out. It would take both wealth *and* strength of character to cope with the feckless Yorkshire Winstanleys.

The first part of the evening passed quickly, and the ballroom rapidly filled. Neither Sophia nor Isabella wanted for partners, though some of Isabella's were rather shorter than she could have wished. She consoled herself with the thought that, in the country dances at least, the difference in height was not very noticeable. If one of the shorter gentlemen asked for the waltz, however, she was determined to make her excuses. For the waltz, it was imperative that a lady have a partner who overtopped her. She caught herself wishing again for a chance to waltz in Amburley's strong arms but quickly pushed it out of her mind. Whatever he might have said, it was stupid to think of it now, since he was not even present.

But in that, she was wrong.

Lord Amburley had arrived late, just before eleven, when the doors were shut against all comers, however august. He had chosen to stand impassively in a dark corner of the crowded ballroom, his hooded eyes taking in every detail of the brilliant scene. He knew he could not expect any enjoyment from this evening's excursion but, none the less, he had decided it had to be done. He frowned darkly as he surveyed the dancers.

Presently, he was spied and joined by his friend Lewiston.

'Leigh! I had given you up. To be honest, I did not really believe you, when you said you would come. Do you dance this evening?'

'But of course. Why else does a man come to Almack's? Not for the quality of the wine, that's certain,' he added, with a grimace.

His friend laughed. 'You surprise me, I admit. Tell me, which of these beauties has found favour with your discerning eye?'

Lord Amburley gave his friend a hard look. 'I thought to try my luck with Miss Sophia.' Ignoring his friend's sharply drawn breath, he continued, 'I told you I should. I am minded to tempt her with a title. It's only a barony, of course, but it may serve to show her in her true colours.' Looking at his friend's expression, he wondered whether he should have avoided such directness. The answer came almost immediately.

'Amburley, that is monstrous!' exclaimed Lewiston, in outrage. 'You propose to trifle with Sophia, just to prove your warped theories about rich débutantes. Why, you—'

'Nothing of the kind, George,' countered his lordship evenly, determined to keep control of his own temper in the face of his friend's anger. 'If my theory, as you term it, is mis-placed, then Miss Sophia will not respond to me at all, and no "trifling" will occur. If she chooses to respond, it is because she is as I have described her.'

'Nonsense! Have you considered that the poor girl might fall in love with you? Leigh, what you propose is not honourable.'

Without uttering a word, Amburley simply stared at Lewiston until the younger man coloured and looked away. 'I apologise, Leigh,' he said at last, rather stiffly. 'That was unjustified.'

Amburley's frosty stare melted immediately.

He put his hand on his friend's shoulder. 'I promise you that there will be no question of love—on either side. Believe me, my intentions *are* honourable. I wish only to—' He stopped short. He had been about to admit that he was trying to save his friend from becoming attached to an unsuitable lady. 'I only wish to get to know the lady rather better,' he finished, lamely. He determined to say nothing more.

Amburley noted that Lewiston had now clamped his jaws tight together. Probably he was trying to prevent another outburst, since it could have led to a rift between them. Then, with the briefest of nods, Lewiston turned on his heel and strode back into the main part of the ballroom. Lord Amburley, apparently at his ease, lounged back against the wall, smiling grimly as he watched his friend approach Miss Sophia and lead her into the dance.

He had to admit they made a handsome couple. Miss Sophia might be spoilt, but she presented a very attractive picture. She seemed most animated, too. Every time the movements of the dance brought the pair together, they exchanged laughing remarks. And his lordship was not the only man watching her progress. He counted at least four more potential suitors watching avidly.

Half an hour later, Mr Lewiston returned Sophia to where Isabella stood in conversation with one of the chaperons, and a spirited discussion ensued about the respective merits of the various country dances. Isabella was pleased to see that all Sophia's earlier misgivings seemed finally to have disappeared. Two dances with Mr Lewiston and, no doubt, a raft of compliments, had set everything to rights again.

The musicians were just striking up for the next dance, when Isabella saw Lord Amburley approaching. Where on earth had he sprung from? She had been so sure that he was not present. She felt her heart begin to race and her colour rise slightly as he reached them. She told herself sternly to stop reacting like a green girl. His lordship was merely an acquaintance. It would be very…pleasant to dance with him again, even though it was not to be the waltz.

His lordship bowed with casual grace. 'Your servant, Mrs Ramsey. And yours, Miss Winstanley, Miss Sophia.' He smiled at them all. Isabella felt his manifest charm envelop them. Out of the corner of her eye, she saw that Mrs Ramsey was looking round anxiously to summon her daughter for an introduction to this most eligible gentleman. Isabella smiled warmly, anticipating his invitation.

'May I have the pleasure of this dance,' began his lordship, 'Miss Sophia?'

If Isabella lost a little of her colour when Lord Amburley led Sophia into the set, she gave no other sign of her inner turmoil. She concentrated with grim determination on pursuing her earlier conversation with Mrs Ramsey and Mr Lewiston whose smile, she noticed, now looked a little strained.

Mr Lewiston does not welcome his friend's attentions to Sophia, she concluded, forcing herself not to think about her own feelings. Mayhap he is more taken with her than I had thought. But Amburley! He is the last man I should have expected to be attracted to a girl of Sophia's age and sophistication. She will not know what to say to him, even if he is merely being kind by distinguishing her in this way.

A tiny doubt intruded. What if he were not 'being kind'?

She was perversely grateful when Mr Lewiston interrupted her wayward thoughts. 'Miss Winstanley, would you honour me for this dance?'

'Why, thank you, sir. That would be delightful.' She placed her hand on his proffered arm, and they made their way into the set.

It was easier to watch Lord Amburley and Sophia from the centre of the dance floor. They seemed to be enjoying an amusing conversation, except when parted by the movements of the dance. Isabella could not help but remember her own dance with his lordship—she had hardly said a word to him. Was it any wonder he preferred the gayer company of a younger girl?

The end of the dance brought the two couples back together, as Lord Amburley returned Sophia to Isabella's side. Isabella fancied she detected a degree of coolness between the two gentlemen. Sophia, however, was all laughter and animation, blossoming in response to Amburley's subtle encouragement. Clearly Isabella had underestimated her young charge— and the effect of his lordship's ready charm.

Mr Lewiston said very little. His expression grew blacker and blacker until, eventually, he excused himself. Isabella did not miss the look that passed between the two gentlemen as he left.

Something has happened between them, she thought. And it concerns Sophia.

She pulled her thoughts back to the present, just in time to hear Lord Amburley offer to take Sophia in to supper. With a sideways glance towards Isabella, Sophia accepted with a smile. Isabella did her best to return it.

'Will you join us, Miss Winstanley?'

'Thank you, sir, but no. I must look to Lady Wycham. If you will excuse me?' Without waiting for his response, she dropped a slight curtsy, turned and made her way to the card-room, where she knew Lady Wycham was to be found. There she spent a slightly uncomfortable half-hour, chatting to Lady Wycham between hands and trying not to think about Amburley and what his motives might be. What was it he had said to her? That he did not dance with 'young and foolish girls'. Had he changed his tune in so short a space of time? Or was there something special about Sophia that had caused him to break his rule? Isabella had no way of knowing, but she thought—nay, feared—that perhaps Lord Amburley might be succumbing to Sophia's youthful charms. Many other gentlemen were pursuing Sophia—why not Amburley, too?

Isabella soon decided that, if Amburley was pursuing Sophia, he was making sure that no one else should suspect it. Following the supper interval, he danced almost every dance and rarely with the same lady. Isabella noticed that most of them barely reached his chest, though they all strained to gaze up into his eyes.

How distasteful, she thought uncharitably. At least, I am tall enough to look at him without making a spectacle of myself.

The next dance was the waltz. Sophia, sitting by Isabella's side, was putting up a brave pretence that she was quite unconcerned about being unable to dance it. She must know she would not be alone, for a great many of the young ladies present had not yet received permission.

A gentleman approached to invite Isabella to dance. Inwardly she groaned. He was much too short. They would look perfectly ridiculous.

'I thank you, sir, but I do not dance the waltz this evening. Pray excuse me.'

As the young man bowed and left, a well-known voice intruded from the other side. 'That is indeed a pity, Miss Winstanley, for I had hoped to have the pleasure myself. However, my good friend Lady Sefton has given permission for Miss Sophia to waltz this evening. Perhaps she will do me the honour?'

An awe-struck Sophia looked up to see that Lady Sefton was smiling encouragingly at her. Without so much as a word to Isabella, Sophia rose, curtsied to the patroness and departed happily on Lord Amburley's arm.

For a moment, Isabella felt totally isolated among the crowds in Almack's ballroom. It was as if an icy hand had clutched at her heart and were slowly crushing it. She sat completely still, watching the couple make their way into the dance, her eyes riveted to his broad back and the shining black hair curling above his collar.

Eventually, with an effort, she dragged her eyes away. What was the matter with her? She was behaving like a love-sick schoolgirl. Love-sick? Oh, God, no! Surely she could not have fallen in love with him? Please, no!

But in her heart she knew it was too late for such prayers. Her heart was given, even though the man of her choice could have no notion of it. She, who had remained immune for so many years, had fallen in love with a man who was clearly courting a girl of little more than half her age.

She glanced again towards the floor. She could see them whirling round, apparently totally attuned to one another. Then, thankfully, they were no longer in view. She let out the breath she had been holding, seemingly for ever, and turned away to seek out Lady Wycham once more.

No one shall ever suspect my feelings, she promised herself as she walked briskly back towards the card-room, least of all he. I may have lost my heart to a man who will never return my regard, but at least I shall salvage my self-respect.

A further shaft of the light of self-knowledge fell on her.

And this time, she vowed, I shall *not* allow my emotions to overcome my judgement. This time, there shall be no quarter given. This time, I shall win.

Chapter Twelve

It was noted by members of the *ton*, during the days that followed, that Lord Amburley was now playing an active part in every possible event of the Season and honouring a large number of hopeful young damsels in the process. It was soon rumoured that he was actively looking for a wife—the tabbies were agreed that he was of an age when he needed to be setting up his nursery. There was less of a consensus, however, on where his choice would fall, for he seemed to have no preferences among the many young ladies with whom he danced and flirted. It seemed to Isabella, sitting disconsolately among the chaperons, that only she noticed how often he was to be found with Sophia.

* * *

One afternoon, some time after that first evening at Almack's, Lord Amburley called in Hill Street, by appointment, to take Sophia driving in Hyde Park. She was certainly flattered by his invitation but, unlike Isabella, she was not ready when he arrived. He was left to cool his heels in the book-room, where Isabella heard him pacing up and down for fully twenty minutes.

When Sophia eventually emerged, she took one look at Amburley's high-perch phaeton, a vehicle with seats some five feet off the ground, and stopped dead in the open doorway. Isabella thought Sophia was about to turn and run. But good manners had been drummed into her since she came to London. She swallowed hard and made her way across the flagway. Lord Amburley helped her in, not without difficulty, and spread a warm rug over her knees. Isabella was sure he must have noticed how pale Sophia had become, but he showed no sign of concern.

When they drove off, Isabella could see that

Sophia was gripping her hands tightly together in her lap, as if determined not to grab for the side of the phaeton. Isabella sighed. She doubted that even Amburley's charm could overcome so much terror.

The phaeton returned to Hill Street much sooner than Isabella had expected. She took one look at Sophia's ashen face and whisked her upstairs to her room and the ministrations of her abigail.

'I am afraid Miss Sophia is not used to riding in a high-perch phaeton, ma'am,' Lord Amburley confided when Isabella returned. 'She found it somewhat unnerving. I do apologise. I should have warned her that I planned to take my phaeton to the park.'

Isabella was far from convinced by his apology, but she felt she must not let the full extent of her annoyance show. 'Indeed, you should, my lord,' she said. 'Very few young ladies are comfortable driving in such a vehicle. You must have known from the outset that she was ill at ease. You should not have gone.'

'I have already apologised to Miss Sophia,

and to you, ma'am. My excuse, such as it is, is that I am not yet in the habit of driving ladies. I had no idea she might react in such a way. The only other lady who has driven in my phaeton certainly did not do so, after all.'

He looked at her for a split second in a way she could not fathom. Then he was all politeness again. 'Will you allow me to take you on that visit to St Paul's soon? On Saturday, if you are free?'

He did not need to mention the wager—it hung between them like a drawn sword. Forcing herself to assume a polite smile, Isabella accepted.

She had no choice.

Lord Amburley drove easily back to Jermyn Street, feeling quite pleased with his progress so far. He was dancing attention on so many women at once, that the tabbies would not know where to turn. No reputations were at risk, he was sure of that.

He had now completed his assessment of Sophia Winstanley. She was just as empty-headed and frivolous as he had supposed. Her entire conversation seemed to consist of second-hand wisdom—from her nurse, he supposed—and naïve gossip about the Season. He found himself feeling rather sorry for her. After all, it was not her fault that she had been brought up in rich idleness or that she had never had an original thought in her life. She was neither well read nor well informed. No doubt her mama had warned her that no gentleman would ever be attracted by such qualities. Such women had much to answer for—in failed and failing marriages—in Amburley's opinion.

But Sophia was not wholly without redeeming features, he admitted dispassionately. She had clearly been terrified from the very start of their drive today, but she had refused to cry off. She had certainly shown courage. And he had noticed during their recent conversations that she showed a degree of concern for Winny, the companion, that he had not expected. A mixed verdict, then—which he must, in all conscience, soon share with Lewiston, if they were to remain friends.

* * *

'I admit I was wrong about Miss Sophia,' he told Lewiston at White's the following day. 'I have conversed with her, danced with her, and supped with her. I have even taken her driving, though that was *not* a success, as I told you. She is conversable, provided you do not stray beyond the commonplace. She is not pretentious, as so many rich young ladies are, so I was probably wrong to call her "spoilt". Frivolous? Well, yes, but they mostly are at that age. She may well improve. As to the title, I doubt if she would have it, not if the price is driving in a high-perch phaeton.'

Lewiston had been as outraged as Isabella about the drive in the park and began to upbraid his friend roundly.

'I beg of you, George, no more! I have already had all of this and more from Miss Winstanley, who clucks over her charge like a mother hen. I do hope the family are paying her well, for she performs her role admirably.'

Lewiston ignored his diversion. 'Do I take it

then, Leigh, that you will not be pursuing Miss Sophia any longer?'

'The odd dance for appearances' sake, nothing more. I must find some other ladies to take out driving.'

'What about Miss Winstanley? She may be only a companion, but she's a remarkably fine-looking woman and unquestionably a lady. Well read too, I should guess, so you would not be limited to frivolous conversation.'

'Miss Winstanley is an enigma,' pronounced his lordship, with a sudden frown. 'She is highly accomplished, rides and drives as well as most men, and yet she stoops to this infamous deception, in spite of her manifest sense of honour. Extraordinary!'

'You avoided my question again, Leigh.'

'Did I?'

Lewiston refused to be diverted again. Eventually, following further prompting, Lord Amburley admitted that he would drive out with Miss Winstanley, from time to time. 'But I have no intention of giving the tabbies food for thought in *that* direction, George. It *would* be dishonourable, were I to make a woman of her station the object of their scandal-mongering.'

That afternoon, it was noted that his lordship was driving in the park with yet another hopeful young lady at his side, but he disappointed them all by failing to appear in the evening at one of the grandest balls of the Season. Instead, he went to his club, to play piquet. When he rose from the table, many hours later, his winnings amounted to over two thousand pounds.

His lordship had not been long abed when a loud knocking was heard at the servants' entrance. The butler, struggling into his coat, stomped down the passage to open it.

'What d'you mean by making that infernal row at this time of the morning, you little runt?'

'Got ter see 'is lordship, quick,' gasped Sam, trying to push past the butler to get into the house.

'Oh, no, you don't,' cried the butler, gripping him by the collar. 'What's your business, eh?'

'I got ter see 'im, urgent,' repeated Sam. ''E told me 'isself, ter come at once, 'owever late it were.'

Still gripping Sam's collar, the butler pulled the boy inside and shut the door. 'Now, then. Just what did his lordship tell you *precisely*?'

Sam merely repeated, yet again, that he had to see Lord Amburley urgently, adding that his lordship would be very angry to learn that his orders had been disobeyed. The butler, clearly preferring to avoid sole responsibility where his master's wrath might be incurred, sent for Peveridge. If anyone knew what his lordship wanted, it would be the valet.

Peveridge took one look at the dirty visitor and pulled him into the pantry, shutting the door on his inquisitive colleague. Barely two minutes later, he came out again, almost colliding with the hovering butler.

'Keep him here, Mr Wilson. I'll fetch his lordship.'

His lordship was not best pleased to be shaken awake by Peveridge in the early hours of the morning. He sat up, cursing both his valet and the considerable amount of brandy he had consumed at the piquet table.

'If this is a joke, Peveridge, I'll wring your neck with my bare hands.'

'Now, m'lord, would I dare? You know I—'

'Peveridge!' thundered his lordship, momentarily forgetting his fragile head and immediately regretting it. 'Peveridge,' he began again, more moderately, 'what the devil is going on?'

The valet, for once, came quickly to the point, explaining about their young visitor.

'Right,' exclaimed Lord Amburley, now fully awake. 'Get me some hot water and bring the boy up here, while I dress. I need to talk to him myself.'

Peveridge's protests were cut short. 'Don't argue, Peveridge. Just do it! Now!' Peveridge made for the door. 'Oh, wash off some of his dirt if you must, but be quick about it. And with my shaving water, too.'

Downstairs, the fire was already lit and water put to boil. The canny old butler had already set about removing the boy's dirt, using the coldest water he could find. Peveridge was greeted by the boy's complaints before he was halfway down the stairs to the kitchen.

Five minutes later, having taken Sam up to his lordship, Peveridge was back again. 'Send round to the stables for the curricle, sharpish. His lordship wants it at the door in fifteen minutes, with the bays.'

Normally, Lord Amburley expected to spend some considerable time over his morning toilet, especially if he were planning to make calls. This morning, he almost reverted to his old military ways, but not quite. In battle, the set of a coat or the turn of a cravat had been immaterial. Now, he felt a need to look his best.

Sam watched as, with amazing speed, Lord Amburley set the immaculate folds of his neckcloth and donned a stylish blue coat. ''Tis well enough,' he said to his reflection, 'especially for the early morning light. Let's be off, Sam.' Leaving Peveridge gaping, his lordship ran lightly down the stairs, his leather hessians clicking on the polished wood. Sam followed barefoot at his heels.

By the front door stood the old butler carrying a tray with a cup and saucer on it.

'Coffee, m'lord?' he asked, as if it were all an everyday occurrence.

His lordship caught up the cup and downed the hot liquid in a single draught. 'Splendid, Wilson. Just what I needed. What a wonder you are.'

Then the door was opened, and he was down the steps in a trice.

'I shan't need you, Brennan,' he said to the waiting groom. 'Go and have your breakfast.' The groom nodded knowingly but said nothing, still holding the restive bays with both hands. 'Up with you, Sam. Right, Brennan. Let 'em go!'

In seconds, the curricle was round the corner and out of sight, leaving much of his lordship's household open-mouthed on the flagway.

It took some time for the curricle to reach its destination for, in spite of the early hour, the City streets were thronged with workmen and tradespeople. At length, Lord Amburley spoke. 'Are you sure it was the same jarvey, Sam?'

'Aye, yer honour.'

'No doubt she has an arrangement of some

sort with him. That makes matters rather more complicated.' He thought for a moment. 'You can recognise him, I take it?'

'Aye, yer honour,' said Sam again.

'Good. Then you must ensure he is not there to meet her when she comes out.' He continued, noting Sam's incredulous expression, 'It's up to you how you do it. Interfere with the horse, foul the traces—it doesn't matter, as long as it works. Are you game, Sam?' He opened his gloved hand in which a guinea was resting.

Sam gulped. 'Aye, yer honour,' he said a third time.

Amburley had to wait some twenty minutes before Miss Winstanley appeared. For some moments she stood, looking round for the hackney. It was nowhere in sight. Amburley fancied that, since the market outside the prison was very crowded, Miss Winstanley was assuming the cab had been held up by the traffic. It was obvious that she had decided to wait.

She drew her dark shawl more closely round her shoulders and seemed to be trying to shrink into her shabby poke bonnet. Since it had no veil, it provided little concealment. Passers-by were beginning to look enquiringly at the lone woman huddled in her shawl. Once or twice, a man made to speak to her, but one sharp look from those grey-green eyes sent them on their way. She began to walk a little, for there was a sharp wind blowing up from the river.

'May I be of assistance, ma'am?'

He spoke from above and behind her. She made no sign of recognition or acknowledgement and continued to walk.

'Miss Winstanley, may I not take you up from this place?'

At the sound of her name, she turned. Amburley, now alone in his curricle, bent towards her and reached out his hand to help her to mount.

She looked mortified with embarrassment. She hesitated visibly.

Amburley reached lower. 'Forgive me, ma'am—I may not alight to help you. As you see, I am without my groom this morning.'

She put her hand into his and stepped lightly

into the curricle. Then she sat silently, drawing her shawl more tightly still with her gloved hands.

Amburley sat silently too, thinking. In his haste to arrange this meeting, he had not had time to plan how he would handle it, once she was in his carriage. But he was not surprised, on reflection, to note that she had taken refuge in silence. She was a wise, calm woman.

He turned to look more closely at her. The terrible clothes did nothing to enhance her face and figure, of course, but she seemed to him beautiful, in a serene, distant way. Her complexion glowed with a rosy blush at his scrutiny. Still she did not speak.

'I hope I may be of service to you, ma'am,' he said seriously. 'I am sure your aunt would wish me to convey you back to Hill Street. Shall I do so?'

She swallowed hard and gripped her fingers together. 'You are very good, my lord. I am in your debt.'

The rest of the journey was completed in total silence. Miss Winstanley offered no explanation, and Amburley could not bring himself to embarrass her further by asking for one. It seemed that, once she realised he would not press her, she relaxed a little. At least, she unclenched her hands. She did not raise her head, however, as if she were relying on the poke of her bonnet to conceal her identity from any acquaintance they might pass.

As they neared Berkeley Square, Amburley broke the silence. 'Where shall I set you down, ma'am?' He wondered whether she had yet considered the effect of being delivered to her front door in such extraordinary circumstances.

'I…' she faltered.

'If you would prefer to approach your house on foot, I could set you down before we reach Hill Street.'

At her grateful nod, he quickly halted his team. She sprang down nimbly, without any pause for assistance, turning back towards the curricle to thank him briefly. Then she hurried away.

Amburley took his time with his team, all the while covertly watching her retreating back. Avoiding the main part of Hill Street, she turned into a street that must lead, he supposed, to the back of the house. Truly, she seemed to be two completely different women—a poor companion skulking out by the back door, and a fine lady stepping into her carriage from the front.

Driving away, he continued to puzzle over her actions. The image which stayed with him was of her slim form standing for a moment on the flagway, as she bade him farewell. She had been flushed with embarrassment. Her smile had been forced. And her eyes had seemed to be pleading.

Chapter Thirteen

None of the household saw Isabella slip in through the mews entrance and up the back-stairs to the safety of her own room. She closed the door and leaned back against it, momentarily closing her eyes and letting out a long, anguished sigh. Dear God, what was she to do now? All the detail of their first meetings flashed through her mind, yet again, as it had done when she first heard his voice outside the Fleet. If he had harboured any doubts about the identity of 'Winny the companion', they had certainly now been dispelled. Her only consolation was the fact that he had been alone. A groom would have spread such a scandal all over London in a trice.

But how could she ever face him again? How could she ever explain?

Mitchell came in from the dressing-room. 'Whatever is the matter, miss? You look as if you've seen a ghost.'

'I suppose, in a way, I have, Mitchell.' She moved away from the support of the doorway, tugging at the strings of her bonnet, which seemed to have knotted themselves to vex her. 'Oh, devil take the thing!' she cried, ripping the knot in exasperation. She threw the bonnet on to the floor and sank, half-collapsing, into a chair. She did not know whether she should rage or weep. In the end, she did neither, but sat staring fixedly in front of her.

'Miss Isabella! What on earth has happened? Miss Isabella! Please!' Mitchell stood uncertainly for a moment, seemingly transfixed by the strange state her mistress was in. 'I'll fetch her ladyship,' she said at length, turning to make for the door.

Isabella came to herself again at the abigail's words. 'Do not concern yourself, Mitchell. I am quite well, I assure you. I had an unfortunate encounter outside the prison while I was waiting for Tom, that is all.'

'I warned you it wasn't safe to go alone, miss,' Mitchell began, but her scolding was cut short.

'Oh, I was quite safe,' Isabella said, with an ironic smile. 'Whatever else he may be, Lord Amburley is a perfect gentleman.' She looked up just in time to see both shock and concern crossing Mitchell's face. 'He took me up in his curricle and brought me home.' She was still smiling the same twisted smile.

'Dear God!' exclaimed Mitchell fervently. 'Whatever did you say to him? How did you explain what you were about?'

'He did not ask for an explanation and, coward that I am, I did not give him one. I shudder to think what his opinion of me now may be. And my disguise on the North Road is certainly uncovered.' She sighed again. 'Lord Amburley is an honourable man, but I doubt I shall escape the strictures of the *ton* over this escapade.' She buried her face in her hands.

'Don't cry, Miss Isabella, please don't. You've done nothing to be ashamed of, nothing to bring censure on yourself. You should have told him the truth.'

'The truth?' cried Isabella, raising her head. She was very pale, but her eyes were dry. 'Already he knows of my deception in the north. That is enough to make such a man despise me. God knows he thinks little enough of women as it is. Would you have me give him more reasons for his disgust?' She would not let Mitchell say a word but continued her tirade. 'No, no! I shall tell him nothing. Let him think what he will. And say what he will of me to all the world.' She buried her face in her hands once more and, this time, her shoulders shook with silent sobs.

Mitchell stood silently for several minutes, considering. She started towards her mistress, but then seemed to think better of it. The abigail's face showed deep concern as she said, 'Why are you so sure he will start the gossip? Surely he has never betrayed the detail of your first encounter?'

Isabella sniffed and reached for her handkerchief. 'What do you mean? There is no reason to suppose he had recognised Sophia's "poor relation" until today, when he met me dressed like this.' She blew her nose defiantly.

'That's as may be. His lordship has all his wits about him, though, and I fancy he already knew. And, what is more, I do not believe he'll betray you.'

'What makes you say so?'

Mitchell seemed to be screwing up her courage. She took a deep breath, waiting until her mistress was looking her squarely in the face. 'Because I know his lordship is a truly honourable man. You could not love him if he were otherwise.'

Isabella let out a long 'Oh!' and turned away. For fully five minutes she did not speak. At length, she rose and began to pace back and forth across the room, wringing her hands. 'What am I to do? Oh, God, what am I to do?' She had never in her life felt so at a loss. Mitchell might be only an abigail, but there was no one else to whom Isabella could turn.

Taking her mistress's hands in her own and forcibly stopping the frenzied pacing, Mitchell looked into the troubled grey-green eyes. 'Forgive my bluntness, Miss Isabella. There are two things you can do. You can brazen it out and carry on as if nothing had happened. Or you can trust him enough to tell him the truth. It is for you to choose.'

'Dear God, might it not be better simply to leave London for a while? I do not think I can face him again.'

'Miss Isabella, you have never run from trouble in your life. I do not believe you will do so now.' She started to the door once more. 'Let me fetch you a glass of wine to restore your spirits. Once you are rested, you will be able to think more clearly.'

As so often, Mitchell was right. Within the hour, Isabella was berating herself for her foolish and emotional behaviour. Thank God it was only her faithful Mitchell who had seen her momentary weakness. She would certainly not flee London, though she could not quite make up her mind about whether to take Lord Amburley into her confidence. It seemed such a fearful risk to take.

'You must decide soon, miss,' chided Mitchell. 'Have you forgotten that you are engaged to visit St Paul's with his lordship this afternoon?'

That reminder almost brought about a further bout of foolish emotion. With an effort, Isabella succeeded in controlling herself, partly consoled by the thought that a peer of the realm would not wish to be associated with a woman who behaved in such an irregular fashion. He was bound to send round some excuse for breaking their appointment. And she would not blame him for doing so.

By two o'clock, there was still no message from Lord Amburley. However unlikely it might appear to Isabella, his lordship did not seem to wish to cry off.

She dressed mechanically for their outing, not noticing what she wore. Only Mitchell's care ensured that Isabella still looked well enough, in spite of her unwonted pallor. Mitchell pinned the jaunty green velvet hat on to Isabella's honey curls, allowing the long feather to curl down to her ear.

'That colour does become you, miss,' she said, with a degree of lightness much at variance with her look of concern.

Isabella came to herself enough to notice what she was wearing. 'Oh, dear. This is the very gown I wore when I first drove out with his lordship.'

'And none the worse for that, miss. Do not say you wish to change it, for there is not time. His lordship will be here in a matter of minutes, and you know you never keep a gentleman waiting. Go along now, do.' Faced with Isabella's passive melancholy, Mitchell seemed to be reverting to the role of nurse.

Isabella had barely descended to the drawing-room when his lordship was shown in, punctual to the minute, as ever. She flushed scarlet as she rose to receive him, stretching out her hand, but quite unable to raise her eyes to his face.

'Miss Winstanley, how do you do?' He took her hand and held it for several moments, further increasing her confusion. 'May I say how splendid you look, ma'am? That is a very fetching hat.'

The unexpected warmth in his voice penetrated where the words themselves did not. She looked up to find that he was smiling down at her, without any hint of ridicule or disdain. She dared to hope that the afternoon might not become the ordeal she had feared. With a weak attempt at a smile, she allowed him to lead her out and help her into the curricle.

Settling the rug around his passenger, Lord Amburley was well aware of the tension in her. It was no more than he had foreseen, when considering his tactics for this excursion. On this occasion, he had taken the time to plan carefully, as a good military man should. He knew he had made a poor fist of their meeting that morning. Indeed, he would not have been surprised if she had cried off from this one, on some pretext or other. Any other woman would have done so. But this one…? This one had a special quality that was beyond definition. Not for the first time, he found himself considering Isabella Winstanley with a degree of warmth that he had rarely bestowed on any member of the fair sex.

His lordship had determined to conduct this excursion as though their earlier meeting had never taken place. Any hint of a reference to it would be bound to drive her into a shell from which she would never re-emerge in his presence. She had certainly been mortified by their encounter that morning. No doubt, she was expecting at every moment to be exposed as a cheat and a hoyden all over London. He had not stopped to ponder over why he was protecting her reputation—he had simply decided on the spot that he, as a gentleman, must do so. He must show her, by polite concern and assumed normality, that her secret was safe with him. It would be difficult, for he could in no wise allude to what had happened, but he believed that she would come to understand his intentions by the end of a light-hearted and enjoyable afternoon.

'Will you drive on the outward or the return journey, ma'am?'

'I beg your pardon?' Miss Winstanley was visibly startled. 'Oh, I see. I fear I had forgot, my lord.'

Amburley forbore to quiz her about her lapse. Her wounds were as yet too raw. Later perhaps, when she had become a little more comfortable in his company. He set the greys in motion. 'They are, in any case, a little fresh still,' he commented, controlling them with practised skill. 'On our return, you will find them less of a handful, if you are minded to try them.'

She summoned up a nod. 'I should like that, my lord.'

Amburley relaxed a little. Now that she had begun to respond more normally to him, progress could be made. He embarked on a totally innocuous conversation about the events of the previous week, noting how her replies became gradually longer and easier. After half an hour of careful work, he reckoned that their rapport was as much restored as it was going to be on this occasion. He was silently congratulating himself on his success, by the time they walked up the steps into St Paul's.

'How long have you known the truth about me, Lord Amburley?' she asked in a low, quiet voice, her eyes fixed on the steps.

For once, his lordship was almost at a loss. He had underestimated her courage yet again, it seemed. 'How long, ma'am?' he repeated, playing for time.

It appeared that, having begun on this perilous tack, she was not about to desist. 'Aye, my lord. When did you discover the truth? For my own peace of mind, I beg you will tell me.'

'When I first met you again in London, Miss Winstanley,' he responded simply. 'You were singing, most beautifully, at Lady Bridge's soirée.'

She blushed and fell silent.

Amburley could not tell if the blush was a result of his compliment on her singing, or of her shame at being thus unmasked. In an attempt to divert her thoughts, he began to talk randomly about the beauties of the cathedral they were entering. Now was surely not the time to ask about her excursions to the Fleet.

She seemed determined not to be diverted. 'Lord Amburley, I must ask you—how is it that the story of my outrageous behaviour is not the talk of London Society?'

'Why should it be so? Only Lewiston and myself are aware of it. I admit that we have been intrigued, but we have spoken of it to no one else. It is not my way to make sport of ladies, whatever they may do.'

She turned away quickly, without a word.

Amburley feared that he had embarrassed her yet again. Although he could no longer see her face, he fancied there was a tinge of a blush on her exposed neck. He should not press her further. And yet…she herself seemed to be intent on confessing her faults. He had assured her he was to be trusted. Perhaps she would confide in him about her visit to the prison? After a moment's deliberation, Amburley ventured a question, knowing that by doing so, he risked all their new-found rapport. 'Forgive me, Miss Winstanley, but I am still puzzled by our…encounter. Will you tell me why you—?'

'Pride, my lord,' she whispered, before he could finish. 'My stupid, stubborn pride.' There was a catch in her throat as she repeated the word. She straightened her back and lifted her chin, but she did not look at him. 'You will have concluded by now, my lord, that I have allowed it to rule my actions, even when my judgement tells me that I should not succumb. You must think me very wrong-headed.'

So she was too proud to admit to having relatives in the Fleet. At that moment, Amburley was in no mood to blame her. All the blame should fall on the person—whoever he, or she, might be—who had persuaded her to visit the prison thus unaccompanied. She should not have agreed, of course, but the principal fault did not lie with her. When she was less agitated, he would endeavour to discover the identity of the culprit, but there had been confessions enough for the moment.

'Who am I to sit in judgement?' he asked calmly, drawing her hand through his arm. 'Come, let us look at the stained glass. Do you wish to mount to the whispering gallery? I have never done so, but I am told it is worth the exercise.'

Then, placing his hand lightly over hers, he added, 'Do you dare, Miss Winstanley?'

* * *

Although the Isabella who drove back to Hill Street was a considerable improvement on the one who had left in mid-afternoon, she was yet finding the encounter uncomfortable, because she could not put aside her feelings for him. She had found it difficult enough to hide them earlier, especially at the moment when she realised how generously he was dealing with her. She had not dared to look at him then, lest he see her love writ boldly in her eyes. It seemed that he was, after all, everything that Mitchell had described—but she must not think of that.

She forced herself to remain practical, to make a dispassionate assessment of what had taken place. Lord Amburley had gone out of his way to restore her shattered spirits, and with a fair degree of success. She had admitted to him that her 'poor relation' pose had resulted from her stubborn pride. Of course, she had not explained why she was so determined to preserve her anonymity—that would have revealed her hidden wealth—but he had accepted her flimsy explanation calmly and had not badgered her for further details. Best of all, he had done nothing, by word or gesture, to allude to their meeting outside the Fleet prison.

Brennan hurried to the horses' heads as Isabella halted the team outside Lady Wycham's house. Lord Amburley sprang down to help her out and escort her to the door.

Isabella felt a desperate need to end their encounter on a conventional note. 'Shall we see you at the opera tonight, my lord?' she asked.

'I have not yet decided,' he admitted frankly. 'Do you all go?'

'Sophia and I are joining Mrs Ramsey's party. Lady Wycham finds the opera rather too taxing for her strength.'

'I see.'

Isabella thought that he looked somewhat distant, for a moment.

'The opera it shall be, then,' he said, with a nod. 'I look forward to paying my respects in the course of the evening. Until then—your servant, ma'am.' With a swift bow, he returned to his curricle.

Isabella went slowly up the stairs to her room. The faithful Mitchell began to help her to remove her velvet gown but did not speak, for which Isabella was grateful. Mitchell always seemed to know when her mistress needed time to collect her thoughts. Isabella sat at her dressing table so that Mitchell could begin to unpin her hair.

'You do not ask any questions, Mitchell?'

Mitchell looked hard at her mistress in the glass, but said nothing. There was a smile of understanding in her eyes.

Isabella turned round to look squarely at the abigail who was probably closer to her than any other person in the world. 'How did you know I loved him?' she asked simply. It was a day for honest questions and straight answers, she had decided.

'Because I know you, miss,' replied Mitchell, equally simply. 'Lots of little things…they just added up.'

'Does *everyone* know?' Isabella had become even paler at the thought of being the subject of gossip in her household and beyond.

'I have said nothing to anyone, miss, nor would I. How can you think so?'

'Oh, Mitchell, I did not mean that. You know I did not. I trust you above all others. No, I meant…if I have betrayed myself to you, others may have guessed also. Tom, for example. He was with me when I encountered Lord Amburley in the park, the morning after the Duchess's ball.'

Mitchell's lips tightened a little at the reference to the meeting in the park. She had probably suspected something of the sort.

'You need have no fears about Tom, Miss Isabella. He's not one to gossip, even if he did suspect, which I doubt. Unless…what did you tell him about this morning? He may well start to wonder, if he knows his lordship took you up.'

'I did not tell him. I said I was forced to hail a hackney to bring me back when he failed to meet me. He was so intent on making me his apologies—a problem with a broken trace or something of the kind—that he asked no questions at all.'

'And his lordship?'

'You have proved a better judge than I. He would have passed the whole afternoon without a single reference to our first meeting or to this morning's, but I could not let it be so. I had to know whether I was to become the butt of the Season. It was as you suspected: he recognised me at Lady Bridge's musical evening—and he has spoken of it to no one, save Mr Lewiston.'

Mitchell gave a small sigh of relief. 'Did you tell him about the Fleet, too?'

'No. In fact, I told him nothing at all. He simply said he had known all along, and it was not his place to judge me. Then he turned the subject. I could not bring myself to a further confession.'

'Even though it might have redeemed you in his estimation?'

'How so? He would not approve of such unladylike behaviour.'

'You cannot know that, Miss Isabella. After all, he finances his mother's good works.'

Isabella did not stop to consider how Mitchell might have come by that snippet of information. 'It is of no moment, in any case, Mitchell.' She took a deep breath. 'I believe he is developing a *tendre* for Sophia. It would be a good match for her. He is strong enough to resist the unreasonable demands of her family, yet able to keep her in relative comfort. I only hope she values him as she ought.'

'I don't believe it, Miss Isabella.' Mitchell sounded outraged. 'What on earth makes you think that?'

'He has been paying a great deal of attention to her of late and seems to be intent on pursuing her. And he was undecided about attending the opera tonight, until I told him Sophia would be there as well as I. It is not so wonderful after all. She is young, pretty and biddable. They seemed very gay in each other's company.'

Mitchell looked unconvinced.

Isabella turned back to the mirror. 'I should warn Lady Wycham, I think. She will need to be ready to tell him of Sophia's prospects when he calls. I doubt that her lack of dowry will weigh much against her other attractions.'

Chapter Fourteen

Preparing for the visit to the opera, Isabella did her best to put Lord Amburley and his feelings out of her mind. Nothing was left to her now except that stubborn pride of hers, and so she resolved to maintain her dignity, at least. She therefore chose to appear very much the *grande dame* for this meeting, in a gown of garnet red silk of expensive simplicity. Its severe lines and complete lack of ornamentation flattered her tall, slim figure but emphasised that she was no longer in the first flush of youth. She further enhanced the effect by filling the deeply cut neckline with her splendid diamond collar and adding matching ear-studs and bracelet. A diamond aigret sparkled in her honey-gold curls. The woman who stared back at her from the mirror looked magnificent, but cold and unattainable, rather in the style of a classical statue.

'My goodness, Isabella,' exclaimed Lady Wycham, when her great-niece came to her room to take her leave, 'you do look splendid. I had not seen you wear your mother's diamonds before. I thought you…' The thought trailed off, unvoiced.

Isabella felt a need to defend her apparent change of style. 'This gown is rather too plain without something striking by way of jewellery. The diamonds are all I have that can be worn with this shade of red.' Even to her own ears, it sounded rather lame.

The younger ladies took a fond leave of Lady Wycham and descended to the hall, where the butler placed Isabella's dark red velvet opera cloak round her shoulders. Sophia donned a white taffeta cape that had once been Isabella's. The contrast between the two could not have been more marked. Sophia looked young, pretty and innocent. Isabella was clearly a woman of the world, sternly handsome, daunting.

Isabella chose a seat at the front of the Ramsey box, as far to the side as possible. From there, she could enjoy a clear view of the stage and also, she hoped, an opportunity to listen uninterrupted to the music.

The first two acts passed all too soon. When the curtain fell, Isabella was recalled to a sense of the present and to the uncomfortable prospect of a meeting with Lord Amburley.

But he did not appear.

The great Neroni was soon producing more exquisite sound from the stage, but Isabella could not succeed in concentrating on the third act. What a hypocrite I am, she thought bleakly. I distance myself from the others so that I may lose myself in the music, but I cannot devote even half my attention to it. The greater part is occupied in wondering why he has not come, even when I know that it is Sophia he comes to meet. A hypocrite, and a fool besides!

Lord Amburley was not among the visitors

to the Ramsey box in the second interval, either. Several of Sophia's cavaliers presented themselves, however, and set about making themselves agreeable. Sophia's laughter carried easily to the nearby boxes.

'Good evening, Miss Winstanley.' Mr Lewiston's familiar voice shook Isabella out of her reverie. 'You are a great lover of the opera, I collect?'

Isabella rose and extended her hand politely. 'Why, yes, sir, I am. Neroni was wonderful, did you not think?'

'I am afraid I have seen too little of the performance to dare to pass judgement, ma'am. My arrival was much delayed.'

'Oh, I am sorry to hear that. You missed a rare treat, I assure you.'

Isabella was searching for something else to say, when Sophia joined them. 'Why, Mr Lewiston,' she said, as they shook hands, 'I had not thought to see you at the opera. Do you have a box, too? Is it not delightful to be able to meet all one's friends with such ease? And Mrs Ramsey has ordered champagne, too. It is quite wonderful.' She beamed artlessly at Mr Lewiston. 'I have not seen Lord Amburley this evening,' she continued, ignoring the slight furrowing of Mr Lewiston's brows at the name. 'I hope we have not offended his lordship, that he fails to come to our box.'

'Why, certainly not, ma'am,' protested Mr Lewiston, driven at last to speak of his friend. 'Amburley is not here tonight. Indeed, that was the cause of my own late arrival. He has left town on a matter of some urgency, I believe. He sent a message to tell me of it, but my good-for-nothing man failed to deliver it. So I waited for nigh on an hour before I discovered what was amiss. It is to that, Miss Winstanley, that I ascribe the blame for having missed Neroni sing.'

'But why has Lord Amburley gone—?' began Sophia.

'We must hope that nothing untoward has called Lord Amburley from town,' interposed Isabella politely. 'Do you stay in London for the rest of the Season, sir?'

'I shall certainly stay for some weeks yet

ma'am. As will Amburley, I believe, when he returns.' With a gentle smile for Sophia, who was looking quite crestfallen, he set about satisfying her curiosity. 'I expect him to return to town quite soon. Lady Amburley summoned him back to the estate, to deal with an unspecified crisis. Probably, she... Well, never mind. I doubt it will take long to resolve. He will be sorry to have missed paying his respects, particularly when you both look so splendid.'

Isabella accepted the compliment with a dignified nod. It was not, she knew, directed at her. Mr Lewiston's eyes had been fixed on Sophia's face.

'Indeed they do,' echoed their host, as he joined them. 'Miss Winstanley looks particularly splendid in red, if I may make so bold as to say so.'

'You are too kind, sir,' smiled Isabella, recognising that her appearance was likely to be attractive only to gentlemen of an earlier generation. Mr Ramsey's extravagant attentions made her feel old enough to be Sophia's mother.

* * *

After a night's sleep, Isabella felt somewhat recovered from the desolation and disappointment of the previous day. Then, she had passed the events of recent weeks under review and had concluded, reluctantly, that Lord Amburley was pursuing Sophia. Now, in the clear light of morning, her conclusion seemed even more logical.

Isabella was sternly resolved to act in Sophia's best interests now. Her own desires were pushed into a dark corner of her mind where she turned the key firmly. No one would learn of her feelings for Amburley—not Lady Wycham, not Sophia…and certainly not the lord himself.

Having despatched Sophia and her abigail for a fitting at Madame Florette's, Isabella moved reflectively up the staircase to Lady Wycham's room, to broach the subject of Amburley and Sophia. It was, for Isabella, a matter of honour.

Lady Wycham accepted the news with equanimity. 'I was fairly sure she would attract the attentions of at least one eligible gentleman, in spite of her want of prospects. Amburley certainly seems to have been paying considerable attention to her of late. But, from what you tell me, his friend Lewiston has been rather particular in his attentions also.'

'That is true,' conceded Isabella, 'but Mr Lewiston shows no sign of wishing to come to the point, even though he has had opportunities—more indeed than Lord Amburley—to attach her affections.'

'Do you think either of them has done so?'

'Frankly, no, I do not. Though there is a degree of rivalry for Sophia's favours between his lordship and Mr Lewiston which has led to a marked coolness between them of late. It must be resolved soon, I think.'

'You say neither has attached her affection, but has she a preference, do you think?'

'I do not know, Aunt. She has not confided in me. In fact, I doubt she has anything to confide. She likes them both well enough, I dare say.' She paused as a vivid recollection came to her. 'I do recall, however, that she once said Lord Amburley frightened her.'

'Did she so?'

'Yes…but that was when she first knew him. I am certain he does not so affect her now.' Lady Wycham looked unconvinced. 'He is a man of honour and, I suspect, of deep feeling. She would grow to value him.'

'Hmmph. That's as may be. We shall see. For myself, I cannot see why he should have developed a *tendre* for Sophia. A singularly ill-assorted couple, in my estimation.'

Isabella swallowed and nodded dumbly. If only Mr Lewiston would make Sophia an offer quickly, before— She stopped that thought in its tracks, admonishing herself sternly. It is not for Sophia's benefit that you would urge him on, she chided herself, but for your own. And what of Amburley? Does he not deserve happiness with the woman he loves, after so much early heartbreak? How can I wish for him to lose his heart's desire again? If that is the extent of my love, then it is no kind of love at all.

Lord Amburley, arriving back in London after an absence of over a fortnight, set about quizzing Lewiston about his relationship with Sophia. 'I saw the report of the Hill Street ball. A resounding success, by all accounts,' he said, as they shared some fine burgundy over dinner. 'I scanned the *Gazette* regularly for your betrothal announcement. Do you tell me you do not intend to make Miss Sophia an offer?'

Lewiston turned the glass in his fingers, watching how the wine sparkled where it caught the candlelight. It was some moments before he spoke. 'To be honest, I cannot decide. She is surrounded by admirers, wherever she goes. I am merely one of the throng. I see no reason why she would look favourably on my suit. I have nothing to offer her.' He emptied his glass and reached for the decanter.

'You do yourself an injustice, George. You have far more to offer her than most of that motley crew of hangers-on. You, at least, are not after her fortune. You have good family, a noble estate—'

'Nothing that she does not have already, Leigh. My only advantage over the others is wealth—which she does not need.'

His lordship sipped his wine meditatively. 'Does she favour any gentleman in particular?'

'Not as far as I can see.'

'Then you have no clear rival. Come, George, look at this in a positive light. If she has not yet formed an attachment, it is up to you to ensure that her choice falls on you. You *do* want her, I take it?'

'Yes,' admitted Lewiston, reddening slightly and staring again at his wine. 'Yes, I do. But I shall not make her an offer unless I am sure she will accept me. I could not take a refusal, Leigh.'

His lordship concluded from this that his friend's case was very bad indeed. 'There can be no absolute certainty in such matters, you know, George. Women are strange creatures, and unpredictable. If it would be of any help, I could try to draw her out a little on the subject of gentlemen in general, and you in particular.'

Lewiston accepted this unusual offer with alacrity. 'I am engaged to ride in the park with the Winstanley ladies tomorrow morning, Leigh. Will you join us?'

'Not possible, I'm afraid. I must go into the City to see the family lawyer in the morning.'

'Trouble?'

'Of a kind. My mother is in need of substantial funds, for which arrangements must be made.'

'I supposed that something of the kind was the cause of your sudden departure.'

'In that case,' replied his lordship, with a shrug, 'you supposed wrongly. When it is a question of money, my mother simply writes to require me to provide it. She went to the trouble of summoning me to tell me my father's uncle was reported to be dying. She wanted me to persuade him to change his will.'

Lewiston's question was written clearly in his eyes.

'No, of course not. I did not go near him. How can you think it? Silas Stansfield is a family tyrant, who uses his wealth as a weapon to enforce obedience from all his relations. He will live to plague us for years yet, but I refuse to dance to his tune.'

'Your mother could make the approach on

her own behalf, I suppose, seeking his help for her good works.'

'Waste of time, George. The old man don't believe in charity, especially when it's organised by women.'

'So Lady Amburley has to turn to you again?'

'It is natural and right that she should do so, George, since I am the head of the family,' responded Lord Amburley, very much on his dignity.

'I did not for a moment mean—'

'No, of course not. I apologise for being so pompous.' Amburley sounded just a little sheepish. 'It's just that she's gone rather far this time—an orphanage is to be built by public subscription, with the costs underwritten by Lady Amburley, so that building can begin before all the money has been raised. The donations so far are pretty meagre. Unless building is to be halted, the Amburley donation will have to be both large and immediate.'

'Perhaps I might make a donation to Lady Amburley's fund?'

Lord Amburley looked hard at his friend.

'You have not the least interest in orphans, George.' He noted how Lewiston coloured, without attempting to argue. 'Thank you, but no. This is a problem I must resolve for myself.'

'Miss Winstanley's debt might help, if you could bring yourself to collect on it,' observed Lewiston shrewdly.

His lordship laughed. 'By God, I've missed your company, George. It's dull as ditchwater in the country at this time of year. Between the bailiff's interminable lectures about the state of the land, and my mother's urgings about Uncle Silas, it was a singularly dreary visit. Tell me how you have been going on while I was away.'

Lord Amburley then listened to a racy account of the progress of the Season, from which he deduced that his friend was paying court to Sophia Winstanley in much too timid a fashion. As soon as he had resolved his own business affairs, it would be necessary for him to take a hand in Lewiston's.

Lord Amburley's visit to the City firm of Dicks & Jenner next morning took much less time than he had expected. The arrangements proved to be remarkably straightforward—just the liquidation of part of his investments in the Funds which, Mr Dicks assured him, was simplicity itself. Even so, the visit might have lasted longer, if the lawyer had been allowed to deliver the homily that was clearly on the tip of his tongue. Like most of his kind, he strongly disapproved of his clients' dipping into their capital. Indeed, he was wont to say that expenses that could not be funded out of income should simply be forgone.

However, on this occasion, the client cut him short. 'Thank you, Dicks, but my mind is made up. Please go ahead immediately, and arrange for the proceeds to be transmitted at once to Lady Amburley. I take it you have all the authorities you need?' Lord Amburley rose from the hard chair on which he had been sitting.

Mr Dicks hurriedly followed suit. 'Indeed, yes, my lord. I shall set matters in hand immediately.'

Lord Amburley nodded curtly, turning to leave. Mr Dicks scuttled round the desk, only just reaching the door in time to open it and bow his noble client out of the inner sanctum.

'Good day to you, Dicks.'

Mr Dicks bowed again as the outer door closed.

Lord Amburley stood on the step, drawing on his driving gloves. Where was his curricle? After a moment's thought, he concluded that Brennan must be walking the horses in the nearby streets, since he would not have expected his master to appear again so soon. His lordship cursed silently. He could have accompanied Lewiston and the ladies on their ride after all, if he had but known how soon his business would be concluded. But it was too late now. Lewiston would already have made his excuses.

He leaned back against the door jamb, lazily surveying the bustle around him. No wonder Brennan had taken the curricle off. If he had remained here, the result would have been chaos, for there was barely room for a single carriage in the narrow confines of the City street. Most of the traffic was perversely slow, too—hand-carts and hugely overloaded vehicles drawn by single horses, fit only for the knacker's yard. If they met traffic like this during their race, the results would be appalling! It would be vital to avoid such narrow streets when they decided on the route. Not for the first time, he found he was grateful that no one knew what was planned. It was likely to do nothing for his reputation as a whip.

He was still musing abstractedly on Isabella Winstanley when his curricle appeared at the corner of the street. Brennan's consternation was evident. He was making excuses even before he was within earshot.

'Spare me the explanations,' said his lordship curtly, but without heat. 'You had no way of knowing I would need you again so soon.' Lord Amburley did not expect his retainers to number crystal-ball gazing among their accomplishments. He sighed resignedly. 'And now, I find I even have an hour or so in hand. I wonder… Ah, I know. Cigars.'

Brennan looked sideways at his master.

Lord Amburley was in a mood to be indulgent. 'I need some more cigars,' he said brightly, 'so we will pay a visit to Fribourg & Treyer in the Haymarket. It is not far out of our way. And someone has to pander to my filthy habit.' He laughed to himself. Cigar smoking was definitely frowned upon in polite society but he, like many of his fellow soldiers, found blowing a cloud much preferable to taking snuff, even if he did have to skulk outside on the terrace to do it. Perhaps, one day, it would become more acceptable.

It took some time to reach the Haymarket, because the traffic was heavy everywhere. It kept reminding him of the risks attached to his race against Miss Winstanley—if luck were against him, he might even lose his precious greys. He refused to consider such an eventuality.

'Shall I walk them up and down, m'lord?'

Lord Amburley shook his head. 'No. I am in no hurry now. Better you drive them round St James's and back again, so that they are not kept standing. I shall be here when you return.' With that, he passed the reins to the groom and jumped lightly down. He had already disappeared into Fribourg & Treyer's by the time his curricle was in motion once more.

Barely five minutes later, he was standing on the flagway with a box of cigars under his arm. It seemed he was fated to encounter only efficient tradesmen today. In normal circumstances, he would have been cursing if they had been otherwise, but today, everything seemed to be conspiring to give him time on his own—time to think—which he would have preferred to avoid. He began to stroll down the Haymarket, glancing idly into the shop windows as he passed. He hardly noticed what they offered, so preoccupied was he with his thoughts.

He had reached the corner of Panton Street before he paused to look around for his curricle. No sign yet. Ah, well. He turned back to look into the window of the shop on the corner.

Lord Amburley was not in the habit of frequenting jewellers' establishments, but Garrard's certainly offered an eye-catching display. The front of the window was filled with unusual items, obviously bespoke, which must have been made for wealthy clients. In addition, there was a tray of quite beautiful rings, some with oriental designs, and all containing the most exquisite stones. For several minutes, he gazed into the window, considering. Then, with a sudden shrug of his shoulders, he strode into the shop.

Chapter Fifteen

In the course of the next three weeks, Lord Amburley and his friend were often to be found in the company of the Misses Winstanley. Initially, the *ton* found it difficult to decide which of the ladies was being pursued, and by whom.

Mr Lewiston was mainly directing his attention to the younger lady, the heiress from Yorkshire, though he treated the elder Miss Winstanley with the greatest courtesy and danced with her often. Lord Amburley drove out pretty regularly with Miss Winstanley, though not more frequently than with other ladies. He did not drive Miss Sophia at all, but he danced with her at every event, sometimes twice. With the elder Miss Winstanley, he never danced at all.

The tabbies concluded, after much enjoyable speculation, that both men were pursuing the heiress, and that both felt they should seek the chaperon's support for their cause. The gossips would not stoop so low as to wager on the outcome—such activity was beneath them—but they did split into factions to argue the merits of their case.

Lady Sefton favoured Amburley's suit. 'Amburley offers a title. Lewiston has only wealth to recommend him, which she does not need. She will choose title and position.'

Mrs Drummond Burrell disagreed. 'She will choose wealth and the younger man, especially once she meets Georgiana Amburley. A young lady of Sophia Winstanley's background and style will never marry a man whose mother is totally immersed in good works. No parties, no entertaining, no London Season? A title is inadequate compensation for pious boredom.' Since she was the only untitled speaker in the group of patronesses, her words did not carry quite as much weight as she might have liked.

The speculation continued and came, inevitably, to the ears of Lady Wycham. 'Isabella, we must do something. Sophia has become the centre of attention since Amburley returned to London. They are all taking sides as to whether Amburley or Lewiston will win her. We cannot allow this to go on. She has the appearance of the most accomplished flirt, leading on two eligible gentlemen almost for the fun of it. I think I should speak to her. Do not you?'

'I do not know, Aunt. She does not flirt in any improper sense, I assure you, though she is clearly flattered by all the attention she receives. What can one say to her, when she is doing nothing wrong? She cannot be asked to choose between them, for neither has yet come to the point. And who is to say whether they will?'

Lady Wycham was silent for a while. 'I believe you may be right, my dear. If she were to discourage either of them, there is as yet no guarantee that the other would come up to scratch. And with her prospects, we cannot afford to offend *any* possible suitor. I shall not speak to her, then—not yet, at least. But when I next see Amburley, I shall ask him about his intentions.'

'Oh, no!'

Lady Wycham looked up sharply. Isabella flushed bright red under her aunt's penetrating gaze. 'Why ever not? He is not a man to run from such an enquiry. And if he once confides in me, he may bring himself to address Sophia.'

'I beg your pardon, Aunt. I… You will do as you think best, of course, only…I suspect that Sophia will feel duty-bound to accept the first eligible offer she receives, for fear there may not be another.'

'Do you tell me she favours Mr Lewiston?'

'I cannot be sure, but I fancy she may do so. Oh, dear, it is all so difficult.'

'Indeed so,' responded Lady Wycham with a shrewd glance at Isabella. 'Very well. I shall leave matters a little, but only a very little, longer. Meanwhile, you, Isabella, must find out what Sophia's feelings are. I shall speak to Amburley at the end of the week, unless you can assure me that she truly favours Lewiston. Are we agreed on that?'

'I shall do my best, Aunt,' promised Isabella.

After Isabella had left the room, Lady Wycham returned to her tapestry work. For several minutes, she set no stitches at all, staring blankly at the canvas. Then, with a little shrug and a long sigh, she began to ply her needle.

Isabella returned quickly to her own room. Her fiery blush had been replaced by a pronounced pallor, and her hands were shaking slightly as she closed the door of her sanctuary. For once, Mitchell was absent. Isabella had only her own disordered thoughts for company.

They were not pleasant thoughts. Three weeks of watching Amburley in pursuit of Sophia had depressed Isabella's spirits.

Isabella herself had had very little real contact with Lord Amburley since his return, except for their regular weekly drives in and around London. Although he had never once referred to her masquerade or to the encounter at the Fleet, it was becoming increasingly difficult for her to retain her composure in his company.

She had often wished she were not committed to their private race. None the less, since it was unavoidable, she remained determined to show him she could be a worthy opponent. Partly for that reason, she had insisted that they avoid the simple, direct route along Fleet Street and the Strand. That would simply be a matter of speed—she would have no chance at all of mounting a respectable challenge.

Lord Amburley had eventually agreed, after much discussion, that a more circuitous route, taking in Newgate and Lincoln's Inn Fields, would be a fairer test of their skill. They had driven it twice now, and the times had been wildly different. The outcome of their race might be purely a matter of chance.

Had it not been for the need to hide her feelings from him, she would have enjoyed their drives. His lordship was a well-read and much-travelled man, whose measured opinions marked his good sense and considerable intellect. Furthermore, he paid her the unusual compliment of discussing serious subjects with her. He knew how to provide

amusing company, besides. His witty anec-
dotes of the lighter side of a soldier's life in the
Peninsula often brought Isabella's laughter
bubbling out, in spite of her inner melancholy.

He seldom spoke of Sophia. When he did, he
seemed to Isabella to be trying to probe for information about her feelings. But, however ob-
liquely he might approach the subject, Isabella
was always on her guard. Privately, she sym-
pathised greatly with his desire for reassurance
before making another offer, but she owed it
to Sophia not to give anything away. In any
case, as she had now admitted to Lady
Wycham, she really had none of Sophia's
secrets to share.

It being Wednesday, she and Sophia were
engaged for Almack's, with Isabella yet again
in the role of chaperon. Isabella was tempted
to play the *grande dame* once more, which she
had not tried since the night at the opera. But
what would it serve? She would look cool and
dignified, to be sure, but it would not make her
the object of his affections. If anything, it
would widen the gulf that was already opening

between them, and she had to admit she did not want that. Being in his company might be purgatory; but losing him forever would be like the loss of part of herself.

She reviewed her situation as dispassionately as she was able. Time was not on her side. She had no choice, now, but to set about discovering what Sophia's feelings were. And if Sophia did favour Amburley, he would no doubt be brought up to scratch by Lady Wycham within a very short time. Thereafter, private intercourse with him would be at an end. He would be Sophia's betrothed. Isabella's only hope was that Sophia might truly favour Mr Lewiston—though it was not a wager on which she would have hazarded much.

Twenty-four hours more, she concluded. That is all I have—tonight at Almack's, and tomorrow, when we drive out into London. Aunt Jemima expects her answer before Friday. Well, I shall endeavour to make the most of every minute. The memories will be all I shall have.

She reviewed her tactics in this new light.

Not the *grande dame*, she concluded, but the beauty. She would be exactly as she had been at the Duchess of Newcombe's ball, even as far as the aquamarines. He had admired her then. Perhaps, just perhaps, he might do so again.

Lord Amburley and his friend dined in Jermyn Street before going on to Almack's. His lordship had very little progress to report.

'It is a little difficult on our drives because of the groom, of course, but I have tried on several occasions to draw Miss Winstanley out on the subject of Miss Sophia's feelings. Unfortunately, she persists in avoiding the issue. Have you been more successful?'

'Not really. Miss Sophia gives me vague encouragement, but nothing specific. And she seems to favour others quite as much as she does me. I tell you, Leigh, I cannot continue this posturing ritual for much longer.'

Amburley refilled their glasses. 'No,' he agreed slowly, 'it must be brought to a head soon. I wonder… Yes, I think that might serve. Provided I can create an opportunity for an uninterrupted private discussion with Miss Winstanley, I think the matter may be managed.' Lewiston looked inquiringly at his friend, but Amburley did not expand on the details of his plan.

Lewiston sounded a note of caution. 'That might be difficult, in the crush. It is so easy to be overheard. Still, you could always dance with her.'

That was treading on very delicate ground. The two men had reached an unspoken under-standing, some weeks before, that they would not discuss Amburley's reluctance to dance with Miss Winstanley. Amburley had chosen to let his friend believe that it was a result of a desire to avoid gossip, particularly during a period when he was driving out with her fairly regularly. To himself, he was prepared to admit that the reasons went deeper than that, but he would not probe them too far. The truth might be painful.

'If it is the only way,' Amburley returned lightly, 'I shall certainly dance with Miss Winstanley this evening. You, I take it, will be dancing with Miss Sophia?'

'If I can. But that will be, at most, two dances and precious little time to woo her.' He sounded almost despondent.

'Come, let us talk of other things for now. There is nothing more we can do about your courtship, until we arrive at the Marriage Mart.' He sipped his wine. 'Lord, how I detest it. So many hopeful young things, swathed in silk and hung with jewels, paraded to tempt the eligible male of the species.'

'What an extraordinary man you are, Leigh. You have certainly changed your tune of late. You make it sound positively medieval—' Amburley's cocked eyebrow indicated that that was precisely what he did think '—but in any case, Miss Sophia does no such thing. She dresses as becomes a young lady just out, and she is never hung with extravagant jewellery. The most I have seen her wear is a locket, or a single strand of pearls.'

'Very expensive pearls,' remarked Amburley sardonically.

'But quite in keeping for a lady of her position. Miss Winstanley, by contrast—'

'What of her?' interrupted Amburley, rather too quickly. 'I have never seen her wear more than aquamarines.'

It was Lewiston's turn to win the war of words over jewellery. 'I'm afraid you missed the spectacle at the opera, Leigh. Miss Isabella Winstanley in a gown of unrelieved red silk and positively dripping with diamonds.' He paused, as shock registered on Amburley's face. 'I cannot imagine why she wore them or, indeed, where she had them. The effect was stunning, I may tell you. She looked like a queen—at least, to those who do not know what she really is.'

'Dear God,' muttered Amburley, half to himself. He reached for the decanter and concentrated hard on refilling their crystal glasses. 'The sooner we can have you safely riveted to Miss Sophia, George, the sooner Miss Winstanley will revert to her proper station and abandon this shameful imposture. I shall see what can be done tonight, I promise you.'

For several moments, there was silence between them. 'Come,' said Amburley at length, rising from the table, 'we had best leave now, so that we have ample time at Almack's. There is much to be done.'

Lord Amburley was set on seizing the initiative at Almack's—and keeping it. Barely had the Winstanley party entered, than he greeted them. 'Good evening, Miss Winstanley, Miss Sophia.' He was delighted to see that his tactics were working. Miss Winstanley had clearly not been prepared to meet him the moment she entered the ballroom. He registered the shock in her eyes as he shook her hand. 'You see us both before you, reformed characters, ma'am.' His gaze warmed as he took stock of her stunning appearance. 'May I have the honour of this dance?'

Miss Winstanley gave a little gasp but made a quick recover, with a forced smile, as she accepted his arm to the floor.

There was not much opportunity for conversation during the country dance. Amburley fancied his partner was remembering the embarrassing silence of their only previous essay on the floor, for she forced herself into light-hearted banter each time they came together.

'You mentioned that you are reformed, my lord. Dare I ask from what wickedness you have turned?'

'Lack of self-interest, ma'am.'

He had surprised her into a laugh. 'I knew I should not ask. I am now even less enlightened than before,' she said as the dance parted them again. They passed down the set and came together again at the bottom, having completed the complex figures. 'Curiosity is my besetting sin, my lord,' she said, looking up at him through her lashes, 'particularly when my partner fails to satisfy it.'

'If you would allow me to borrow your favourite epithet, ma'am, I should say "outrageous",' he said, ruthlessly stifling his natural desire to laugh. 'But then, it would be outrageous in me, so to describe a lady.'

'Oh!' She was trying to assume an expression of disapproval, but it was totally unconvincing. Her eyes were sparkling, and her lips twitched as she tried not to smile.

Amburley gazed down at her. She looked so radiant that he caught his breath. For a moment, he could think of nothing at all to say. 'One of the benefits of an early arrival at Almack's, ma'am, is the opportunity to ask for the hand of a beautiful lady for the waltz.' He had to clear his throat before he could continue. 'Will you do me the honour, after the supper interval?'

He felt her hand tremble a little in his. She failed to meet his eyes as she replied huskily, 'Thank you, my lord, I should be delighted.'

The dance ended then, and he led her from the floor, turning the conversation to everyday matters while he tried to fathom what on earth had come over him. He had fully intended to waltz with her later, but what had possessed him to say such a thing? Madness! An inner voice whispered that there had been hidden meaning in her reaction too, but he refused to listen to it. He must hold fast to his purpose.

Isabella left the supper room on the arm of a middle-aged admirer, unable to say what she had eaten or what she had said or done. Since that dance with Lord Amburley, his words kept running round and round her head. She could not stop seeing his face and the warm glow in his chocolate eyes. She could not imagine why he now wished to dance with her. She tried to tell herself sternly not to hope.

Lord Amburley came to claim her for the waltz. She was perversely pleased, this time, to see that she managed to control the quivering of her fingers when she touched him. She had promised herself, besides, that she would not stare in silence at the perfection of his cravat—but she still found it immensely difficult to open the conversation.

'You waltz most elegantly, ma'am,' he began politely, expertly guiding her through the whirling throng. 'It is a pleasure to have such a partner. And it is a pleasure, too, to have an opportunity of private conversation with you.'

She looked up at him, suspicion beginning to cloud her sparkling eyes.

'I need to speak frankly on a delicate matter, ma'am, and you are the only person who can advise me.'

Isabella's heart was sinking rapidly in the direction of her silken slippers. She forced herself to keep a smile on her lips, politely assuring him that he might continue.

'It concerns Miss Sophia, ma'am, as I think you may have guessed. Forgive my plain speaking, Miss Winstanley, but tell me, I beg you: will Miss Sophia favour Lewiston's suit?'

Isabella felt as if an iron hand had gripped her, so that she could not breathe. She had known he was pursuing Sophia but, somehow, particularly here in his arms, she had allowed her hopes to overcome her reason. Now, all was clear. He was waltzing with her, not for the pleasure of her company, but callously, to create an opportunity to quiz her about whether Sophia favoured Mr Lewiston over himself.

Her confusion must have been evident. And it was some moments before she found her voice. 'You are very blunt, my lord,' she said, in a strained tone. 'But your confidence is misplaced, I fear, for I cannot answer your question.' She had become rigid in his arms by the end of this little speech.

'I see,' he responded tightly. 'Forgive me for my impertinence, ma'am, I had thought you… I beg your pardon.'

Their dance continued in stiff silence. Isabella breathed a sigh of relief as he returned her to her party and took his leave. Thank God that was over. Being alone in his company had become unbearable. But how could she avoid it? They still had not completed their race. Oh, God! Tomorrow she was engaged to drive out with him again. Surely she would never be able to face him?

For a moment, she toyed with the thought of feigning illness on the morrow, but she soon dismissed that idea. She could not be such a coward. Drawing on all her inner resources, she smiled benignly on the gentleman who approached to invite her to dance. Whatever else Amburley may think of me, she vowed, he will never find me craven.

Chapter Sixteen

When Lord Amburley returned from his early morning ride next day, he found Sam shifting impatiently from one foot to the other outside his front door.

"Ere, guv'nor, I got what yer wanted at last. She—'

'Not here, Sam,' interrupted Lord Amburley sharply. 'Curb your impatience just a little longer, lad.' He gave the reins of his huge grey into the hands of the waiting lackey and led the way inside. 'Bring some madeira to the book-room, if you please, Wilson, and a pot of ale for young Sam.'

Sam made to blurt out his news as soon as the book-room door closed behind them, but

Lord Amburley cut him short. 'Have you *all* the information this time, Sam?'

'Aye, yer honour, the 'ole fing. She's—'

'I suggest you wait until you've wet your whistle a bit and then give me it all from the beginning. Ah, splendid, here's Wilson with the madeira.'

By the time his lordship had poured himself a glass of madeira, Sam had emptied his pot of ale and was obviously itching to embark on his tale. But Lord Amburley would not be rushed. He wished to prepare himself for intelligence that he rather feared would be unwelcome. With deliberation, he took his accustomed place behind the mahogany desk and looked searchingly and sternly at Sam.

'Very well, young Sam. Now, tell me everything you have learned, from the beginning, if you please.'

Sam swallowed. 'Well, yer honour, like I told yer last week, the gentry-mort visits the Fleet at least once a se'enight, sometimes more'n once. Always ever so early it is, when she gets there. An' always with the same jarvey, 'im what I fixed when yer honour wanted 'im out o' the way. I got in under 'is 'orse an' cut 'is trace. 'E didn't even know I were there.'

'Go on,' encouraged his lordship, not wishing to interrupt Sam's flow, even though he was repeating facts from earlier reports— and boasting of his successes.

'She always wears them dark togs, wi' the shawl an' bonnet an' all. An' the jarvey comes back to meet 'er, by arrangement like, when she comes out again. I 'itched meself on the back o' the 'ackney outside the Fleet last week. Weren't worth the trouble. Went right back to the gentry-ken what she started from.'

Amburley's fingers were now starting to drum impatiently on the arm of his chair, and his stern look had developed into a frown. He was going to have trouble controlling his temper, if Sam did not soon come to the point.

Sam swallowed again. 'Yer honour wanted ter know 'oo the gentry-mort were visiting in the Fleet. I managed ter find a cove from inside last week, guv'nor, an' 'e agreed to watch 'er on 'er visits. Cost me 'alf-a-crown,' he added hopefully, looking at his lordship.

'Your expenses will be paid, Sam, *provided* you come up with the goods. Now…'

'This cove in the Fleet, 'e took a terrible long time ter find out about 'er doings, but 'e struck lucky t'day. The gentry-mort visits a cove name o' Graham.'

'What do you know of him? What sort of man is he?'

'Don't rightly know, yer honour, 'cept 'e's quite young an' well togged-up in a dreary sort o' way. Black, mostly.'

'You've seen him?'

'Aye, yer honour. 'E left just after the gentry-mort came out ter meet the jarvey.'

'He *left*?' repeated his lordship in surprise. 'I see. Do you know where he went?'

'Course I do. Followed 'im, di'nt I?' Sam gave a satisfied smirk. 'Went in ter that big church near the river.'

'Not an inmate, then,' deduced Lord Amburley, 'and, by his dress, a parson.'

'Dunno about that, yer honour. Di'nt fink

yer honour'd want ter know that. Thought it were the gentry-mort you was after.'

'I do want information about the lady, certainly. And for a lad who claimed to have "the whole thing", you have provided precious little so far.'

'I ain't finished yet, 'ave I?' countered Sam indignantly.

Amburley had to laugh at the defiant face of the urchin before him. 'I beg your pardon, Sam,' he said in mock contrition. 'Pray, do continue.'

Sam gave him a knowing look. 'I dunno whether this 'ere Graham cove's a parson or not, but I 'ave found out what they do in the Fleet.'

Lord Amburley leaned forward in his chair, tension apparent on his face.

'The cove's started a school for the nippers in the Fleet, them as is in there wiv their parents, like. The gentry-mort comes to teach the girls ter sew an' such like. I'd o' found out afore, only I never thought but that she were seeing someone in there more permanent, so ter speak.'

His lordship cut short Sam's recital of why

he had taken so long to solve the riddle. He wanted, above all, to be alone, to think through this remarkable intelligence. 'Here.' He dropped two golden guineas into the grubby palm. 'Now, I'm going to send you down to the kitchen to get a square meal into that scrawny body of yours.'

Sam had hardly begun to voice his astonished gratitude by the time the butler appeared, summoned by Lord Amburley's bell.

Amburley let out a long breath as the door closed behind them and poured himself another glass of madeira. Sipping it meditatively, he began to piece together what he now knew.

She went to the Fleet to teach the wretched children there. Not surprising, really, in view of her passionate defence of Christian charity. She might be a penniless companion, but she would recognise that there were many who were even more disadvantaged than herself and, yes, she was the kind of woman who would wish to do something about it. Her wealthier sisters would simply give money to salve their conscience—if they had one.

Isabella Winstanley was denied that easy option. She would give of herself. He should have guessed as much.

He smiled a little as he sipped the golden liquid. It was almost the colour of her hair. Unconsciously, his hand went to his waistcoat pocket to finger what he carried there. Her image rose in his mind as he had seen her last evening, a vision in the exquisite gown of gold and jade. She was beautiful, he admitted to himself, though not in the recognised sense. Hers was a more elusive quality that defied description. Beauty of soul, perhaps? He shook his head at such high-flown words and wondered, not for the first time, how it was that he had become so impractical of late.

After a moment more, he rose and began to pace the room. Doubts assailed him once more. If it were merely a piece of charity work, why had she not explained, when he picked her up outside the Fleet? The question nagged at him. He could not help wondering whether there was more than a shared interest in the education of hapless children between Miss Winstanley and the Reverend Mr Graham.

When he returned to Jermyn Street some hours later, having vented his frustration on various opponents at Gentleman Jackson's boxing parlour, there was barely time to change his dress before he was due to leave to collect Miss Winstanley. In a surprisingly short space of time, he was back in the hallway, impatiently slapping his gloves against his leg, while he waited for Brennan to return from the mews with the new team harnessed to the curricle.

No sooner had they appeared, than he was off.

'They're very fresh today, my lord,' said the groom, surreptitiously gripping the edge of the seat as Lord Amburley feather-edged the corner. 'Not best suited to town-driving, if I may say so.'

His lordship looked, for a second, as if he were about to deliver a very sharp retort, but then thought better of it. Brennan had served him too long to be the butt of his temper. 'I shall need you to walk the horses when I reach Hill Street.

But I don't take you with me this afternoon. You can walk back to the stables.' Brennan did not attempt to argue. He always knew when his master was not in a mood to be crossed.

In spite of Amburley's hair-raising driving, they arrived in Hill Street a minute or so behind time, which certainly did not improve his lordship's temper. Brennan sat mute, a little pale around the mouth. 'What's got into you, man?' snapped Lord Amburley, losing patience at last. 'Go to their heads, dammit, I'm already late enough.' Brennan scrambled to obey.

As usual, Isabella was ready and waiting, dressed in the rich green she so often wore. If she looked a little pale, she hoped it would be attributed to her late night at Almack's. 'Good afternoon, Lord Amburley,' she said, rising to meet him and extending her hand. 'Punctual as ever.'

'That may be said of you, Miss Winstanley, but not, on this occasion, of me. I fear I was delayed by some business and am a little behind my time. Pray, excuse me.'

Isabella thought that his voice sounded a

little strained. He could not, surely, be as tense as she was about this meeting? Unlike her, he had no cause.

Having settled Isabella comfortably in the curricle, Lord Amburley took the reins himself and, with a brief nod to his groom, let them have their heads. They were still very fresh, and it took considerable strength to hold them.

Isabella sat calmly with her hands clasped in her lap, admiring his skill and in no way incommoded when he took the first corner with barely an inch to spare. 'If you drive like that in our race, my lord, I shall certainly not best you, however generous the time allowance.'

Lord Amburley checked and slowed the greys a little. 'I beg your pardon, ma'am, I did not mean to alarm you.'

'But you have not done so,' protested Isabella, sitting totally composed.

That provoked a sidelong glance from Lord Amburley. 'I see I must beg your pardon yet again, Miss Winstanley. In my defence, I can only say that you seem to have nerves of steel, at least by comparison with my groom, who was not even trying to conceal his fright by the time we arrived in Hill Street.'

'An interesting comparison, my lord,' murmured Isabella, noting a slight tightening of his jaw at her veiled suggestion of impropriety. She chose to soften her strictures a little. 'I can well understand his feelings,' she continued. 'After all, he must do as he is bid, whatever your behaviour. I have always the option of asking you to modify it.'

'And do you so choose, ma'am?' he asked tartly, deftly steering his team through a gap that looked too narrow to accommodate them.

'Not at present, my lord.'

Perhaps it was her teasing smile, perhaps it was his own self-control, but, from that moment, he visibly began to relax. The horses seemed to sense their master's change of mood almost at once and became noticeably less skittish. They drove on in comfortable silence, until they reached St Paul's.

'As this is to be our last outing before the race, ma'am, I thought you might like to drive the route a second time. The corners between

Newgate and the Fleet are a test of any whip, especially at speed.'

Isabella felt a little uncomfortable at the mention of the prisons, but she did not attempt to speak, merely nodding her assent. She took the ribbons and the whip from his hands and gave all her attention to her team, setting them in motion at a good but not cracking pace.

His lordship watched approvingly as she completed the circuit of the cathedral and started up Newgate Street. 'You are not planning to demonstrate all your skill today then, ma'am?'

'You shall not tempt me so easily, my lord,' she replied, expertly flicking her leader with her whip. 'I do not yet know what manner of time you will set me next week. It would certainly be foolish in me to give you an early indication of what I can do. Behold me, serious and sedate.'

'Indeed, ma'am,' he agreed, 'as you always are.'

Isabella could not immediately hit upon a suitable riposte, but her smile must have told him his barb had struck home. She was concentrating on threading her team through the traffic around the prison.

'The City seems very busy today,' he observed. 'It will not be much of a race if we face this again next week.'

'At this pace, I dare say we shall need wellnigh an hour more to reach the Abbey. Does the traffic depend on the day, my lord? Markets or some such?'

'It certainly varies from day to day, ma'am, but I am at a loss to account for it. In London, there are markets almost every day.'

Although the traffic had eased somewhat, and Isabella's team had picked up a little speed, she was forced to go carefully in the narrow lane skirting the prison. When the Fleet itself came in sight, her hands tightened a little on the ribbons, making the greys resume their earlier restiveness as they made the turn into the main street.

'If you will forgive my saying so, Miss Winstanley,' began his lordship gently, 'your tension is conveying itself to the horses.'

'Oh!' gasped Isabella. 'Are you regretting

your decision to permit me to drive them, my lord?' Her tone became even more haughty as she added, 'I shall of course return the reins to you at once, if you have the least concern for the welfare of your team.'

'No, ma'am, pray continue. I have not the slightest desire to take them from you. If I have a regret, it is only that you do not trust me enough to tell me what it is that so troubles you about this place.'

Isabella coloured and then grew very pale. Tension was now evident in every line of her body. 'You seek my confidence, my lord?' she asked at length, in a very low voice.

'Only if you are prepared to entrust it to me, ma'am. I pray that you will. I should like to help you if I can.'

Isabella's brain was in turmoil. She did not know what his offer of help might mean, but she warmed to the note of genuine concern in his deep voice. Her heart longed to tell him everything, to confess every outrageous action and throw herself on his mercy. Her head warned her that there might be no mercy.

Besides, why should a man in love with Sophia take such pains for her spinster cousin?

Her innate sense of justice reminded her that she *owed* him an explanation, whatever his motives for asking might now be. He knew she visited the Fleet in the guise of the poor relation. He could have pressed her for an explanation at the time; or he could have made her the subject of wicked gossip. Yet he had done neither, proving surely that she might trust him?

She slowed her team to a sedate walk while she made up her mind. She saw that he was smiling at her, beguilingly, so that her heart turned over and she was lost. 'I think I do owe you an explanation, if you wish for it, sir.'

He nodded encouragingly.

'It is a complicated tale, I fear,' she began hesitantly. 'I told you once before that my actions had been driven by foolish pride. Nothing can now be done about that, and I beg that you will forget about it.' She looked at him for some sign of understanding.

She could see that he was hesitating. She could not wonder at it. It would be difficult for any gentleman to overlook conduct such as hers. She held her breath, waiting.

After a moment, he seemed to reach a decision. 'I can undertake to indulge in an appropriate lapse of memory, if you wish, ma'am.'

'Thank you, sir,' she whispered, closing her eyes for a second, before looking gratefully up at him. 'Pray, why do you smile so?'

His lordship considered a moment more. 'Well, ma'am, you have spent the last several weeks in studiously addressing me as "my lord". Until now, that is. I hope your reverting to the less formal mode of speech is a sign that I may be winning your trust.'

Isabella was now completely at a loss for words. She had not consciously chosen any particular mode of address, but it seemed that her formality had rankled. The unconscious change, she supposed, had dated from her discovery of her own feelings for him and her natural desire to salvage her pride in the face of his indifference. How difficult it was to deal with him. And how relieved she would be when these meetings were at an end.

She swallowed hard. 'You have asked me to confide in you, sir, and I shall do so. I feel that I owe you an explanation, I freely admit. Your forbearance has been more than I dared to expect.' Seeing that he was not about to make any reply, she screwed up her courage and plunged into the recital of her iniquities.

'You chanced to encounter me one morning outside the Fleet prison, my lord, dressed as I had been when we met on the North Road. You have, no doubt, wondered about that incident. I must tell you, first, that I was waiting for a hackney that should have been there to meet me, but was delayed by some slight accident.'

Lord Amburley nodded.

'What you will not know, sir, is that I was outside the Fleet because I had just been inside it.' She glanced up at him then, but he said nothing. 'You do not ask why, my lord?'

'I see no need, ma'am. I feel reasonably confident that you intend to share your motives with me.'

'As you say, my lord. I should tell you, first

that I chanced to make the acquaintance of a curate, a Mr Graham, who is also a chaplain to the Fleet. His uncle is the rector on my brother's estate. Mr Graham is a man of great qualities, who burns to do good in the world. He has been much impressed by the beneficial changes which have been brought about in the felons' prisons, such as Newgate, by the Christian charity of a Mrs Fry, from the City. She is in fact a Quaker, I understand, and the wife of a banker. It would not normally be expected that our paths would cross and, indeed, I have never met her myself. But I know that she has wrought miracles among the Newgate women, in turning them aside from drunkenness—and worse.

'The position with the Fleet is not, of course, so dire. Some of the debtors there live in relative comfort by comparison with Newgate. But the women and children—some of them live in such squalor and want! Mrs Fry teaches a woman's skills to the females awaiting deportation. In the Fleet, nothing has been done. The little girls have no one to help them learn the skills they will need, if they are ever to earn an honest living.

'The prison needed someone who could teach them to sew and to mend, and the dozen other skills that most women learn at home at their mother's knee. Mr Graham besought me to find a lady who would undertake the role. I could not charge another with… Suffice it to say, I took on the task myself and, oh, I am glad of it, whatever other difficulties it may have created.' She ventured another glance at him then, but there was nothing to be read from his expression.

'I visit the Fleet in the early mornings, once or twice a week, dressed as you saw me. I go alone,' she added, with a note of challenge in her voice, 'though I do not want for chaperons once inside. And, except on the single occasion when you took me up, my lord, I am carried to and fro in a hackney driven by my old groom, Tom.

'There, sir, you have it all,' she concluded, staring fixedly at a point between the horses' heads.

'It is surprising, perhaps, that the story of Miss Winstanley's good works has not got about,' he observed.

'I do not use my own name in the Fleet, sir. There I am Miss Winter.'

'Very wise.' He paused, obviously digesting this new information. 'Miss Winstanley, I…I am grateful that you have felt able to confide in me. It is an edifying story. I wonder only why—forgive my presumption, ma'am—why you did not tell me at the time. Your reticence was bound to make me seek a much less laudable explanation for your presence at the Fleet. And I might have shared my ill-founded suspicions with others, to your detriment.'

They had reached Lincoln's Inn while he was speaking. Isabella tried to concentrate on her horses, pulling them to the side of the road and bringing the curricle to a gentle halt. She turned to face him then, for the first time since she had taken the reins at St Paul's. Her cheeks were a little flushed as she looked up at him, unable to read the veiled expression in his eyes.

'I had already made you one confession that

day, my lord,' she conceded, almost in a whisper. 'I did not have the courage to make you another.'

Chapter Seventeen

When she arrived back at Hill Street some time later, Isabella had still not regained her composure. To be sure, she and Lord Amburley had reached a tolerable accommodation over her exploits in the Fleet prison. He had even gone so far as to look favourably on her charitable impulses, though she fancied he did not approve of her methods. She had no doubt that his Sophia would never be allowed to jaunter around town in a common hackney, or to venture into a den of iniquity such as the Fleet, however charitable the aim.

His Sophia! Oh, God! She had only a few hours left in which to find out whether Sophia returned his regard. Aunt Jemima might be beholden to Isabella for the upkeep of her establishment, but on matters of social propriety, her rule was absolute. Lady Wycham would speak to Lord Amburley precisely as she had warned.

Refusing to allow her feet to drag, Isabella climbed the stairs to her room to change her dress. 'Is Miss Sophia at home, do you know, Mitchell?' she enquired presently. Even the most distasteful interviews had to be faced.

'No, miss. She is gone out driving with Miss Ramsey and has not yet returned.'

Isabella was not sure if such respite were welcome. Would she be able to keep her courage?

'I shall rest for a little while before dinner. But I do wish to speak to Miss Sophia, as soon as she returns. Be so good as to bring me word immediately, Mitchell.'

Sleep was impossible, of course. Her mind was in total disarray, with unrelated snatches of their conversation running round and round—images, too, like the quizzical lift of his eyebrow, or his strong hands controlling the greys with practised ease. And always—

always—the clean scent of his skin whenever she was close enough to touch him…as she so often longed to do.

Now, faced with the prospect of losing him irrevocably, she at last admitted to herself that he would have been precisely the husband for her. He had a thousand good qualities. They could have shared so much together, laughed together over so many private jokes. He was, admittedly, a little taciturn in company, but that was surely to be preferred to the vacuous fribbles with which London abounded? So well suited. And she knew she could have made him happy, if only…if only he had loved her and not Sophia.

This melancholy reverie was interrupted by a message that Sophia had returned. Isabella hastily donned a dressing-gown and allowed Mitchell to restore some semblance of order to her hair.

'Shall I ask Miss Sophia to come, miss?'

'No, Mitchell, thank you. I shall go to her, I hink.'

Sophia spent the first ten minutes regaling sabella with the details of her day and her hopes for the ball they were to attend that evening. Isabella listened with only half an ear, absently watching the clever fingers of Sophia's abigail re-dressing her mistress's hair for the evening.

'That is most becoming, Sophia, dear. In your new blue gown, you will look lovely, I am sure. Have you some flowers for your hair?'

'Oh, yes. Madame Florette sent some silk ones, in shades of blue. And I have received such a pretty blue posy.' She rose to fetch it. 'Look. It will be exactly right, do you not think?'

'Why, yes,' agreed Isabella, eyeing the posy suspiciously for a sign of who might have sent it. 'But you will need some jewellery to wear also. Would you like to borrow my pearls again?'

At Sophia's eager nod, Isabella despatched the abigail to fetch them from Mitchell, who would know instinctively to hold the younger woman in conversation for a while.

'From whom did you have the posy, my dear?' Isabella then enquired nonchalantly. 'Someone who knew what colour you planned to wear to the ball, I collect?'

'Oh, no! This one was from Mr Elworth, I think. There were several others too, but mostly pink or yellow, which would not do at all.'

'I see. And do you favour Mr Elworth?'

'Lord, no!' exclaimed Sophia. 'Why, he's as old as my father!'

Isabella frowned a little. Her charge's relative youth could not excuse such dangerous naïvety. She must learn to understand the importance of small gestures, where gentlemen were concerned. 'If you do not favour him, my dear, do you not think it a little unwise to choose his flowers over all the rest?'

Blushing, Sophia admitted she had not thought of that.

'Come, let us see what else you have. Perhaps one of the others may be made to suit.'

There were five posies altogether, two pink, two yellow and one white. 'Well,' said Isabella uncertainly, 'the yellow is clearly impossible, but the white would serve. And the pink also, if you were to change the flowers for your hair. May I ask who sent these posies?'

It transpired that one of the pink posies was from Mr Lewiston. The white one was from Lord Amburley.

Sophia hesitated self-consciously, touching first one posy, then another. 'Mr Lewiston's flowers are very pretty, to be sure. But these tiny white rosebuds in Lord Amburley's bouquet are exquisite, do you not agree? And I could add some of the blue ribbon from Mr Elworth's posy to the white one, which would make it quite perfect.' Sophia was beaming at her own ingenuity.

Isabella was determined that Sophia should not make her choice lightly. 'Lord Amburley will be gratified that your choice has fallen on him,' she said gravely. 'You are sure you should not favour Mr Lewiston, rather?'

'Oh, no! Decidedly not.' Sophia sounded very sure. 'Besides, he will need no explanation, when he sees that my gown is blue.'

Their discussion was interrupted by the return of Sophia's maid with the promised pearls. There would be no opportunity for any further conversation of a private nature before the ball. Isabella would have to rest on what little she had managed to glean.

She hurried away to Lady Wycham's room. 'She has not told me in terms, Aunt, but she has chosen to carry Lord Amburley's flowers tonight, in preference to Mr Lewiston's, even after I explained what could be read into her choice. Perhaps she does prefer Lord Amburley after all? Certainly, she cannot now dislike him. Even she must know better than to carry the flowers of a man she would wish to avoid.'

Lady Wycham nodded sagely.

'I should be better placed to judge this evening, I fancy,' Isabella continued, trying to keep all emotion out of her voice. 'I mean to observe them both closely, when he sees Sophia has accepted his posy.'

'And also Mr Lewiston, I suggest, when he sees that she has not,' observed the sharp old lady. 'Come to me after the ball, dear, and tell me what you have seen. I shall not be asleep, I promise. Now, you had best go and dress. It wants but half an hour until dinner.'

It did not take Isabella long to change into a splendid new gown of gold-spangled silk over an ivory underdress. The shimmering ensemble was completed by her gold filigree jewellery and a spangled scarf over her bare arms. She was critically assessing the overall effect, when a footman appeared at the door with a florist's box. Inside rested a tiny posy of exquisite rosebuds in ivory and gold.

'How on earth can this be?' exclaimed Isabella, searching for the card. 'Surely this cannot be coincidence?' She stopped in disbelief, holding the card in her fingers. It contained only a firm black signature—'Amburley'.

'Oh!' breathed Isabella, unable to tear her eyes from the card.

'What is it, Miss Isabella?'

'Just for a moment, Mitchell, I thought… But no matter. He sends me flowers in hopes that I may help him to win Sophia, I believe, that is all. She had a splendid white posy from him earlier. This, I think, was an afterthought.' With that painful conclusion, she went down to dinner.

* * *

Watching both Sophia and Amburley, when they met at the ball, was rather more difficult than Isabella had supposed. She could see all of Sophia's face; but part of Amburley's was in shadow.

Sophia was smiling brilliantly at Amburley and thanking him for the flowers. Isabella wondered whether the radiant delight arose from meeting his lordship, or from being at the ball. With Sophia, it was always difficult to tell.

Amburley was smiling down into Sophia's face with what seemed, to Isabella, to be real warmth and love. She was unable to see the expression in his eyes, but she was not at all surprised, a moment later, to learn that he had asked Sophia for the first waltz. A lover was bound to ask for the waltz, after all.

Mr Lewiston frowned a little, Isabella noted, on hearing that his friend's flowers had been preferred, particularly when Sophia naïvely admitted to having changed the ribbons on the white bouquet.

He thinks she could as well have added blue

ribbons to his pink posy, Isabella concluded. As, indeed, she might have done.

Mr Lewiston's disappointment did not prevent him from securing Sophia's hand for the second waltz, however. Clearly, he was not yet prepared to give up hope.

Considering the situation, Isabella was beginning to feel more than a little sorry for Mr Lewiston, when Lord Amburley appeared by her side to interrupt her train of thought. 'A penny for them, ma'am,' he said.

'Oh! I beg your pardon, my lord. I fear I was wool-gathering. And I have not yet thanked you for the beautiful flowers. I admit I was quite astonished to receive a bouquet which exactly suited my gown.' She raised the posy to inhale the exotic scent. Something more to remember.

'I collect that you believe that ladies have a monopoly on intuition, Miss Winstanley,' responded his lordship smoothly—omitting to mention that he had bought the information from Florette's man.

Isabella had no answer for him. She merely

smiled and breathed the heady perfume once more, while trying to think of something to say.

His lordship was before her. 'Will you honour me with the second waltz, ma'am, if you are not already engaged?'

She had not expected that. After all, he no longer needed to contrive moments of privacy with her, in order to further his cause with Sophia. For her own peace of mind, she should refuse him—but she could not bring herself to do it, even while she continued to wonder about his motives. He scribbled on her card and was gone.

Although the ball was a splendid affair, Isabella was not enjoying it much. She had to spend too much time spying on Sophia and her cavaliers. By the time supper was announced, Sophia had danced twice with Lord Amburley, including the first waltz, and once with Mr Lewiston. She seemed to stand on terms of intimacy with both gentlemen, which Isabella found puzzling, though she fancied she detected something special in the way Sophia looked up into Amburley's eyes. When

Isabella herself danced with Mr Lewiston, she felt he was rather less at his ease than he had been previously. She supposed it must be jealousy. Poor Mr Lewiston.

Isabella was beginning to feel sick with apprehension as the second waltz approached and Lord Amburley came to claim her for, perhaps, the last time in her life.

'The privilege is mine, I believe, ma'am,' he said politely, offering his arm.

She hesitated before taking it. The sensations, she knew, would be just as before—strange feelings of heat throughout her body, and weakness in all her limbs. When they took the floor, she began to feel light-headed, even though she had taken no wine all evening.

He waltzed beautifully, guiding her securely but effortlessly round the floor. 'Are you looking forward to our race next week, Miss Winstanley?' he began abruptly. 'I must tell you, I am beginning to feel some qualms at the prospect of losing my favourite horses to you.'

'Fie, my lord! I do not believe for one moment that you expect to lose.' She had responded with more spirit than she had thought possible.

Lord Amburley looked a little guilty. 'Expect to lose? Well, no, ma'am. But, on the other hand, I am not wholly confident that I shall win. You are much too good an opponent for that.'

'Thank you, sir. From you, that is a compliment indeed.'

He then proceeded to explain all the details of the first leg of the race, which he would drive. Isabella mutely agreed to everything he proposed. Her own turn could take place at any time in the following three weeks, he said. Again, she simply nodded. She did not choose to tell him that she had privately resolved to be done with it as quickly as possible, certainly within the week.

As the waltz neared its end, Lord Amburley switched the conversation. 'How is Lady Wycham, ma'am? I note she does not often accompany you to engagements of late. I trust she is not indisposed?'

'Thank you for your kind enquiry, my lord. I fear Lady Wycham is not quite herself at present. She is recovering from a sharp attack she suffered a week ago and does not yet venture out.'

'Pray, give her my best regards. Indeed, if she is receiving visitors, I shall call myself to deliver them.'

Isabella glanced up sharply at that, but apart from the faintest gleam in his eye, his expression was unreadable. Devil take him! 'Lady Wycham received some callers today, I believe, my lord, while you and I were…otherwise engaged.' She smiled a little as her tiny arrow hit home and—if she were truthful—at the memory of their afternoon together. 'It is a great pity she is not yet herself again,' she added, after a moment's further deliberation, 'for she particularly wanted to accompany us to Richmond tomorrow. Unfortunately, it is not to be. Are you engaged for the party to Richmond, my lord?' she asked innocently, though perfectly well aware that he was not.

'No. I fear I shall not have that pleasure, ma'am. My friend Lewiston will be there, I believe,' he added. He seemed not at all concerned that Sophia might be stolen almost from under his nose. Then, leading Isabella from the floor, he looked into her eyes and added softly, 'Thank you for the waltz, Miss Winstanley. It has been my pleasure.'

On this last occasion, Isabella found that she wanted to believe him. But she could not—his motives were all too obvious.

By the time she arrived back in Hill Street, long after midnight, Isabella no longer doubted that Lord Amburley intended to offer for Sophia. She had watched the pair covertly for the rest of the evening. All his actions seemed, to the knowledgeable observer that Isabella had become, to betray the lover. Indeed, she wondered why there was, as yet, so little gossip about their burgeoning love affair. And, to cap it all, he had danced with Isabella, simply to find out whether and when he might approach Lady Wycham for permission to pay his addresses. Odious, odious man! She wished she might never set eyes on him again.

Isabella was soon sitting on the edge of Lady

Wycham's bed, sipping (at her ladyship's insistence) a glass of warm milk. She had schooled her features to show nothing of what she felt. 'I spent the evening watching them, Aunt. I am as sure as I can be, that Sophia returns his regard, at least enough to accept an offer from him. *His* feelings are beyond doubt, I believe. There is such warmth and love in his face when he looks at her. He even created an opportunity to extract information from me about when you might be well enough to receive him.'

'Did he, indeed? And how did he contrive that, my dear?' Lady Wycham sounded rather sceptical.

A slightly bitter laugh preceded Isabella's reply. 'I own to having trapped him, ma'am. I baited my trap with the information that Sophia and I were going to Richmond tomorrow without you. I think you may expect him to call in the course of the day.' Her face was inscrutable as she pronounced the death sentence on her own love.

The old lady nodded. 'Well, at least it should

be a more pleasant interview than my last, when Gradely came to seek *your* hand.'

Lord Amburley waited on Lady Wycham at noon next day. She fancied he seemed less than his normal assured self. Strange, for he had no grounds for concern, surely? An eligible gentleman, titled and fairly comfortably circumstanced, about to offer for a penniless chit barely out of the schoolroom? Sophia's father would welcome him with open arms.

Lady Wycham took pains to put her visitor at his ease, but she did not truly succeed. He declined her offer of refreshment. And he perched precariously on the edge of his chair. Lady Wycham smiled encouragingly.

'Lady Wycham,' he began, then paused to clear his throat. 'Lady Wycham, I seek your permission to pay my addresses to Miss Winstanley.' He sounded a little strained.

'It is a joy to me that your choice should have fallen on Sophia,' responded Lady Wycham, with a generous smile.

His lordship stared. 'Why, no, ma'am. I fear

you are mistaken. I have no desire to wed an heiress. No, indeed. It is the regard of Miss Isabella Winstanley I seek to earn.'

'Isabella? Oh, dear…'

Lord Amburley launched into what seemed to be a prepared speech. 'Lady Wycham, I know her position is awkward, but my intentions are wholly honourable, I assure you. I am perfectly able to keep Miss Winstanley in a comfortable, though not an opulent style. She would be—'

Lady Wycham could not let him continue. 'Lord Amburley, forgive me, but you are labouring under a terrible misapprehension. I do not quite understand how it may have come about—and it is most distressing that I should have to disabuse you in such…delicate circumstances. I must tell you, sir, that Sophia is not an heiress. She has no expectations at all. Neither, to be precise, has Isabella.' She stopped, looking very concerned. 'Lord Amburley, I have to confess that Isabella and I have given currency to a falsehood, in order to protect Isabella herself from fortune-hunters. Since you ask for her, I must now tell you that she is *already* a very rich woman in her own right.'

Amburley looked stricken. After a moment, he excused himself and walked to the window where he stood immobile for some minutes, apparently lost in contemplation of the beauties of the house opposite. When he returned to his seat opposite Lady Wycham, his face was pale and set.

'I have made a grave error, Lady Wycham, for which I can only apologise. I pray you will allow me to take back what I have said to you today and to withdraw.'

Lady Wycham was astonished. 'Do you mean to tell me you do not wish to offer for Isabella after all? Such is not the conduct I should have expected of you, sir.'

His lordship flushed but stood his ground. 'I am no fortune-hunter, ma'am. When I marry, *I* shall be the one to provide for my wife. I ask you to try to understand my position, ma'am. To continue now would be impossible.'

Her ladyship was much touched by this honest appeal, in spite of an overwhelming desire to box Amburley's ears. How could a grown man be so stubborn?

'I ask you to grant me one favour, ma'am,' continued Lord Amburley, in a low voice. 'It is that you forget everything I have said to you today and, especially, that you say nothing of it to Miss Winstanley.'

'And you expect me to agree to this?'

'I ask it of you for Isabella's—Miss Winstanley's—sake, ma'am. Whatever her feelings may be, it can do nothing but harm for her to learn that I wished to make her an offer—but could not.'

Lady Wycham nodded.

'I should prefer to say, simply, that I called to ask after your health, as I promised I should. Will you do this—for her, Lady Wycham?'

'Yes, I will. But you will permit an old woman to tell you that you are a fool, my lord,' she added, shaking her head sadly. 'All kinds of a fool.'

Chapter Eighteen

None of the Hill Street ladies saw Lord Amburley for the better part of a week. According to Lady Wycham, he had called on her merely to enquire after her health. According to Mr Lewiston, he had departed for the country later that same day, presumably following another urgent summons from his estates.

Isabella could not understand it at all. Not for the first time, she taxed Lady Wycham on the subject. 'Do you tell me, Aunt, that he gave no hint at all of wishing to make an offer?'

'Isabella, it is quite unlike you to persist in asking questions that I have already answered. What are you about? Lord Amburley was not here above fifteen minutes. He asked after my health. He could quite easily have asked my permission to offer for Sophia. Indeed, I did what I could to encourage him to speak. He *chose* to make no offer for Sophia. Now, I hope that you will be satisfied at last, and that we need not return to this subject again. Speculation about what might have been achieves nothing.'

'Perhaps he is gone to Yorkshire?' ventured Isabella.

'I take leave to doubt that. Why should he go to her father, when he was already in my house and could ask leave of me? I imagine he has been recalled to his estate, or some such. No doubt he will return ere long.'

Isabella knew better than most that Lord Amburley must return, for he was due in London on the morrow, for the first leg of their race.

On the following morning, Isabella prepared with some care. She knew she must be practical in this, for the curricle would be moving at considerable speed through some of the least salubrious parts of London. It would be dirty and dusty; and if it should chance to rain, they would, no doubt, become thoroughly mud-spattered as well.

She ought to wear something eminently serviceable, of course, but she found herself laughing out loud when it occurred to her that the most appropriate costume would be 'Miss Winter's' hideous brown dress. Lord Amburley would certainly have some barbed comment to make about her appearance, if she wore that!

After lengthy hesitation, Isabella donned her newest walking dress, in Prussian blue with black frogging at the neck and cuffs. It was heavy enough to keep out the worst of what the weather might do and, if it did become covered in dust and dirt, it would no doubt brush clean. Isabella considered her reflection in the glass. She had to admit that her matching shako-style hat looked most becoming—but, at the last moment, she cast it aside in favour of a rather less daring blue bonnet. Unlike the shako, the bonnet could be securely tied under her chin.

By the time she was finally satisfied, it wanted but five minutes to the hour, and so she made her way downstairs, to await Lord Amburley's arrival. Somehow she knew he must come, that he would not cry off without sending her word. She was not surprised, therefore, when he was announced, promptly at the hour agreed.

'Good morning, my lord,' she said affably, shaking hands with him. 'I hope you have not interrupted your business out of town, simply to keep a frivolous engagement with me?' She observed with concern that his smile did not quite reach his eyes. He was troubled; but he was taking pains to conceal it.

'Nothing short of force would have per-suaded me to fail you, Miss Winstanley, I assure you. Especially,' he added, with a rather more genuine smile, 'as my greys would then have been forfeit.'

Isabella laughed. Then, purposefully drawing on her York tan gloves, she led the way to the door.

The first part of the journey to St Paul's was completed in almost total silence. Lord Amburley seemed to be too preoccupied with his team to make any conversation. And Isabella, feeling suddenly both nervous and a little embarrassed, could think of nothing to say. She concentrated instead on the varied sights around her. Normally, they drove out together in the afternoon but, on this early morning excursion, the light made everything seem very different—Isabella found herself noticing things that she had previously overlooked.

It would be impossible to overlook St Paul's, of course, for its huge dome dominated all the City around it. Isabella promised herself that, if Lord Amburley still had not spoken by the time the dome came in sight, she herself would find something to say. She found herself looking out for it much too soon, as they threaded their way past the King's Mews towards the Strand. So far, the weather was being kind; the sky was blue and the sun was now shining directly into their eyes. Isabella was half-blinded, in spite of her poke bonnet.

Lord Amburley had his team well in hand now, since the fast trot along Piccadilly had taken the edge off them. He had been lucky with the traffic thus far, Isabella knew. Even the Haymarket had been less crowded than usual. She refused to think about what that did to her chances of winning, when her own turn came.

The Strand became more and more crowded, however, the closer they came to St Mary's church. The street was slightly wider there, but the buildings were much too tall for Isabella to catch even a glimpse yet of the great dome. And Lord Amburley still sat silent, his gloved hands delicately steering the greys between coal carts and carriages.

Isabella had to admire his skill as they inched past a laden cart—a very tricky manoeuvre, which she was not sure she could have undertaken herself. Just as they cleared the obstacle, a man ran out from behind a street-stall, bellowing something totally incomprehensible at the top of his voice. The nearside horse, startled, made to shy, but Lord Amburley controlled it instantly, and without apparent effort.

As he pressed on towards St Clement's, Isabella found herself saying, 'That was a very fine piece of driving, my lord.'

Lord Amburley half turned towards her, but he did not look her in the eye. 'Thank you, ma'am,' he said, before falling silent again.

Isabella was beginning to feel that she ought to be annoyed at his want of manners; a gentleman really should make some effort in a situation such as this. But she could not speak just then, for they were approaching Temple Bar— the entrance to the City. Lord Amburley had to rein in his horses to negotiate the narrow gateway, which left Isabella almost within touching distance of the fly-infested meat stalls at the roadside. She looked away quickly, trying to ignore the overpowering smell of blood.

Once through the gate, St Paul's was soon visible in the sunlight, its gold cross glinting and its dome forming a massive backdrop to the elegant black spire of St Martin's. Now, she must force him to speak.

'With so little traffic about today, you will certainly record a good time, my lord,' Isabella said calmly. 'You picked a favourable day, indeed. Another example of male intuition, perhaps?'

Her banter seemed to go wide of the mark.

Amburley's jaw clenched visibly, and he seemed to be in the grip of a sudden passion. He turned on her with cold anger. 'Do you suggest, ma'am, that I play other than fair in this?'

Isabella was shaken by his harshness, but she responded immediately. 'Of course I do not, my lord, and you know perfectly well that I would not do so. I declare, you seem determined to pick a quarrel with me today.'

Her counter-attack deflated his anger. 'I beg your pardon, ma'am,' he said stiffly. 'I have offended you. Pray, excuse me.'

What on earth was the matter with him? Her teasing had never before provoked such a response. He must be under considerable strain to forget himself in such a way. Isabella resolved to tease no more that day and lapsed into silence again, while the curricle made its way up Ludgate Hill, finally drawing to a halt by the statue of Queen Anne in front of the cathedral steps. For a moment, Amburley sat taut, staring ahead; then he seemed to relax a little and turned towards Isabella.

She smiled generously at him, looking up

into dark eyes that seemed to warm, just a little, in return. 'I had forgot to ask you when we last met, sir, about how the timing is to be done. There are rules about such things, I collect?'

'Indeed, there are, ma'am.' He took his watch from his pocket and handed it to her. 'It is for the opponent to give the word to start and to take charge of the timing. It is perfectly in order, too,' he added, with a hint of sarcasm in his voice, 'for you to wait until my way is barred by traffic before you pronounce the "off".'

'I should not dream of doing so,' protested Isabella. 'I shall win fairly or not at all.' She threw him a challenging look.

He did not reply. He simply looked at her with frank admiration for a long moment. Her flush of wrath was in danger of becoming a blush of embarrassment. An awkward silence reigned yet again.

Isabella fixed her eyes on the watch, determined not to look up at her companion. Out of the corner of her eye, she saw him straightening the reins in his fingers. 'I am ready whenever you say,' he said curtly.

Isabella waited. She had decided she would give the word as soon as the minute hand reached the quarter, but the hand was moving so slowly it seemed to be stuck. She looked up at the clock tower to check. It showed the same time. She forced herself to concentrate again on the watch.

All around her, the noise and bustle of the churchyard seemed to intensify. Every word spoken, every tradesman's cry seemed to be magnified until she felt as if they were resonating in her mind like pealing bells. At her side, the warm, vibrant body of her companion was a magnet to her fingers; she had to clasp her hands more tightly around the watch to prevent them from straying towards his arm. His male scent filled her nostrils, overpowering even the memory of the earlier sickening stench. She closed her eyes. The effect of his presence became stronger still.

The quarter hour chimed. 'Now!' she cried, without pause for thought.

The horses leapt forward with such power that Isabella was thrown back in her seat almost dropping the precious watch in the process. If his lordship heard her shocked gasp, he gave no sign of it. He was concentrating on his team.

In the relatively light traffic, the curricle moved fast, taking the corner of the cathedral with barely any slackening of speed and overtaking slower vehicles with ease. A movement opposite caught Isabella's eye: by the time they had rounded the second corner and were racing north towards Cheapside, several wide-eyed boys were staring down at them from the cathedral school window, pointing excitedly. Isabella cringed inwardly.

She had forced herself to resume her normal, upright position. She was both exhilarated and dismayed, for she knew she herself could never drive through town in such a fashion, however exciting it might seem. And they were already attracting far too much attention—not only from schoolboys, but from almost everyone else around. Two men on horseback had pulled up to stare. So much for Amburley's 'private race'. Unfortunately, there was nothing she could do or say now. He would slow down if she asked—she had no doubt of that—but that would not be fair. He would slow down, too, if he thought she was frightened—but she would not stoop to such a stratagem. She might as well live for the dangerous moment.

Isabella focused on the spire in front of her as they came up to the busy cross-roads. She could not remember the name of the church, which vexed her immeasurably, but she allowed herself a moment to admire the simplicity of its steeple. That reflection would help her to retain her calm during Amburley's headlong dash.

The junction was too busy to allow any vehicle to pass at more than walking pace, however skilful the driver. Horses and carts seemed to be crossing in all directions. Some of them were laden with freshly killed carcasses. Isabella swallowed hard. It was the first time she had seen traffic of this kind. By afternoon, she supposed, the market trade was usually long over.

It seemed that Amburley, too, had not reckoned on such heavy market traffic. He had slowed his team, perforce, but the set of his shoulders suggested that he was more than a little annoyed at the delay. Isabella found herself thinking that, if her own drive took place in the afternoon, she might have an easier run. Perhaps Amburley was thinking the same.

The curricle was forced to a standstill while yet another huge meat-cart made its way across the junction and into Cheapside. Amburley's hands tightened on the reins and he muttered something to himself. The horses had become rather skittish—probably unsettled by the smell of blood all around them.

Amburley's deep voice began to soothe them gently. It soothed Isabella too, she had to admit, for she had been getting as edgy as his team.

At last they were clear into Newgate Street, though progress was not much faster there. It seemed that every other entry led to a tippling house of some kind—one stumbling drunk almost fell under the horses' hooves. And then, here were the innumerable meat stalls to contend with, so close to Smithfield market. Thank God their route would avoid the bloody excesses of Skinner Street!

The curricle had barely edged above a walk by the time they reached Christchurch. Isabella dared to take a deep breath as they passed the neat vestry house. How could anyone live there among the noise and the appalling smells? Perhaps one became accustomed. After all, when she had first entered the Fleet, the stench had made her ill. Now, she barely noticed it.

Beyond Christchurch burial ground, the street narrowed once more, with high buildings and market stalls on both sides. At the corner, the looming walls of Newgate cast a deep shadow across the junction towards St Sepulchre's great church. Isabella was perversely glad that she had remembered the name of this one, at least.

They were approaching the turn when it suddenly occurred to her that she had no idea what might confront her when they rounded the corner of the prison. This, after all, was where public hangings took place. She forced herself to think rationally. Hangings took place at eight in the morning—it was now nearly ten. Besides, there would have been a huge crowd around the prison gate for a hanging, and St Sepulchre's bell would have been tolling. She looked up expectantly at the church, but the bell remained stubbornly silent. Surely sometimes the corpses were left to hang on the gibbet, as a warning? What if—?

Amburley feather-edged the corner into Old Bailey, travelling rather faster now. Isabella immediately shut her eyes, momentarily afraid of what she might see. Then, feeling the increasing pace, she realised that any obstructions outside Newgate must have been removed. Somewhat ashamed of her weakness, she forced herself to look. All that was to be seen was the gaunt expanse of Newgate's walls. Of course.

They were heading due south now, in the shadow of the prison. Isabella shivered in the sudden chill but refused to let it overset her. Instead, she raised her eyes to the blue sky. She could just see the wedding-cake tower of St

Bride's over to her right, glistening white in the sunshine. She smiled in recognition.

In a moment, the curricle must make the turn from the breadth of Old Bailey into the narrow confines of Fleet Lane. If Amburley were very lucky, he might have a chance to race along its winding length; but they had never yet managed to do so on any of their practice runs. On every occasion, they had encountered at least one vehicle blocking their path. Isabella fancied they might soon be brought up short.

In the event, Amburley made the turn rather faster than prudence dictated. The turn itself was gentle enough, but the entry into the lane was blind. Isabella managed to overcome her instinct to grab for the side of the curricle—but she did shut her eyes again for a few seconds. Amburley would not be aware of her weakness; he was fully occupied in controlling his team.

The lane must be empty, Isabella thought, eyes still stubbornly closed, as the curricle gathered speed once more, racing down the slope to the first bend. It was really cold now, for the lane was so narrow that hardly any sunshine eve penetrated between its high walls. She forced herself to master the urge to shiver, even as she forced her eyes open once more. The lane was indeed empty as far as the bend. Once they rounded that, anything might happen.

Isabella steeled herself, feeling suddenly ashamed of her earlier weaknesses. It did not matter that Amburley was unaware of it. Isabella Winstanley should not show fear, even to herself! She resolved that she would do so no more, however recklessly his lordship might drive. She would *not* cling on to the curricle—and she would *not* shut her eyes like a frightened child.

Amburley had not said a single word to her since they left St Paul's, apart from that unintelligible muttering at the Cheapside junction. As they neared the bend in the lane, Isabella heard him snatch a sudden breath and start to rein in his horses. A lumbering cart had just reached the end of the lane that joined from the right, barely thirty yards ahead of them. It was making to turn across their path, to precede them down Fleet Lane. Isabella fancied she heard a murmured oath; then the horses were whipped up again. Obviously, Lord Amburley had decided to squeeze through the diminishing gap between the turning cart and the stone wall. If he made it, they would probably have a clear run to the end of the lane. If he failed…

He must be mad, Isabella concluded. And I must be mad too, to be here with him. I have never known him to behave so rashly. What can have happened to make him behave so? It cannot be just the risk of losing his horses. Surely—

They were barely ten yards from the cart when the driver heard them. His head jerked round sharply. The vacant expression on his face changed to horror, as he registered the curricle bearing down on him. In a split second, he had thrown all his weight on to the reins, yelling to his horse to stop. Isabella had a momentary feeling of sympathy for the poor old animal, pulling such a huge load. No wonder it stopped at a word.

The gap between the corner of the cart and the wall did not look wide enough for the curricle to pass through, but Amburley gathered his pair and pushed them on, almost without a check. The carter's shouted abuse followed them down the lane. Isabella was glad she could not make out his words.

She felt Amburley throw a quick glance at her. She hoped—nay, she knew—that she was sitting proudly erect, showing no fear. She had determined long ago to salvage her pride, if nothing else. She thought he smiled, briefly.

Amburley's watch was still tightly clasped in her gloved hands. They were nearing the Fleet prison now. Its high walls were already visible on their left, behind the ramshackle houses in the lane. Isabella judged they had covered about a quarter of the total distance, but she had no idea of how much time had elapsed. She had rather lost track, because the watch cover had snapped shut when she almost dropped it. She must find the catch to open it again.

She could not quite see where it was. The watch was quite large, but delicately made. It was certainly not intended to be opened by heavily gloved hands. She began to fumble awkwardly, then paused, wondering whether she should remove one of her gloves. But how was she to do so without dropping the watch in the process?

Amburley's team continued to pound along the narrow lane to the turn into Fleet market. Isabella continued to fiddle with the watch, trying one last time to spring the catch with her gloved fingers.

The curricle reached the corner of the prison. The road ahead was clear. Amburley took the turn at a cracking pace. The horses started to gather even more speed.

Isabella had barely noticed where they were. She was still struggling with Amburley's benighted timepiece.

'Look out!' cried a man's voice.

A small girl had strayed into the roadway in the path of the oncoming curricle. For a moment, it seemed she must fall under the pounding hooves. But Amburley was quick to see the danger. He wrenched his horses sharply over, almost overturning the curricle on the muddy surface. For several seconds, it seemed to hang in the air, precariously balanced on one wheel. Then it came to rest again on two. Lord Amburley, the child, and the greys were unscathed.

But Isabella—concentrating on the watch and unaware of any danger—had been tossed out on to the roadway where she now lay, still as death.

With a groan of despair, Amburley leapt down from his place, flinging the reins to the nearest bystander. He dropped to his knees beside her inert body and gathered her in his arms. His face was ashen. 'Isabella! Oh, God, what have I done? Isabella!! Speak to me, my love!'

Her body lay limp in his arms. She was intensely pale, with a tiny trickle of blood at her temple. It was impossible to tell whether she still breathed. Amburley himself was breathing very fast now, trying desperately to find a pulse, some hint of life, however faint. He laid his cheek against her lips, praying for a sign that he had not lost her. There seemed to be none.

'No, no!' he whispered, through clenched teeth. 'Please, God, do not let me lose her now!' Pushing aside her bonnet, he stroked her hair back from her pale brow, cradling her head in his arms as if she were the most precious thing in the world. 'Isabella! Come back to me! Do not leave me, my love!'

For a long moment, he simply gazed down at her mask-like face, his own contorted with anguish. Then, at last, as if in answer to his prayers, her eyelashes flickered a fraction, though her eyes did not open. She stirred a very little in his arms. 'Wh…what did you say?' she whispered, her voice barely audible.

Amburley was transformed as he looked down at her. In an instant, he seemed to have recovered his normal upright bearing, and the colour had returned to his face. 'Isabella. Oh, Isabella,' he responded gently, drawing her even closer into the protection of his encircling arms. 'Thank God you have come back to me. Try to open your eyes, my love. Please, try.'

She struggled to comply and finally succeeded. She felt dazed. Her eyes could not focus properly on his face, so near to hers. His seemed to be radiant with love, but that could not be, surely?

'What did you call me, sir?' she whispered

again, striving just a little to be released from her compromising position.

'Lie still, my love,' he replied, with a brilliant smile of relief. 'I can see that you are yourself again, but there is no call to struggle. I have you firmly now, and I mean to keep you.'

Isabella closed her eyes and sank back into his comforting embrace. Her mind was in a whirl. Had it not been for the warm pressure of those strong arms, she would have known she was dreaming. As it was, she simply stopped trying to think at all and gave herself up to feeling.

The curious crowd gathering around them was growing ever more pressing. There was clearly an urgent need to remove Isabella from the roadway. 'Do you think you are sufficiently recovered to be taken home, Isabella?' he asked anxiously.

She knew he was willing her to respond. When her eyes opened this time, her dazed look had been replaced by a glow of so much love that it almost took his breath away. 'Yes, my lord, if you will just help me to stand.' She made a move to rise.

'Be still, woman!' he commanded lovingly, smiling more broadly, now that her recovery seemed assured. He stood up with her in his arms and carried her to the curricle, where he placed her tenderly on the seat, supporting her back and head while he climbed in beside her. Tossing a shilling to the urchin who had taken charge of the greys, he collected them with practised ease and then set them in motion towards the Strand, very gently, with Isabella resting against his shoulder.

They had barely gone a couple of streets before she drew away from him to sit upright in her place. Her head was spinning, her bonnet was askew, and she knew she looked a fright. Amburley removed his supporting arm and gave his attention to his horses, watching her covertly from the corner of his eye.

Isabella, more or less recovered now, set about bringing some order to her dress. If she had been seen, all dishevelled, driving in a open carriage with Amburley's arm around her and her head on his chest… Suddenly, it burst upon her that she did not care. He loved her. He loved her! Above the noise of the London traffic, she would swear she could hear birds singing.

The journey was accomplished in silence until they reached Hill Street. Isabella was floating on a magic cloud, afraid to speak lest she break the spell. But when he halted his team and turned to look down into her eyes, she knew the spell was forever. 'My lord—' she began.

'Isabella,' he interrupted, in long-suffering accents, 'I will not be saddled with a wife who persists in addressing me by my title. Unless you can bring yourself to call me "Leigh", I shall have to withdraw my proposal.'

'But you haven't made one!' she protested. Then, at the sight of the wicked mirth on his face, she began to laugh. 'Ouch, that hurts,' she cried, putting her hand to her head.

'Forgive me, love. You are far from fully re-covered. Let me bring you into the house. The other matter,' he added, giving her a meaning-ful look, 'can be resolved later.'

She made only a half-hearted protest, when he lifted her down from the curricle and carried her into the house and up the stairs to the drawing-room, where he laid her gently on the sofa. Having removed her bonnet and gloves, he knelt beside her, holding her hand until Lady Wycham appeared in response to his summons.

'My lord, what has happened?'

Amburley relinquished Isabella's hand and rose to meet Lady Wycham.

'Pray do not alarm yourself, ma'am,' he said swiftly, taking her outstretched hand. 'There was an unfortunate accident. A child ran under the horses' hooves. The child escaped un-scathed, but Miss Winstanley was thrown out of the curricle. She landed rather awkwardly and sustained a nasty blow on the head, I fear.' Lady Wycham gasped and put her hand to her throat. 'I believe Miss Winstanley has taken no lasting harm, ma'am, but you will wish to see for yourself.'

'Do not worry, Aunt,' interposed Isabella from the sofa. 'I have the headache and some bruises, that is all. His lordship has been kindness itself. I am sure I shall be quite well by tomorrow.'

After a brief examination of her great-niece,

Lady Wycham pronounced that it did not *seem* serious, though she doubted Isabella's hurts would mend in a day. 'I have some excellent salve upstairs. If you would be good enough to bear Isabella company for a few minutes, my lord, I shall fetch it.' Without waiting for a reply, she hurried away, closing the door behind her.

Amburley laughed softly, turning back to Isabella. 'I shall say it before you do, my love,' he commented, with a glint of mischief in his eyes. 'Outrageous to leave us together thus, without a chaperon. Do you think she is trying to compromise us, so that I may be forced to marry you?'

'I no longer know what to think,' replied Isabella, with as much of a smile as she could muster. 'Forgive me, Leigh, but my head aches so, I cannot—'

'Hush. Lie still,' he urged softly, dropping on one knee by the sofa. 'We have all the time in the world before us. What matters now is that you get well.' He raised her hand to his lips and kissed it. 'When you are a little recovered, I shall call to make my proposal in form. My token, then, shall be just what custom demands. For the present—' he turned her hand over and dropped a feather-light kiss on her palm '—I have a different token to leave with you.' He pressed a small metal object, warm from the heat of his body, into her hand and closed her fingers over it, just as Lady Wycham re-entered the room. 'Be sure I shall return,' he whispered. With the briefest of bows to Lady Wycham, he was gone.

Lady Wycham might not have known, at first, what to make of it, but now she was clearly in no doubt at all. She drew a chair up to the sofa and sat quietly by Isabella, helping her as she struggled to raise herself a little.

'Oh,' whispered Isabella in a long drawn-out breath, looking down at the object in her hand. Tears began to trickle down her cheeks, though she smiled as they flowed. 'Oh, Leigh!'

In her hand lay a tiny rectangle of gold and enamel, inset with rubies. A perfect miniature of the queen of hearts!

Chapter Nineteen

Lord Amburley called next day but, in spite of his protests, Isabella would not consent to see him. Lady Wycham received him in Isabella's stead, in order to reassure him about her niece's recovery. The interview soon progressed, of course, to Amburley's sudden change of heart—Lady Wycham professed herself delighted, but mystified. He had been so adamant that he would never marry where he might be branded a fortune-hunter. And Isabella was no less wealthy now than before.

Much embarrassed, Lord Amburley had no choice but to explain exactly how he had discovered the depths of his own feelings for

Isabella—and of hers for him. 'I would gladly have taken her with nothing,' he said, 'but I was being totally selfish. I saw it as a grand gesture to raise my love from penury, without ever stopping to consider how she would feel.' He grimaced. 'Then I learned of her fortune, and I thought only of what the world would think of *me*—when I should have been thinking of what I ought to do for *her*. Lady Wycham, I was blind until I thought I had lost her; and then I understood, at last, that nothing mattered except Isabella's happiness. Her money is of no importance. We shall find a way of dealing with it—together.'

Lady Wycham nodded, smiling her agreement. 'Very well, sir, you have convinced me. And I must tell you that I am delighted to learn that your regard for Isabella is as deep as hers for you. I really did believe, at one time, that it was Sophia's hand you sought.'

'Why, no, ma'am,' he began quickly, clearly much embarrassed, 'that was never in my mind.' At Lady Wycham's rather sceptical glance, he looked even more embarrassed.

'My friend Lewiston is… somewhat diffident, I fear, in spite of his wealth, and so I—'

'You did your best to help his suit.' Lady Wycham finished his sentence for him with a smile. 'And you have succeeded, I am glad to say. Sophia accepted him this morning. I suppose you knew?'

Amburley's expression was a mixture of pleasure and surprise. 'No, I did not. I am afraid that I have not seen Lewiston at all since I returned. But I am very glad to hear it. He is to be congratulated.' He, too, was smiling broadly now. 'I take it that Isabella is pleased by the news?'

'Yes, sir, she is. And when she is recovered, she will see them both to congratulate them. For the moment, however, she will see no one—not even you, my lord.'

With that, he had to be content.

For two more days, Isabella continued to receive no one. Lord Amburley called every day, impatient for sight of her, but she was always denied. On the fourth day, however, he marched straight past the butler, ignoring that worthy's protests, and mounted the stairs. He came face to face with Lady Wycham on the landing.

'Where is she, ma'am?' he demanded curtly, totally failing to observe the normal courtesies.

'In the drawing-room, my lord,' responded Lady Wycham, hastily adding, 'but you may not see her. She still has a black—'

It was too late. He had already thrown open the drawing-room door.

'A black eye,' finished Isabella, rising from her seat to confront him. 'How dare you force your way in, sir, when I expressly forbade all visitors? Is this the high-handed treatment I am to expect at your hands?' In spite of her stern words, she could not conceal her joy at seeing him.

'No, ma'am. You would be wise to expect much worse,' he grinned, striding forward and taking her in his arms.

Behind them, Lady Wycham quietly closed the drawing-room door and hovered, protectively, on the landing.

For a long moment, neither spoke; they

simply clung to each other. Isabella felt deliciously warm and cherished in the circle of his arms. She was sure he must be conscious of the rapid beating of her heart through her fine cambric gown.

'Isabella, my love, queen of my heart, will you be my wife?'

She smiled at him, a little crookedly. 'Yes,' she whispered, looking up at him through her lashes. 'Yes, my dearest love. I will.'

The glow in his eyes at her words was almost more than she could bear. How could she ever have mistaken his feelings towards Sophia for love? She continued to devour him with her eyes, until forcibly distracted by his taking her left hand to slip a magnificent sapphire on her finger.

He lifted her hand to his lips to kiss it. He kissed her lips next, gently at first, being mindful of her bruises, but then more passionately, holding her wrapped tightly in his arms. By the time they broke apart, both were breathless and Isabella's knees would barely support her. Her dreams had never promised anything as overwhelming as this.

He guided her to the sofa, where she instinctively made to tidy her hair. 'Do not,' he said, removing her hands and raising them to his lips once more. 'You look—' he smiled, feathering a kiss into her palm '—enchantingly dishevelled. It reminds me of spring in Hyde Park.' Ignoring Isabella's rosy blush, he kissed her other palm and closed her fingers over it, just as he had done with the queen of hearts.

'You, sir, are a quite outrageous flirt.' She was trying to look—and sound—nonchalant, but she knew she was not succeeding. And she had not uncurled her fingers.

Amburley simply smiled at her. It was the kind of smile that made her insides quiver in response. The look in his eyes was so soft, so loving, so open, that she felt as if their souls reached out and touched. She should feel embarrassed, but she did not. She had given herself to this man completely and forever. She would conceal nothing of herself from him.

He put his arm around her, drawing her into the shelter of his arm and resting his cheek on her tumbled curls. 'Mmm,' he murmured contentedly, stroking her cheek with his free hand.

Isabella felt so safe, so surrounded by love, that she wanted to melt into him. She closed her eyes to drink in these feelings and the wonderful scent of him. For a moment, she was sure she could hear birds singing again. But surely there were no birds here, in a Hill Street drawing-room?

Without warning, there were tears flowing down her cheeks. Amburley's stroking hand pulled away as if it had been burned. He straightened to look anxiously at his love. 'Isabella, what is the matter?'

He looked so very concerned. She would have told him if she could, but the truth was, she had no idea what had caused her tears, unless it was pure happiness. Heavens, the practical Isabella Winstanley was become a watering-pot!

She scrabbled in her pocket for her handkerchief. There, her fingers encountered the little metal plaque which she had gazed at for so many hours in the last few days. She sniffed and blew her nose, trying not to look at him. Then she presented him with the little gold jewel, face up, on the palm of her hand.

'Have you an explanation for this, my lord?' she asked, trying to sound stern and forbidding.

He had the grace to look a little sheepish. 'Oh,' he said. There followed a long pause.

Isabella fancied he was trying to concoct a story to save her from embarrassment. 'It's easier to tell me the truth, you know,' she said, with a valiant attempt at an impudent grin. 'I shall, of course, accept whatever plumper you choose to tell me, but can you be sure you will remember to tell the same story on a future occasion?'

He seized her hand between his larger ones as if to capture the offending jewel and hold it fast. 'Madam,' he said, 'once we are married, I shall command that you believe every single word I say, even if I contradict myself in the same breath.'

Isabella laughed, without trying to free her hand. She said nothing, but her eyes looked her continued enquiry.

'Oh, very well,' he smiled, 'I yield. And the

truth is not so very bad, after all.' He uncurled her fingers gently as he spoke. The little queen seemed to wink up at them both. 'I chanced to see a display of enamels in a jeweller's and ordered this for myself, in memory of a lady who plays a remarkably fine game of piquet.'

Isabella knew she must be blushing. She was glad that Amburley was looking at her hand, not at her face.

'I had never intended to show it to anyone, least of all you. It was just that when you were lying there, all battered and bruised—and by my doing, too—it came into my mind that I needed to show you that you had always been in my thoughts. I had nothing else to offer you,' he finished simply.

She bowed her head. 'That game of cards— you knew what I had done.' It was a statement, not a question. She felt, rather than saw, his gentle nod. 'I fear that women are strange, un- accountable creatures, my lord,' she whispered.

He drew her back into his arms. 'And women in love are even stranger,' he said, pushing up her chin with his finger so that he could start to kiss her again. His lips fastened on hers and the queen of hearts fell into the lap of her gown as Isabella raised her arms to encircle his neck, drawing him closer. Since the day she first set eyes on him, she had longed to push her fingers into his thick, curling hair. But the joy of caressing him was quickly overtaken. The impact of his mouth on hers was so much more thrilling, as he teased her lips apart with the tip of his tongue, darting it into the honeyed recesses of her mouth. Isabella clung to him, feeling as if her whole body was on fire. She was quivering in the strangest places, which seemed to be linked to her mouth by strings, like a marionette. She could not suppress a groan of pleasure.

Amburley raised his head. His eyes seemed to be out of focus. 'What is it, my love? Have I upset you? I go too fast…'

She was shaking her head before he had finished. 'I had not known…' she began uncertainly. 'When you kiss me, I feel so…' She did not know how to complete the sentence. She did not have the words.

His lordship looked suddenly very proud. He moved a little away from Isabella, leaving her space to compose herself, watching as she brought her emotions back under control. They sat in companionable silence for a moment.

Suddenly, Amburley frowned and took a deep breath. 'I have a real confession to make, Isabella,' he began very seriously, taking her hand in his once more. 'And you will have every reason to be furious with me when I have made it. I ask you only to hear me out before you vent your wrath on my head.'

Isabella nodded, bemused.

'I would have proposed to you before. Indeed, I was on the point of doing so, when I found out about your fortune.' He pressed her hand as she made to intervene. 'I had believed, you see, that you were precisely what you appeared on the North Road, a penniless companion. I came to love you, and I thought I could offer you the kind of life that would otherwise be denied you. But when I approached Lady Wycham…' he would not meet her eyes '…when I spoke to Lady Wycham and she told me about your true position, I realised that I could offer you nothing but a title, and a minor one at that. I could not face the thought of being branded a fortune-hunter by the polite world, or by you…and so I withdrew.'

Isabella's face betrayed her shock, but she did not try to interrupt his recital.

'I had determined to leave London, to return to my estates, but of course I was honour-bound to complete our race, even if I lost my greys to you in the process. I behaved abominably in that race. No—do not try to defend my actions. There can be no defence. I was so stupidly determined to win, to best you there, at least, because I could not aspire to your hand. I behaved like a scoundrel!' Isabella was shaking her head vehemently, but he would not stop. 'It was only when you were lying in the roadway and I thought you might be dead, that I came to understand that nothing else mattered but my love for you. At that moment, I should not have cared if all the doors in London had been closed to me, provided I could hold you, alive, in my arms. Isabella, my dearest love, can you forgive me?'

Isabella's dazzling smile showed he had nothing to fear. 'Having made so many mistakes of my own, how could I refuse?' It was clear from his puzzled expression that he did not know what she meant. 'I promise to explain,' she said, squeezing his fingers, 'but later. We have to decide now what to do about my accursed fortune.'

'Nothing at all,' he replied blithely. 'Do with it as you have always done. Or give it to my mother. She would soon spend it. We shall have no need of it.'

This was going to be more difficult than she had thought. 'Might we not invest some of it in the estate, Leigh? It would be for our children, after all.' She coloured a little at mentioning such things. She still had not recovered from that devastating kiss.

He pulled her back into his arms, resting his chin lightly on her golden hair. 'Fortune has smiled on me, my love, in the most peculiar way. My great-uncle Silas, the family miser, died on the day after your accident. Oh, do not offer condolences, I beg of you. He was roundly hated in the family. I learned only this morning that his last act of defiance was to disinherit all those who had fawned on him over the years and to leave his entire estate to me, who refused to have any truck with him. I fear I may now be even wealthier than you are.'

In spite of herself, Isabella found she was laughing. 'Oh, dear,' she gasped, 'how can I behave so? I should be ashamed.' She giggled again.

'It does create one difficulty, I fear.'

Isabella's laughter ceased abruptly.

'As his heir, I am obliged to observe the mourning period. It will not be possible for us to be married until it is over, nor may I escort you to balls and assemblies and waltz you round the floor as I long to do. I had hoped for us to be married within the month,' he admitted wistfully, caressing her gleaming hair, 'but Uncle Silas has had the last laugh on me there.' A thought seemed to strike him. 'Unless, of course…' He let the words hang in the air.

'Unless what?'

'We could be married quietly now, by special

licence, and travel immediately to the continent. There the mourning could be forgotten.' At her sharp intake of breath, he hesitated. 'But no. How could I suggest such a thing? It would be wrong to deprive you of the wonderful wedding you deserve. We shall spend the time in preparing a ceremony of suitable splendour.'

'Shall we, indeed? And if I do not want such a lavish affair? What then?'

'Isabella, do you mean that?' His voice had become a tense whisper.

Her shining eyes tried to tell him that she did.

'Rash woman. You shall be my wife within the week.' He kissed her again, long and lovingly, to seal their bargain.

'How can you possibly want to marry a woman who is covered in bruises?' she asked at last, drawing a little away from him.

'Are you? I can see only a black eye.' His gaze roamed caressingly over her slim figure. 'You mean there are more, that I cannot see?'

'You, sir, are outrageous. How dare you say anything so improper?'

'Madam, I wish only to be assured that my

wife-to-be will be able to…fulfil her role.' He grinned wickedly at her.

Isabella's insides turned airy somersaults at his words. Nor could she control the fiery blush which spread to the roots of her hair. What a sight she must look, part red, part purple, part yellow—yet he seemed not to notice. 'Leigh—' she began.

'Ah, that's better.' He kissed her again, first on the lips, then on her good eye, then ever so gently on her bruises. 'I promise to be outrageous only when you forget my name.'

* * * * *

É